THIS OUR FAITH

BY JOHN LESLIE HART

Jacob
Marley
PUBLICATIONS

THIS OUR FAITH

Alma 44:3

©Copyright 2020 John Leslie Hart 1-9057862191

ISBN 9781733940764

Library of Congress Control Number: 2020924001

Second Edition

Printed in the United States of America

Contents

Chapter 1

Sydney clung to a sloping surface, about to slide off the earth into who knows where. The world, its ashen sky and helpless stars, loomed off to one side not at all where they should be; gravity itself became terribly confused.

Shock and pain racked his body. The heaviness of all outer space rested on his chest and kept him from even breathing. He tried to move. Again, he tried to breathe – he tried, but air wouldn't come.

"This is what it is like to die," he thought. Now he couldn't breathe or see the stars.

"I am certainly going to die," he thought, free falling into his vortex of blackness. "I can do nothing about it."

"Sydneeee! LaMarrrr!"

Sydney heard his father's shout in a strange, husky voice. He tried again to breathe; air wouldn't come. He heard his father's heavy work shoes clomping across the highway. He wondered if he would live to see his father, or if they would find his body lying there. Off the road. Dead as a door nail.

He heard Dad still shouting, searching the wreckage. Sydney lifted his head. Air hadn't come. His chest felt flat and wooden and worthless beneath tons of outer space. Darkness closed in again. Even if Dad found him, what could he do? Sydney gulped. This time a slight bit of air leaked into his lungs. He sucked again so gratefully. More air came. He sucked more, and more. And more.

Then the world came back into touch. Stars streaked back overhead where they should have been all along. The earth righted itself.

He could see now. Breathing slightly eased his shock. He moved and found he could sit up. He started to stand, but sharp hurt pulsed his ankle and he caught himself, half standing. He fell back watching helplessly as Dad searched. He could see the shadow of the ruined farm wagon in a lonesome heap shoved forward from the wrecked car.

"Sydneeee! LaMarrrr!"

Dad's dark figure shouted without his stopping, jerking wheat-bundle-shaped shadows from the heap. Swinging and shoving away bundles he'd earlier cradled to the rack, Dad paid no attention to whether kernels fell off or not. Sydney climbed to his knees as Dad reached down to heave up on something too heavy to move. He saw his Dad's hands lift, then Sydney heard fall free the broken, splintered end of a pole. Dad threw it away with his left hand into the barrow pit.

"Sydneeee! LaMarrrr!" Dad yelled again.

"Dad," cried Sydney, now able to speak. "Daddy! I'm hurt!"

Dad stood at his side. "Sydney!"

"I couldn't breathe!"

His father's hands slipped from gloves and patted over Sydney's body.

"My ankle," said Sydney. Dad's fingers touched the swollen ankle.

"Ankle big as an ox," he said. "Anywhere else?"

"No."

"You got the wind knocked out of you. Your ankle may be broken."

Sydney felt himself being cradled up as easily as if he were a wheat bundle. His skinny legs dangled as Dad packed him across the road. Dad hugged him. Dad's closeness, his smell of sweat, his grime, a brush of whiskers, enveloped him. For a brief second, he hugged back. He couldn't remember the last time he hugged Dad.

Sydney felt himself being lowered into the long-stemmed rye and timothy grass next to where the tractor puttered to a stop.

"You must get by, Magpie," said Dad. "I got to find LaMar. I heard something scream – sounded like wire snapping down a long line. LaMar screaming."

Sydney winced at the pain in his ankle and blinked back tears. A minute ago, LaMar held to him. But he hadn't been able to hold on. Nowhere could he see LaMar.

"Where is he?" asked Sydney in panic. "Is he hurt?" Sydney shivered and sat up to see more. He tried his ankle. He pulled himself up on his good leg. He limped a few steps and his ankle felt like a spike had been driven through it. Across the road a light winked on inside the offending car, well behind the heap of wagon. Dad ran to it. Sydney struggled closer and saw the shadow of a man seated inside his car.

"Try them lights!" ordered Dad. The man halted and stared dumbly at him.

"Try them lights," repeated Dad, this time at point-blank range. The man slowly moved. First the windshield wipers batted on. Finally, a single headlamp tunneled through the darkness spotlighting one corner of the wreck.

3

In the light, Sydney could see the broken wagon had dropped its belly on the road. Entrails of gilt gushed out. Under one corner of the rack, Sydney noticed, kernels dribbled into a cone-shaped pile, perfectly thrashed.

"LaMarrr!" shouted Dad.

"LaMarrr!" cried Sydney.

Dad trotted back and began again to paw through bundles now reduced into straw. He tossed armfuls of chaff wildly back, glittering as it fell through the soft tunnel of light. Dad's still-gloved hands cleared a pathway that he opened wider with his shoulders. He continued burrowing until a pole stopped him, the other end of a long, wired-on corral pole. He tugged on it and the shaft twisted with a springy sensation.

"My boy!" cried Dad. Sydney hobbled next to Dad. Dad dropped to his knees and bent low over the rubble. He stroked straw back from the pole's buried end. He whipped his gloves off; he brushed chaff from a small object – a boy's unpolished, puggy work shoe.

"LaMar!" cried Sydney, his voice cracking. "It's LaMar!"

Dad pushed more straw off and uncovered LaMar's legs and body. Dad's hands were again stopped by the pole. It rested fully on LaMar's hips. Sydney leaned forward and accidentally blocked the tunnel of light. Dad's arm pushed him roughly to one side. With the light restored, Sydney also dropped to his knees and stared in a helpless, hopeless trance.

Dad stood and gripped the raw wood in his bare hands. He hefted upwards. His back locked into the lift; his chin thrust out. He moaned lowly from the stress. His legs rose

4

like levered springs. The entire end of the wagon, wheels, and mounds of straw stirred as he heaved. Bundles of wheat shifted. Up came the wagon; bundles slipped down into the pea gravel – plash, plash. The load settled backwards . . . plash, plash, plash. Then the pole jerked free. Dark-tipped, splintered, it rolled down the roadside. Dad fell to his knees and brushed loose straw from LaMar.

"LaMar." He said it begging, not like himself at all. "Oh, my LaMar!" He lowered his head and held his ear against the boy's chest and listened.

Sydney bowed, and waited crookedly in the straw.

"He's alive," Dad half whispered to Sydney. "Oh God! Please keep him for us." Dad pulled off his battered, frowning cowboy hat, bowed as he covered LaMar's head with one thick hand. "I'm not much of a one for church," he prayed. "But in the name of God, please keep him alive for us – in the name of Jesus! Amen."

"Amen," whispered Sydney.

Dad's hands moved from LaMar's head and explored the small and motionless body. He felt LaMar's neck and patted along the plaid shirt and denim-clad body. At LaMar's hips, where the pole had fallen, Dad brushed back more straw. A dark blotch soaked the boy's middle. Sydney flinched as Dad picked straw and splinters from the blotch. He flipped them aside, showing in the vague light as angry red splinters against gold. Dad stood and unbuttoned his work shirt. He shook it vigorously to one side, then draped it over LaMar's middle. Immediately, blood soaked through it. The black splotch grew, following the weave of Dad's shirt. Behind them, Sydney could hear windshield wipers beating evenly. Beyond stretched the vacant road. An empty river of darkness.

"Nothing coming," said Dad. "We've got to get this boy to the hospital."

"Nothing's coming," repeated Sydney helplessly.

The Moment refused to move onward. Straw littered asphalt, the smell of chaff mixed with the smell of automobile oil. Headlamp light illuminated a corner of the wreck and cast its yellow on only one side of the low straw heap. The rest of the world spread away in darkness and silence. Dad stood still for a long Moment. His hands opened and closed helplessly. Sydney looked anxiously back and forward along the highway.

"There's lights," said Sydney, pointing. In the distance, pinholes pierced the vast canopy of black.

"Maybe prayers are answered," Dad muttered. He picked up his hat from the straw and trotted out to meet the oncoming car. It approached and he began waving his hat in wide arcs. As the car drew nearer, tires squealed and Dad's hat and undershirt glowed bright in the lights. Instead of stopping, though, the car pulled inside, toward the wreckage.

"My LaMar!" shrieked Dad. "You'll hit him again!" He dashed into the car's path. "Stop! You'll run over him."

Lights blazed on him. He swatted with his hat the way he would at a runaway cow. Rubber howled and the car slid sideways around the wagon with its lights away from the wreck. The tractor in the barrow pit lit up for an instant like a flash camera took its picture. The car recovered slowly. Brake lights brightened and the car paused. Then it resumed its journey. Sydney watched in disbelief as the automobile, at first near enough to set a hat on, drew away from reach.

"No," bellowed Dad. His hands came up to hold the small size of the diminishing car from growing any smaller. "You can't pass me up! No!"

Sydney stood, paralyzed. Tail lights slowly diminished into twin red dots.

"Why did he do that?" asked Sydney. "Didn't he see us at all?" He limped and pain shot through his ankle, quavering his next words: "But another car's coming – see it?"

High beam headlights moved slowly along the road toward them.

"Yeah," said Dad, smothering a sob in his voice. "Just what I need. Another car like the other two. My son broken, my outfit wrecked. The bills…." He coughed heavily, smothering his sob. "You feeling any better?"

"My foot's not broke," said Sydney.

Dad's hands dangled, then curled into fists. "That's another prayer not answered," he hissed. He crashed his fist against the dented fender. "God just won't listen to me!"

From the impact of his blow, the tunnel of headlight wavered and shrank into darkness.

The wrecked car's driver spoke for the first time: "See what you have done. Gone and broke the lights." His blond head poked out of the car and then retracted. They could hear him rolling up his window.

"He's gone silly," said Dad. He took a deep breath. "Nobody is going to help me out of this one. I got to do it myself, as always." He replaced his hat on his head and pulled the brim low. "So much for praying. I never could

7

rely on that." Now he sounded altogether like himself. He
strode to wrecked car and began gently rocking the dented
fender. As he did so, the tunnel of light winked and
flickered back on. The car's tail lights also lit up. Dad's
thick arm penetrated inside the car. Its driver lifted his arms
to protect himself.

"Don't," he pleaded. "I didn't mean to. I didn't get
much sleep last night."

"I won't knock you silly," growled Dad's angry voice.
"I would, but somebody beat me to it." Dad fumbled for the
light switch. He began turning it off and on, off and on.
Immediately the approaching car responded by slowing,
then pulling to a halt with its high beams showing fully on
the broken wagon and injured boy lying on the asphalt.

A door of the car opened and a man limped into the
headlights. Another figure also climbed out.

"It is Arsle Klaybill, and Carn, too," said Sydney.

Carn's hulking frame partially eclipsed the lights as he
walked to the small, limp figure in the straw, ogling.

"We've got a hurt boy here," said Dad, the authority in
his voice stopping both of them and taking over their old
Ford, used in the field while the new Buick remained in the
garage. "We've got to get him to the hospital. Now!"

Dad waved toward the car. "Hold the back door
open," he said. Arsle limped back to the Ford and opened
its rear door. He leaned in, switching on the dome light.
Sydney walked closer. In the car's light, Sydney could see
Arsle's knotted face and the blue veins that mapped his
nose.

"I'm ready," said Arsle, picking up Dad's urgency.
"Let's get him into the car and go."

Dad returned to LaMar and slid his arms under the boy's body. One hand spread under his middle. Sydney followed.

"Steady his legs."

Sydney felt his lips tremble as he knelt and slid his arms under his brother's legs, like toting kindling sticks. Dad and Sydney arose together, Dad hunched over, Sydney stretched up. They walked carefully bearing LaMar. Sydney's ankle sagged in unspeakable pain at each step. The car's dome light shone over its rear seat draped with a turquoise and red and white Indian blanket. They eased LaMar on the blanket. Straw littered the seat.

"Don't mind the straw," called Arsle, walking to the front. He manipulated himself behind the wheel and the car started. Dad paid no attention to the straw but climbed in next to LaMar.

"Stay here and take care of things," he ordered Sydney. "See the cows are milked. Save that wheat in the gravel for the chicks."

"Never mind Carn," said Arsle as he started the motor. "We'll leave him here to help out."

"I ain't staying here alone," called Carn from the other side where, oblivious to Sydney, he gawked at the wreckage.

The door slammed.

"Hey," yelled Carn, from where he still gaped at the broken wagon. "Don't leave me here."

In answer, the car drew away into the night.

Chapter 2

Sydney watched Carn's vague form running and running after the car. Carn's lopsided boots crunched more and more faintly in the gravel flank of the highway as he ran. Finally, Carn's dark form slowed and stopped. He returned, his footsteps gradually came back within hearing, gravely clompings in the night. Sydney leaned against the corner of the hayrack and waited. He began shivering and couldn't stop. He heard Carn coming nearer. He watched Carn's dark form walking toward the wreck and inspecting the now-dark heap; only dimming, red-blinking brakes of the broken car showed light. Fall's night cool almost hurt through Sydney's long-sleeved shirt. He watched Carn reach out and touch the hayrack, drumming his fingers over its dismembered wood.

"Thought you were running away," said Sydney, breaking the silence.

"Unnnnh!" yelled Carn, jumping back. "I didn't see you." He peered at Sydney. "I figured they left me by myself, again, as usual."

"I am here by myself," said Sydney. "My Dad took off and left me. I thought you were running away, too."

"Running home," said Carn. "But home is too far." He peered anxiously at Sydney. "I forgot to ask. Was you hurt? I don't see no blood nor nothing on you."

"My ankle might be broke," said Sydney. "I might be bleeding to death under my skin."

Carn studied him. "Maybe you had ought to sit down."

"I can stand it," said Sydney, holding his arms over his stomach against the coolness. "I already almost died." Then to be certain Carn knew, he added, "But I didn't."

Carn reached out and held onto the corner of the hayrack. "Do you think your brother will pass beyond?" he asked quietly.

"Naw," said Sydney. "He'll be better."

"He might," said Carn. "It knocked him out cold. Sometimes people pass beyond after they are knocked out cold."

"Naw," said Sydney.

"Unconscious," said Carn. "He didn't move. Sometimes people pass beyond when they are unconscious."

"Naw," said Sydney. "He'll come to at the hospital. What hospitals do is bring unconscious people to."

"I wonder what it is like to pass beyond," said Carn. "Do you ever wonder what it is like to be dead?"

"Nope," said Sydney. "Never do. Even though I almost did. Be dead, that is. But I didn't," he reminded Carn.

"I wonder about it sometimes," said Carn. "Do you suppose the spirits of dead people in the beyond can fly?"

"Huh?"

"Can dead people's ghosts fly? I am scared if I get up high. If I were a ghost, could I fly? What do you think?"

"Never thought about it," said Sydney, shivering more, remembering that a few minutes ago, he thought he'd pass into that beyond. "Never expect to again."

"I will tell you something if you promise not to laugh," said Carn. He stepped closer, suddenly intimate in the darkness that hid him from the world with all its cruel minds and words.

"I don't care if you tell me or if you don't," said Sydney. "I am sure I will not laugh tonight." He looked homeward and saw headlights coming from town.

"I am not afraid to go beyond," said Carn. "Sometimes I even wish I could."

"What?" said Sydney. "You must be crazy."

"I am tired of people making fun of me all the time. And scaring me." He hurried his words to be finished before the lights arrived. "My Uncle Arsle gives me lickings. Uncle Mafe teases me. They don't pick on anyone but me. I am tired of it. I wish I could just stay asleep. No one bothers me when I am asleep."

Sydney could feel the intensity of his look.

"Know what?" Carn said. He leaned so far forward he almost fell frontwards. "When I saw your brother, I wished it were me instead of him. I wished I could go beyond."

"You're crazy," repeated Sydney.

"Don't tell anyone. You said."

"I won't," said Sydney, himself confiding now. "You know," he spoke cautiously, quieter. "I knew this would happen. I had a real feeling days before that it would."

Carn stared at him in the murky, indistinct light of oncoming headlamps.

"That would be scary. But I won't tell anyone," he promised.

"Thanks," said Sydney. "It is scary to be like this."

They waited in silence for the headlights that came towards them. Vehicles pulled over and gleamed high beams on the wreckage. A cattle truck parked first. A hawk-faced man not much taller than its fenders stepped out.

"It's Neeter," said Sydney. Carn stepped away.

Neeter began with questions. As soon as he asked one, he answered it, then asked another.

"Whose outfit is this?" he asked. "Spengs, I reckon. What happened? Car hit it, I s'pose. Dark as a coal cellar at midnight. Anybody hurt? The little guy." Probably why Dallern is gone. He turned to Sydney. "You hurt, Nat?"

Sydney waited for him to answer his own question. He didn't. Sydney finally answered. "I'm Sydney. Nat's my big brother. Wind knocked out of me, maybe broke my ankle, that's all."

The man stepped up to him. Sydney felt the raptor nose pointing at him and blinking, beady eyes searching him. "See if you can walk," said Neeter.

Sydney took a limping step. He put his weight slightly on the ankle and his face writhed at the biting pain.

"It ain't broke," said Neeter. "You couldn't walk like that if it was broke. I learned that in the rodeo. Get in the truck and rest if you want to."

Other vehicles stopped. They remained with engines running, and each, as if copying the others, shined headlights on the wreckage. More lights made the scene smaller. Men climbed out of their pickups and began to swarm.

Neeter turned to Carn. "You in charge of this clean up? What should we do?"

13

Carn stared at him without answering.

"So?"

"Dunno," said Carn. "Guess we better find a bucket somewhere."

Neeter laughed. "Yeah, a bucket, a really tall bucket."

Other vehicles arrived, parked and directed their lights on the sight. Drivers walked over and heard how the wagon wrecked, and repeated it to the next drivers. They stood reverently at the spot of blood where LaMar had laid.

"Someone could drive up any minute and say LaMar had passed beyond," Sydney said toward Carn. "Or maybe he already has and I won't know about it for hours."

"Naw," said Carn. "He ain't."

"He bled a lot," said Sydney. "It could happen."

"Naw," said Carn. "He'll make it."

"My Dad gave him a blessing, sort of," said Sydney.

"Oh?" asked Neeter, standing near.

Sydney didn't say more.

"Huh?" said Neeter.

Sydney didn't answer.

Oncoming cars on Highway 89 slowed and waited in a growing line. Every once in a while, someone stepped into the beaming lights and waved them on through. Soon a dozen men milled about and peered at it like wreck inspectors. After a few more minutes a dump truck pulled up alongside the heap of straw, bundles and broken wagon. Men pitchforked and shoveled fractured wheat stalks into the truck bed. Watching them work, Sydney felt dizzy and shivering. He climbed into the cab where he pulled an old coat over his shoulders. He leaned back on the seat and his awareness narrowed into the dull chrome button of the

14

cattle truck's glove compartment, and he dreamed of flying.
Then he began falling and falling.

He jolted awake suddenly, jerking as he caught
himself. His ankle speared pain up his leg. Through the
dusty windshield he saw the wrecked car reared up behind
a tow truck. Rotating red lights of a police car played over
the littered site. In the center stood the county sheriff.
Lights showed him to be a big man with jaw thrust forward
and head tilted to a slight angle. A gold name tag above his
shirt read: Houghton. He spoke loudly to the driver of the
wrecked car:

"No, I won't. I certainly won't. You were speeding and
you sped right into one of our farm wagons."

Sheriff Houghton held a board with a reflector nailed
on, one side with a thick, barely pounded screw. He shook
it in the face of the driver.

Sydney heard the driver mumble something and
everyone stopped to watch as the sheriff answered loudly:

"I'm the sheriff here. You were speeding." In the
light, his left eye closed more as he grew angrier. "Look at
those skid marks."

The driver mumbled again. The sheriff answered even
louder, his left eye nearly shut:

"If you say one more thing, I will issue you a speeding
ticket." He gestured back to the skid marks. "If I ever catch
you speeding through this town of Bloomington again, I
will issue you the biggest ticket you've ever seen. Do you
understand me?"

The tow truck driver revved his engine and the blond
driver turned angrily and climbed into its cab. The tow
truck pulled into the night, with the wrecked car's single

headlight tunneling on, bobbing upward, spotlighting tops of telephone poles in its vague illumine.

Sydney watched from the nether-lands of sleepish-wakishness. Nothing felt real; rather his nightmare continued and he hoped he would wake up soon and find everything changed back to the way it always was. He awoke a little more when Arsle's car pulled up and Arsle climbed out, favoring his game leg a bit more than usual as though it were he who had been injured. Men clustered around. Sydney opened the truck door so he could hear.

"The boy has a broken pelvis and ruptured spleen and some arteries near the spleen were severed," said Arsle. He spoke loudly, a mentally rehearsed speech. "Doc Mooley said how he survived to get to the hospital is a pure miracle." In a lower, more solemn voice, he said, "Mister came and gave him a blessing, afterwards. Doc operated to remove the little guy's spleen. He says if no infection sets in, the little guy will be up and running before the end of the year." Arsle stopped.

"That's good news," said Neeter. He let go a deep breath and a wave of relief passed over the others, all fathers with their own children.

Sydney felt the shock of the news and twirled the bits of it through his mind to understand better: "How he survived … a miracle … operation … up and running around."

Arsle limped closer and continued: "He's a tough little guy to survive a wagon pole breaking over his hips." He paused. "The next twenty-four hours will be rough, though."

When Arsle stopped talking, the men muttered among
themselves, shaking heads and whistling low. They felt as a
single person, a communal Dad whose son might pass
beyond.

"I'll go milk his cows," said Arsle, rubbing his nose.
"Anybody know about his system?"

"I'll get them," interrupted Neeter.

"I can milk them," continued Arsle, limping deeply. "I
haven't milked cows by hand for a few years, but I can still
do it."

"I'll get them," said Neeter.

"I can usually get a herd milked in decent time," said
Arsle. "Usually."

"I'll get them," repeated Neeter. "I've milked them
before. I know his system. Nat over there can help me."

"I'm Sydney," said Sydney.

"Thanks," said Arsle. "I 'preciate it."

Sydney felt an arm across his shoulder. Neeter's arm.
"Stay in the truck and rest," he said. "We're going to load
the rest of this busted-up wagon into the truck. Then we
will milk your cows. You can show me where your Daddy
parks them."

Sydney watched from the cab as the men finished
picking up from the road. Into the back of the pickup, they
tossed timbers from the broken wagon. Somebody lifted the
corral pole with its dark-tipped, splintered end. He called
out and held it in the light for others to look at. Then they
carried it almost reverently, like a casket. That hushed
them. When they'd completed the job and scooped wheat in
the gravel into a bucket without being told to, Neeter

17

climbed into the cab with Sydney, and the truck rumbled toward home.

At the Speng place, the vehicle pulled near the barn, and parked.

"I'll get the cows," said Sydney. He felt unreal and very cold as he opened the truck door and climbed down, touching only his good ankle.

"Stay there," said Neeter. "I'll get them."

Sydney collapsed to the running board, watching Neeter's short form make his way across the street toward the milk cows, disappearing until just his hat showed nodding above the hilly horizon, and then that, too, bobbed into shadow. Sharply awake now, Sydney became keen to his silent surroundings. Night wind stirred the scene with its cold breath, and he sensed its gentle pressure of uncertainty. Flowing air breathed across his face and he felt its uneven texture. In that stillness of the dark and harmful night, time itself became caught up in the movement of the air; the traveling atmosphere moved also in instants – threading itself into the breeze and passing incessantly in swirls and gusts. He felt its touch sweeping his neck and flicking beneath his collar. Again, he felt frustration at time's passage and the direction it had taken.

He felt, for a split second, that if he could clasp the air between his fingers, he could clutch time. A guy could stop the wind, maybe he could even stop time, seizing minutes between his fingers. If he could stop it, he would turn it back a mere couple of hours and change its direction so that the wreck didn't happen, dissolving that cruel point of trauma, and scoot those two hours along a different rail fork, to a usual safe ride home, where nothing changed, where life simply continued as it should have and had always been. Sydney closed his fingers on the wind and held them closed. But nothing changed.

Lowing of the family milk cows lining the road finally brought him up.

"Come on," yelled Sydney, but his voice quavered. "Come on!" he yelled again. The cows stopped and stood staring at him. He hopped awkwardly from the cab and opened the big barn doors.

"Stupid cows," he yelled. He meant "stupid time," but how do you fight that?

Inca, Mom's cow, walked toward him. He watched the file of cows trailing her, seeing their whitish, inflated udders bulging, swinging from side to side beneath shadowy cow torsos, eager to be eased.

He stepped closer to Inca to stroke her side. She stopped and Sydney nestled his head against her flat, sleek neck; in the dark, sheltering him from the wind and brutal passage of time, she comforted like a mother creature. Then he stepped back and called again to the others following in a long line to the milking stable. Last walked Aida, Nat's cow. Her udder hung like a giant balloon and pressed against both flanks as she walked. Aida aimed a mild kick at Sydney from a safe distance.

"Come on, magpie bait," he said.

"I will take it from here," called Neeter from behind. "Just tell me: Are any of them skittish?"

"Only the last one," said Sydney. "Aida. The one with the big bag. She kicks at anybody. And she gives almost two buckets of milk. Dad is just starting to get her settled down."

"I'll hobble her. By the way, do you have any wire bale ties around?"

Sydney shrugged and yelled back, as he limped toward the house. "By the chicken coop."

He passed men unloading wheat and piling wagon wreckage. Sydney didn't stay to help, but hobbled past them.

"Get some rest," one said.

"Everything will work out," another called.

"It will all be fine," said another. "We make it through these things."

Sydney nodded.

Busy as the yard was with men working, the house stood empty, dark, silent. Having a yard full of men but the house empty made it even lonelier. He hobbled in through the kitchen, the door's loose glass window rattling. He slowly climbed the tall stairs to his room, hopping, one foot and one step at a time. Often resting. Clinging to the banister. Wide awake, he shed his greasy long-sleeved shirt and overalls. He knelt briefly at his bedside and ran a prayer as a string of words, adding a few for LaMar, hoping, like casting dice when playing Monopoly.

Climbing into his side of the sway-bellied bed, he left plenty of room for LaMar on the other side, just in case he made it home tonight. Sydney lay still for a long time before sleep would come.

Chapter **3**

One move – agony fired in his ankle and shot through his leg, exploding into the remembrance of last night.

Sydney clenched shut his eyes to push it away. He fervently wished he could make it a different day when this didn't happen. He tried not to think at all. But everything about the wreck flashed back and hurt – LaMar, the wagon, wheat blasted over the highway, Dad's strange voice, the sleepy driver, the wrecked car, the people helping, Sydney's whole body.

He moved again – moving jarred him wide awake. His shoulders and back throbbed like he'd been whacked very hard all over.

Sunlight, plenty of it, streamed through the windows. Across the room, covers rumpled on the empty bed of his older brother, Nat. The other side of his bed remained empty, too. LaMar's side. No sign of LaMar.

"LaMar! Where is LaMar? How is LaMar?" he asked, speaking loudly in his panic. No one answered.

He had to know. He pulled on yesterday's school clothes, buttoning the shirt crookedly, and, after one glance at his engorged ankle, not bothering with socks. Clinging to the banister, he half-slid and hopped one-footedly down the long staircase. He skittered to the kitchen and supported himself heavily on a chair's back, holding to its top arched over lean pegs.

Stirring a kettle at the hotter-than-usual kitchen stove stood Madge, his older sister, a slim and attractive young woman of sixteen with pecan-colored hair and matching pecan-colored eyes; this morning with unbrushed hair. A smaller version of Mom, she wore one of Mom's aprons and held a spoon delicately as she mixed wheat mush and watched over the family.

Across the room at the chipped, imitation marble kitchen table sat Bartholomew, three. Chubby-cheeked, with his hair cut in a bowl shape just above large ears, he waited for his mush by rolling a marble around the bottom of his empty dish. Both looked up when Sydney entered, struggled across the room and folded into a chair. He extended his ankle so everyone could see his injury.

"You're hurt! declared Madge. She leaned the spoon against the side of the large kettle. "How are you feeling?" Her eyes ran over him and stopped at his injured ankle. "Your foot! Is it broken?" She slid the mush pot to the back of the stove and the spoon fell into its boiling lava.

"I didn't die," Sydney said. "How is LaMar? Where is Mom? Where is Dad? Where is Nat?"

Madge rushed across the room, knelt and ran her fingertips over his swollen ankle. "It is extremely swollen."

"That's just muscle," said Sydney, recoiling at her touch.

"Muscle," said Madge.

"How is LaMar?" Hurt sounded in his question.

Madge waited until she returned to the stove to answer. She studied the mush kettle for any sign of sunken spoon and carefully answered, "He survived through the night. They said it took a miracle to make it." She reached

22

for another spoon to lever out the one that disappeared. "Dad waited up all night. Now Mom's staying with LaMar. Nat's out milking. Mom may come home this afternoon."

"But is he going to be all right?" asked Sydney.

Madge stopped stirring and moved the mush to the back of the stove. She wiped her hands on a dish towel. She looked at Sydney.

"Nothing is going to be all right," she said. "You know I help Mom and Dad with the math. I know our situation. We're in trouble with the bank already, and now LaMar is hurt so bad we don't know if he will make it."

Sydney studied his sister's moistening eyes.

"He will make it," he said. "Everything will be fine. You will see."

"The whole wagon on top of his little hips!" She daubed at her eyes with the dish towel. "And all those doctor bills. We can't come close to paying our bills."

"Maybe the church will help us," said Sydney, trying to change the subject.

"That's the only way we can make ends meet," said Madge. "But we simply can't count on that."

"Dad never goes to church. I don't know if they would even help him."

The kitchen door banged open and in raced Prielle, six. Her sun-bleached hair frowzled in a page-boy cut.

"A terrible, bad wreck happened," she shrilled. "It happened right in the yard!" she looked puzzled. "How did they wreck over there by the chicken coop?"

"The men brought the wreck from the highway to the yard last night," explained Madge, still fishing with a second spoon for the first spoon.

"How is he this morning?" asked Sydney. "Did you hear anything else?"

"We don't know," she replied. "We just don't know if he will be all right."

"Everything will work out," said Sydney.

"Don't you get it?" exclaimed Madge. "We're in trouble. Nothing adds up now. It can't be all right because nothing adds up to all right." She stepped closer to Sydney. "It's like nobody in this family can do the math." She shook her head in frustration.

"I don't think my ankle is broken," said Sydney, changing the subject away from Madge's home economics.

Prielle walked over to Madge. "Can we go see LaMar?" she asked.

"Not for a while," Madge replied. She eased the kettle without a hot pad to the stovetop's burning center and lifted up first spoon with the second spoon. Heat of the stove seared her fingers and she dropped the second spoon also. Madge used a hot pad to push the kettle to the back of the stove. She grabbed a third spoon and lifted at the other two, but both slipped down.

"Never mind," she said, leaning the third spoon against the side of the kettle. She wreathed the mush kettle with a dish towel and, as she hefted it to the table, the third spoon also fell.

"This is so hot," she warned as she poured mush into four of the six bowls clustered there. Bartholomew snatched his marble back just before it would have been submerged by the thick, beige substance of goose flesh texture.

Sydney eagerly took a bowl. "This mush has lumps," he complained. He began spooning lumps from his mush to the table top.

"Next time you stir it," said Madge. She ran cold water over her fingers.

Sydney fished a rocklike chunk of brown sugar from the lidless sugar bowl. With a butter knife, he whittled flecks of sweet into his breakfast. Madge put the mush kettle back on the stove. She took a fourth spoon into her hand to begin another fishing expedition. She set it down to fold her arms.

"Prielle, please ask the blessing," she said.

Prielle happily obliged, but before she finished, shrieks from Bartholomew drowned out her hallowing voice. Everyone looked at Bartholomew: great tears rolled down his cheeks; his tongue poked far out.

"Poor Bartholomew," said Madge. "I told you mush is hot. And anyway, you shouldn't eat during the blessing." She handed him a cup of cold water. "Poke your tongue in this." He thrust his tongue into it and sadly rolled his big eyes up.

"Hush," she said. "You'll wake Daddy. He stayed up most of the night."

"I'm awake," called a voice from the adjoining bathroom. With shaving cream smeared over half his face, Dad pushed open the door. The family watched as he returned his face to the bathroom sink and shaved it carefully with a straight edge razor, then rinsed his face. When finished, he walked into the kitchen with his face still dripping.

"Prielle, please say the blessing," he said. Madge and Sydney traded surprised looks.

Sydney shrugged as if to say, "Don't ask me."

Prielle folded her arms and prepared to re-say the blessing.

"Someone's coming," interrupted Sydney. "Front door. I can hear them on the lawn."

"Imagination again," said Dad. But they paused.

A few seconds later someone rapped at the front door. "It's the thresher man," said Sydney, peering up the hallway. "Rindell. Rindell Imagination."

Dad grabbed a dish towel and wiped the drippings from his face. He stepped quickly to the front door, the formal entry. "I'm ready for Rindell, at least for the grain check. What's left of it." On the way out he tossed the towel at Sydney. "All the kids in the world and I end up with the smartest Alec of them all."

He slipped outside to talk to the thresher man. Madge picked up a spoon and began at fishing spoons from the large mush kettle. Prielle climbed on a chair and peeked out the window at the two talking.

"Look," said Prielle. "It's the leaf society lady coming now."

Madge glanced quickly through the window toward the back door. "It's Arsle's wife, Mona Klaybill, the Relief Society president over the women," she announced.

Madge forsook her spoon-fishing expedition, brushed crumbs from her apron, and whispered, "She's checking up on us. To see if we need help, or food or somebody's old clothing."

A gentle knock sounded on the kitchen door, the family door. Madge's expression transformed from panic to Sunday School a she opened the door. Sister Klaybill entered. She'd knotted her scarf neatly around her head, her smile stretched across her face. In her hands she held a white enamel baking dish under tight wax paper. She placed the casserole dish on the table, near mush dishes loomed over by a short pitcher of thick cream. Her eyes swept the cluttered room and rested reassuringly on Madge.

Madge smiled.

Sister Klaybill smiled.

"I am so sorry for LaMar," Sister Klaybill said. "It's such a hard thing."

Madge stepped to the stove. She pushed the large kettle to a cool place, deciding not to fish for sunken spoons in front of company.

"We hear he is doing better this morning," Madge said. "We all feel so blessed."

Sister Klaybill stood and inspected Sydney's thrust-forward ankle. She gently touched it, studying it very thoroughly. Like a nurse would. "I hear you are limping worse than Arsle. At least you'll get better." She smiled broadly. "Put a heat pack on it and the pain will go down."

She looked directly into Sydney's eyes. "Now is a good time for you to get your testimony," she said. "You must pray for LaMar."

"I do pray," said Sydney. He withdrew his ankle from view. "I pray for LaMar. But God doesn't listen to me. I said my prayers and we wrecked anyway."

"My Sunday School boy saying that!" she said, shaking her head and loosening her scarf. She turned back to Sydney. "God listens to everyone. He certainly saved LaMar." She waved her hands expressively. "Doc Mooley couldn't explain why LaMar didn't bleed to death." She looked around to challenge anyone who didn't agree with her. "This family has a miracle. Don't discount a miracle when you see one."

"We wrecked, didn't we?" said Sydney, looking down.

"Prayer is more than slinging off a line or two of words," she said. "You must connect with the other side." She looked deep into Sydney's eyes. "We feel you also were preserved."

"Yeah," said Sydney. "I am preserves, pickled beets preserves."

"My laws," said Sister Klaybill. She shook her head and turned to Madge.

"We're in the Lord's hands," reassured Madge. "I am sure He will take care of us."

Sister Klaybill smiled again. "You sound more like your precious mother every day. Now, I don't want you to argue, but we've arranged a little food."

"Oh no!" exclaimed Madge. "I mean, we don't need help. We'll get along fine."

"The part of the gospel most of us have trouble with is the receiving part," said Sister Klaybill, peeved. "No one wants to receive." She said it like she'd said it many times before. "How can other people give if no one wants to receive?"

"We will get along fine, but thank you, thank you so very much," said Madge very, very sweetly.

"I am so proud of you all," said Sister Klaybill. "You are doing so well."

The door rattled and Dad entered through the kitchen door. But the door hid Sister Klaybill from his view.

"Rindell is doing our place next, thanks to the Klaybills being late as usual. That's two favors they've done us." He stood in the doorway, blind to Sister Klaybill being seated out of his view. "But don't talk to the bishop about our thrashing, or he will get all the high priests in the valley here. I don't want all the high priests in the valley. I'll get Neeter, and us short priests will do the job."

Dad puzzled, trying to understand Madge's veiled look. His eyes moved slowly across the kitchen. He spied the white ceramic dish on the table. He stepped further into the room and closed the door. There sat Sister Klaybill. Her smile turned as hard and white as her baking dish.

"Sister Klaybill's here," said Madge in a tiny voice.

"Oh," said Dad. He straddled a chair backwards and held its slender pegs as to milk them.

"How do you do?"

"Fine, thank you."

"I sure 'preciate Arsle taking us to the hospital last night," he said without letting go of the chair.

"He gladly did it. He ran about an hour late when he came by."

"He and the others helped a lot last night. Must have been twenty of them." Dad took a deep breath and stared at her, signaling Sister Klaybill to leave now.

She changed the subject midstream. "Dallern," she said. "This would be a good time for you to practice a little faith. The doctor said that LaMar miraculously made it to the hospital."

Dad coughed a little and turned away. He spotted the mush bowl on the corner of the stove.

"Have you eaten breakfast yet?" he asked politely.

"Thank you," she said. "I ate earlier."

"Too bad," he replied. He reached the pan and tilted it. The uneaten substance within cooled solid. "At least it's not lumpy. It's just one big lump – of cement."

Sister Klaybill leaned forward. "You child's life is at stake," she pleaded. Her hands shook. "It's time to quit living in your pride. I beg of you, for LaMar's sake. We all love him so." Tears slipped down her cheeks.

Dad settled back in his chair and tilted the mush kettle over an empty bowl. The rubbery substance within flopped out over his bowl, retaining its kettle shape. He lifted it again by one of the sunken spoon's handles, and put it back into the kettle. He tried spooning a corner out, but hit spoons at every probe.

"This here is cement," he said, "and it's full of rebar."

Sister Klaybill tried to smile. The children didn't make a sound. Sydney turned in his chair away from Sister Klaybill. Dad's hands tightened on the back of the chair and one of the pegs snapped in his big hands. The snap echoed like a gunshot.

"Pride," he growled loudly. "I will tell you about pride. This town is filled with pride. People are proud of their goodness, proud of how strong they are, proud of their pioneer grandparents. They are proud about giving help to people, anybody they can find to help. You can even hear it in their prayers. Prayers of pride."

"It wouldn't hurt you to do some praying," said Sister Klaybill in half a voice.

30

"My prayers aren't answered," he said loudly. "If
LaMar is saved, the doctor will have to do it."

"You've had one miracle already," said Sister Klaybill,
her voice growing smaller and smaller. "What does it take
to make you believe in miracles?"

"I believe in the miracle of modern medicine," said
Dad. "The miracle of Doc Mooley. He saved LaMar, and
he did it all by himself." The angry tone in Dad's voice
ended the visit.

White and trembling, Sister Klaybill stood. She re-tied
her scarf, loosely this time, managed a half-smile to the
children, turned and walked out of the kitchen.

Glass rattled as the door closed and Dad looked at the
white ceramic casserole dish. He still held the broken shaft
of wood in his big hand. He hurled it to the floor and it
bounced across the faded blue tile.

"She wants to help us so she can be proud of herself,"
he hissed. "But we don't need help from the church, do
we."

"No," said Madge in a hurt voice.

"Huh-uh," said Prielle. "Shall I say the blessing now?"

Dad poured cream directly into the kettle and began
eating slabs of mush, picking for his bites between the
embedded spoons.

"Don't bother," he said.

31

Chapter 4

Leaning on his good ankle after limping to the schoolroom, Sydney studied white porcelain door knob, shiny on top, grimed beneath by decades of pupil hands. Before turning the knob, he listened. Mister's voice sounded distantly.

"Miss Lutty," Sydney heard him say, "What do you have for the first answer?"

"Math," Sydney thought. "I'll wait just a minute."

He heard Addie blow her nose and reply in a far-away nasal voice, "16 times 27 equals 436."

That's not too bad, he thought. He twisted the door knob to pupil-grime-up position, and pulled the door open a crack. A nebulous, resinish whiff of oiled wood floor seeped from the room, blending with a sharper, more pungent aroma of white paste. The blanket odor of school in session seemed layered, first the paste, then the oil, then the duller smell of twenty pupils, grades fifth through eighth.

"That's close," said Mister's voice, louder through the slightly open door. "But you've made an error. Let's find your error."

Sydney entered, limping deeply on his bad ankle.

"Oh!" said the front fifth grader, looking up from her book. Instantly every eye turned on Sydney. He stepped forward. And limped again.

Another "ohhh" escaped the class. Mister, in a white shirt and tie, leaped forward to help. He took Sydney's elbow. Sydney glanced at Mister's face. He expected to see a saggy teacher face, poised with authority. Instead he saw his own pain mirrored in Mister's eyes and a trembling lip.

"Now he cares," he thought. "Where the heck was he last night?"

He felt Mister lift him toward his seat. He felt Mister's closeness; he came even with Mister's face and saw his teacher's Adam's apple bobbing in a sea of wrinkles. Sydney shuddered inside. He twisted away and lapsed gratefully into his desk. He pulled his arithmetic book from his desk and held it up like a shield.

"A report," Mister said right through the book. "Sydney, give us a report of what happened last night. We've already talked about praying for LaMar."

"I get in a wreck and I have to give a report?" Sydney wondered, looking incredulously at Mister. "Will he grade me for this?" He began to rise but Mister waved him down again.

"You may give this report while seated," he said.

"If I can sit, that's not so bad," muttered Sydney.

He recounted for them what happened. He tried to avoid looking back at glassy holes in heads, hungry eyes, piercing eyes, besieging eyes; eyes willing to devour him. All stared. Some mouths hung open. Sydney finished his report, eyes asking for more. But Mister raised his hand like a policeman and stopped their staring. Mister told them to pray for LaMar and finish their arithmetic.

A silent study period followed in which Sydney stared at his book without seeing any numbers. When recess began, doors opened to the outside and the sharp odor of paste receded to the flow of fresh air. Two eighth-graders, cousins Melvin and Bleu, approached Sydney's desk. The stares changed to words.

" 'Lo, Speng," said Melvin. His face sprouted a few black whiskers above his mouth. "You are a lucky kid. You could of been awful dead, you know. My Dad said that car smashed the hayrack to match sticks."

"My Dad said blood spilled all over the highway," said Bleu.

Sydney swallowed. "Yeah," he replied. "I saw it."

"Did you see Mister?" said Bleu. "How upset? I swear he about bawled."

"He left early last night is why," snitched Sydney. "He is slower than coal tar going up a hill in January."

"He looked guilty," said Melvin.

"He looked guilty," repeated Bleu. Corners of his mouth curled around like the tail of a restless gopher snake.

"We don't mean to be rude," said Melvin. "But we think LaMar will probably die like that Diertmond kid from Lanark did."

"Naw," said Sydney. "He won't. He's getting better already."

Mister interrupted them. "Sydney, you may skip recess. But Melvin and Bleu, go ahead on outside and get some exercise."

When Mister turned away, corners of Bleu's mouth flickered up and down.

"Sure, you old potlicker," he said under his breath. They slowly walked away. Melvin looked back and he and Bleu laughed loudly. Sydney wished he'd heard what Melvin called Mister.

Recess dragged on, and when it ended, the rest of the afternoon crawled on, a throb a second.

"Bleuford," said Mister, "You're not participating."

"Lost my pencil," said Bleu, ignoring the long, newly sharpened one lying in the pencil slot on his desk.

"Here," said Mister. He handed Bleu a can filled with sharpened pencil stubs that he kept on his desk. Bleu took the tiniest, barely an inch long. He held it between his thumb and finger and made a game of trying to write with it.

"Melvin," said Mister. "You are not participating."

"Sprained my thumb," he said. "Milking my cow too hard, I guess."

The older boys ducked their heads to laugh. The girls looked at them trying to guess how that could be funny.

Sydney stared at a book without turning its pages. His thoughts turned inward and backward, around and around. Nothing in the school's words answered his inner questions. His questions kept tumbling forward, upside down, backwards, and forward again, as if following an infinity sign.

"That thought of the future – where did it come from?" he wondered. "Why did it come, anyway? Did having thoughts about the future mean I should try to change the future? Could I get my feelings to tell me more?

He wondered again. "Where did it come from? Did other people know? Maybe I am the only one on the planet earth who knows certain things certainly happen."

Just at that Moment, a pronouncement of everyone's favorite two words interrupted his thoughts: "You're excused."

35

Sydney paused, wondering how he would get all the way home on his sore ankle. He considered finding a stick to rest on, or an old cane somewhere in the attic for tomorrow. He remained sitting.

Across the aisle, he saw Onga. Everyone in school knew Onga's system. She heaped books into a stack on her desk, enough that if she added some mortar, she could build book wall. This is Onga's way of working against possibility of being held back: if she took all her books home each night, surely she would be ready for high school by next year. She carefully hoisted her books, wrapping her arms around the uneven stack. As she did, Melvin brushed by and caught her elbow with his own book, a book everyone knew would not be used at home. Melvin's single book clattered Onga's entire assortment to the floor, including her binder. The binder flew open and broadcast papers across oiled wood. Each paper that she scrambled to collect from the floor had only a single sentence, or a single math problem, written on it.

Melvin strode quickly on past until stopped by Mister's voice.

"Melvin!" said Mister. "A gentleman says he's sorry. A gentleman helps a lady pick up her books."

Melvin stopped. "A gentleman doesn't run off before quitting time," he said. "No gentlemen around here."

Bleu tittered.

"Help her with the books," ordered Mister, glaring ineffectively at Melvin, and reddening. His bright crimson almost reflected on the faces of nearby pupils, but Melvin enjoyed it. He picked up one book and set it on Onga's desk. Onga stopped collecting her mostly blank papers to smile up at him.

"Thank you very, very much," she said. She resumed picking up papers, smiling to herself.

Melvin glared at Mister.

Bleu chimed in, repeating, "No gentlemen around here." Lusty laughter came from the two as they left the room.

In the quiet that followed, Sydney's thoughts returned to his questions for which he knew no answers, questions that cycled continually through his mind. He didn't answer any of these questions, but pondered the feeling of how the troubling idea appeared and then vanished as mysteriously as it came, like a breeze.

This wasn't the first time, either. Once before, he saw the sad future. He'd walked with his new puppy, Prince, when an old cattle truck rumbled by, and just then he knew what would happen. He knew his dog would be run over. And it happened, just so according to mind pictures, just so the way he'd seen it. That numbed him for weeks afterward. He couldn't explain it. In his head, Sydney continued searching those mind pictures of his dog, over and over. But nothing changed, and he refused to have another dog.

"The feelings are always about bad things going to happen. The next time one of those bad feelings comes, I will test it to see if I can change the future," he reasoned. "That has to be why I can see the future, so I can change it. That is what the thought is for." Sydney's resolve grew as he watched pupils leaving the classroom.

"I bet I can do it."

Then he also thought: "If I had changed the future before, LaMar might be here now."

Sydney pulled his good leg beneath him and stood.

"Sydney, I'll drive you home tonight," said Mister firmly.

"You don't have to," said Sydney taking a faltering step. "I can walk."

"I'll be glad to." Mister used his school teacher voice. "I have to clean up a little here first."

His schoolteacher voice kept Sydney waiting. Other pupils dawdled at their desks.

Voyle, who sat in front, turned around quickly and, expressing his sincerity by imitating the grown-up voice and supposed thoughts of his father, said, "I hope your brother LaMar will be all right."

"Thanks, Voyle," said Sydney.

Voyle quickly left.

In front of him, Addie blew her inflamed nose and tucked away her wadded, soggy handkerchief.

"Bye Rudolph," said Sydney. "Don't join in any reindeer games."

She ignored the jab. "I'm so sorry for LaMar," she said. "I will be praying for him."

Sydney started to say more, but he could feel that she really did care, and something in her eyes looking at his eyes stopped him.

"See ya," he said.

She smiled shyly and pulled out her wadded handkerchief to wipe her nose again.

When Mister came to help him walk, Sydney slipped away and limped alone despite the sharp pain, carefully keeping ahead of Mister. Pupils from the younger classes stopped to watch. Mister's poised authority in a white-shirted, coat-and-tie pressed the pupils backwards.

"Look out here, look out," said Mister in his bass school teacher's voice.

Outside, Sydney, feeling captured, slowly descended the concrete steps beneath an awning suspended by chains. He walked beside Mister on the wide path toward the car. The ochre-bricked school's false pillars stood like bars across the front. Windows peered between bars solemn as convict countenances.

Sydney climbed into Mister's 1953 Studebaker as he would a paddy wagon. A new-car smell remained on the seats, even after four years. He looked out the windows at pupils staring from the school grounds, growing smaller as the paddy-baker glided away.

The Speng home, a large pink and yellow pioneer brick building, rose above a carpet of dead leaves. Stubs of weathered boards protruding through the bricks midway up showed its century-long wait to be finished.

When the car stopped, Mister remained at the wheel. Sydney hesitated. He knew Mister planned to say something he didn't want to hear.

"Now Syd," said Mister. "I want you to let me know when there is something your family really needs. I owe your Dad plenty, and this would be a good way to pay him back."

"We're fine," said Sydney. "We always provide for ourselves."

"You always have," said Mister. "But now we have a new set of circumstances."

Sydney didn't know how to answer that.

Mister insisted on taking Sydney's elbow and helping him as they crunched across the lawn through dead leaves. Sydney stopped at the door as a signal for Mister to leave. Instead, Mister pulled the kitchen door open, rattling its glass. Inside, mush dishes piled still unwashed in the sink. The mush kettle rested on the near edge of the table with a little mush still agglutinated to the cream-lined latticework of spoons on its bottom. Chairs of Sister Klaybill and Dad remained in situational confrontation. The broken wood peg had not been picked up. Sydney sat down in Dad's chair and Mister sat in Sister Klaybill's chair. Sydney didn't know what to say, so he tried to make a grown-up conversation.

"Mom is glad you gave LaMar a proper blessing," he said.

"Oh?" said Mister. "And why wouldn't he get a proper blessing?"

"I didn't mean that," said Sydney. "I just meant – well – Dad tried to give him a blessing, a sort of blessing. Not like other blessings. Dad didn't give a proper one. I know that."

Surprised, Mister leaned forward. He bumped the handle of the mush kettle and it bounced to the floor without losing any of its contents or spoons. A little cream dripped out. Mister jumped up and placed it carefully in the sink.

"Bartholomew, is that you?" called Mom's voice from the bedroom.

"It's me," said Sydney, planning his escape. Taking no chances of another mishap, he added, "Mister's here, too."

In a minute, Mom entered, with her hair down, her puffy face showed the effects of daytime sleep. Rounded features of her face with a slightly irregular nose indicated firmness of character without meanness.

"Hello, cousin," she said to Mister. He hugged her warmly. Then she came over and hugged Sydney, really hard. It almost felt good to him and melted away some of the rawness. He hugged her slightly back with one hand.

"I am so grateful you are safe. I thank the Lord that He watched out for you," she said like she gave her faith testimony in the kitchen. "I am so grateful you weren't hurt."

"Maybe I was," said Sydney, pulling away. "How would anyone know? I might be really badly hurt."

Mister and Mom laughed. Sydney scowled.

Mom turned to Mister. "You were so kind to come to the hospital last night. I took such comfort in your words that LaMar would live to be normal."

"Sydney here said Dallern tried to give him a blessing last night out on the highway," said Mister. "It wasn't a proper one, but that would account for the miracle that we had before he arrived at the hospital."

"Did he?" asked Mom. "I know he is an elder and holds the priesthood, but I find it very hard to believe that Dallern would ever try to give a blessing."

"Let Dallern change if he will," said Mister. "Maybe he is opening to change."

"Not the way he treated Sister Klaybill this morning," said Mom. "He did everything but kick her out of the house."

41

"She may have pushed him," said Mister. "Bless her sweet heart, she can be pushy."

He turned back to Mom. "If he opened the door once, perhaps he'll open it again." He turned to Sydney. "Now, what about this blessing? What exactly did he say?"

"I must have dreamed it," said Sydney. He stood and left them talking. As he limped heavily, he heard Mom's "Oh!" He faltered more to the living room, to the old mouse-colored –and infested – couch where he slid beneath a blanket covering its frequent holes. Mom and Mister followed him into the living room.

"Do you need to see a doctor?" she asked. "And tell us about this blessing."

"I just dreamed it," said Sydney, firmly. "I feel kind of sleepy. Maybe sleep will make my ankle better." He flipped the old blanket but it missed covering him up.

"I am so sorry I left early," said Mister. "I slipped so far behind on my math preparation…. Some people are talking again."

"They'll always talk," soothed Mom.

"What do they say?" asked Sydney, determined to change the subject. "About flunking kids?" He flipped the cover again and again it missed. Mister stood and lightly covered Sydney with the blanket. Sydney curled and re-adjusted the blanket. He lay his head down and Mister nodded to Mom and left the room. Sydney heard the glass in the kitchen door rattle and was soon asleep. He didn't wake until he dreamed of being back at the wreck. He dreamed Dad carried him to the barrow pit, to the timothy and rye grass alongside the highway. But when his thoughts realized wakefulness, it was Nat, not Dad, who carried him. Nat lowered him into the big overstuffed chair.

Nat, his older brother, was a senior in high school. His blond hair cropped short on top, combed long and back on the sides. Nat's high cheek bones sloped toward a sharp chin. He lived close to jokes, often finding one lurking nearby, waiting to be told or pulled. Funny bones made up Nat's skeleton, his fingers twitched in wait to tickle whatever younger brother or sister stood near. People who knew Nat could never figure out LaMar, who spoke only bluntly.

Dad talked: "Come in here, Bishop Lutty," he said. "Sit down on the couch."

Sydney blinked awake and straightened up in the chair. Someone returned the blanket to the couch and he grew cold. He bunched himself together for warmth, leaving his swollen ankle outward for everyone to see.

Bishop Lutty looked at Sydney's ankle. "Stay off it a few days," he said. "Ice it."

Following Bishop Lutty came Larkins Perkin, one of his counselors, Voyle's Dad.

"Wrap in it rag strips," said Larkins. "That's what we always do."

Bishop Lutty settled on the piano bench. Bishop Lutty had a square, even boney, jaw and deep-set and always serious gray eyes.

Larkins Perkin stood taller, balding. His prominent nose defined his face. He carried a battered, dark felt cowboy hat, nervously switching it from one hand to the other. He sat, sinking deeply into the couch.

Dad pulled up a chair with one peg back missing and straddled it from behind.

"Tough blow you've had," said Larkins. He plopped his hat over one knee.

Dad nodded.

"We feel like the Lord protected your boys," Larkins continued. "It could have been a lot worse. We saw your wagon."

"Busted to smithereens," said Dad. "I don't know how fast that guy drove. Maybe fifty miles an hour."

After a shaking his head, Larkins plopped his hat on the other knee. He looked at Bishop Lutty, who cleared his throat and lowered his chin.

"Dallern," said Bishop Lutty. "You've been a good neighbor. You've helped half the people in town at one time or another."

Dad looked at the floor. "Never done that much," he mumbled.

Bishop Lutty continued: "Your wife, Nelda, is always the first one there with food whenever anyone is sick." Bishop's face looked kindly, but he'd seated himself between Dad and the door on purpose. His legs bowed and his feet tucked like he would jump up if Dad tried to leave the room. Dad must have felt it, because his hands curled into fists around the thin parts of the chair. Sydney wondered how the back would stay on the chair if Dad busted another wooden peg from it.

"We'd like to repay some of your kindness and help you with the hospital bill."

Dad, half standing, loudly interrupted. "I won't take charity." His voice grew more intense. "We are not a needy family. I don't need help, not openly, not secretly, and not in some cantilevering, bushwhacking way, either."

"I won't go behind your back," said Bishop Lutty. "I respect you too much for that. Whatever we do, we'll come right to your face. What you say, we will do."

Dad's hands uncurled at little at that. He settled back on the chair.

"When are you going to get your wheat thrashed?" asked Larkins. "I hear the Klaybills are behind as usual."

"Soon," said Dad. "Half of it got thrashed out there on 89. But I've got my own crew together and we are ready to go." He turned toward Bishop Lutty. "I won't need your high priests, Bishop. Neeter and I and the other short priests will do the job."

"Short priests," said Bishop Lutty, laughing without humor. "That's a good one."

"Short priests," laughed Larkins. "Neeter is a short priest, all right."

"I'll move my herd into the big field, now that it's cleared," said Dad, making conversation. "That little pasture wouldn't hold them one more day. We'll move them before my breechy, lop-eared cow comes off the range. If she'd been in that little pasture, she'd have been through the fence a dozen times by now."

Larkins laughed again. "She don't like fences. Some people are like that."

Dad looked at him.

Larkins quickly looked down at his hat without speaking.

Bishop Lutty made one last effort. "The church farm is looking for some help for a week or two. Would you be interested?"

"Too much going on at my place," said Dad. "Thanks, anyway." He stood. "My kids are doing fine. Madge is just like her Mom. Nat can milk cows, whenever he's not out blowing his trumpet. Sydney here, he isn't completely worthless, skinny as he is."

"Sydney helped Brid Neeter a bunch last night," said Larkins. "He'll grow up to be a bishop someday."

"I think Arsle should be the bishop," said Sydney. "Why don't they ever make him a bishop?"

Bishop Lutty jerked a little. Larkins shook his head and Dad laughed.

"Why not?" asked Sydney. "He knows everybody."

"He'll have to start coming out a little more," said Larkins.

"It's a great idea," said Bishop Lutty. "I'll suggest it to him. Maybe he'll start working on it. I'd love to see him working on being a bishop."

"I thought everybody came to church," said Sydney. "But I'll never be bishop. I'd rather be constable."

"So would I," said Larkins, "but they didn't ask me."

"Thank you for coming," said Dad, still standing. Bishop Lutty arose reluctantly and Larkins almost jumped to his feet. They made a point of shaking hands with Sydney and mussing his hair and clapping him on the back.

Dad walked them to the door and stood waiting for the sounds of a pickup starting and pulling away.

"Twice the same day," he thundered. He stormed up and down the kitchen and living room. All the children were quiet. "Who do they think we are, boxcar tramps?"

"It wouldn't hurt you to be a little more polite," said Mom.

"Why can't they just let us alone?" asked Dad. "They'll be back. They never let this thing go. They have too much pride in helping the needy." He strode into the kitchen.

"Why don't you just let them help us a little?" asked Mom. "That is what the gospel is about – loving and helping each other."

"I won't be helped," barked Dad. "That is all there is to it. Neither you nor anyone else will change my mind. Now I don't want to hear another word about that from anyone in this family in this house."

He strode to the living room. "If I pay off the hospital, that will get rid of them," he said. "If I can pay off the hospital." He thought for a Moment. "Doc Mooley said he would take his payment in beef. I am going to give him beef. I am going to give him your beef. That will clear him up."

"Beef is beef," said Mom. "Beef we can do without. But what about the farm, the land? You know how far behind we are with them."

Dad didn't answer, but strode into the kitchen and studied the stove.

"We don't need their help," he repeated. He smacked an open palm with a closed fist. "Next thing you know, they'll be bringing over boxes of second-hand shoes."

"Some of the kids could use some shoes," said Mom.

47

"Hummph!" said Dad. "The Federal Land Bank will wait another year when they hear we've had a wreck."

"Don't you dare," said Mom. "We're already in big trouble. They are threatening us."

"We've had an accident," barked Dad. "I got to do what I got to do. And what's got to be done ought to be done quick."

"Don't you dare," said Mom.

Chapter 5

"Little lamb, who made thee?" swirled cursive chalk letters propelled across the board by the slim fingers of the young substitute. Mrs. Clonerson's younger sister, Miss Ingrid, taught during Mister's doctor appointment.

"Think of the imagery here," she said. "Now contrast it with this," she swirled in chalk,
> *"Tyger, Tyger, burning bright*
> *"In the forests of the night."*

"Can't you just see them in your eye of the mind? Can't you just picture them?" Miss Ingrid emphasized her point with her open, gesturing hands.

"I can see the tiger taking care of that lamb in one bite. In the night," said Melvin, laughing at his own humor. When the young substitute looked at him, he asked, "Is there a verse about the tiger taking care of that lamb in one bite?"

"Different poems," she said. "Sorry."

"Some poet he is," said Melvin, scratching the few black whiskers above his lip.

Bleu worked on a spit wad, chewing and packing and shaping. His mouth curled as he worked. His patience with poems and chalk and lambs and schools at an end, he hurled with it all his frustration at Sydney. An "Oooh!" escaped the sixth-grade girls as it landed a woody clack on Sydney's collar. Miss Ingrid pivoted back to the class in time see Sydney return the missile at Melvin, who with one hand deflected it, bouncing to the floor where it rolled to a stop at her slender ankles.

"Well!" she said. "Well! I see who doesn't care for poetry!"

Later that afternoon, when Mister came back into the class, he read the names slowly.

"Sydney."

"Bleuford."

"Melvin."

"Beautiful handwriting," he said. He turned to where the three sat studying only the floor. "I don't ever want you to throw spit wads again. It is entirely ungentlemanly. You disrespect to your teacher."

No one said a word. "William Blake is a fine poet," continued Mister. "You will stay tonight and copy one of his poems."

All three of them chose the tiger poem. Melvin volunteered to add a verse about it getting the lamb, but Mister declined his generosity. Later, they filed quickly out.

"Old Potlicker thinks he is so good," said Melvin, walking eagerly toward home. "I am so sick of him."

"This whole town is sick of him," said Bleu. "Except for Sydney here, who loves him."

"He's my dad's partner, not mine," said Sydney angrily. "He's my Mom's cousin."

"Everybody in this town is somebody's cousin," said Bleu.

"He left us early, before the wreck," repeated Sydney.

"This whole school is a wreck," said Melvin, reaching the schoolyard gate. "It needs to be closed. That's what my dad says."

"Just because I don't do math well, he thinks I am stupid," said Bleu.

"Math isn't that hard," said Sydney. They walked rapidly down the sidewalk. "You just have to think about it."

"Huh! You've never flunked," said Melvin. "You don't know what it is like to come home after the last day of school and your dad is waiting for you, excited to hear how you did, and you have to tell him that you have to take the eighth grade over again because you are too dumb to pass."

They walked in silence.

"My dad almost cried," said Bleu. "I disappointed him so bad."

"Don't worry," said Sydney. "You will be in high school next year, for sure."

"Just so you are on our side against Mister," said Melvin.

"Sure," said Sydney. "He's my mom's cousin, not my friend."

"Don't you forget it," said Melvin.

"I won't," said Sydney. He turned on the sidewalk toward home, leaving the others and walking fast so Mister would not come along and give him a ride. At home, when he entered the kitchen, Mom waited.

"You're late," she said. Sydney hobbled across the kitchen using the backs of chairs for a cane. "It pains me," he murmured.

Mom ignored his ankle. "You're late," she repeated, waiting for an explanation.

"It pains me," said Sydney, sinking into a chair.

"Your ankle must be healing. It's been three weeks. Now tell me why you are so late getting home."

"It keeps on hurting," said Sydney. "Maybe I am not all right."

"Why are you late?" demanded Mom. She stopped her work at the stove and dried her hands on her apron. She faced Sydney.

Sydney didn't answer.

Mom stepped closer.

"Made me stay after," said Sydney in a low voice. "Somebody threw a spit wad at me," he muttered even quieter.

"If you threw a spit wad at the teacher, I will take a belt to you," said Mom in an angry voice.

"I didn't," said Sydney, shrinking back. She reached out and swatted Sydney hard across the cheek with the back of her hand.

"Any more of that and next time it will be a belt," she said. "Spengs do not misbehave in school."

Sydney ducked his head and rubbed his cheek. He turned and made his laborious way into the living room.

"LaMar is recovering faster than you are," said Mom. "He shows improvement every day."

"He's in the hospital. He has a doctor," said Sydney. "I never had a doctor. Maybe I am not all right. No doctor ever looked at it," he repeated.

"We'd better have Nat do the chores again," said Mom. "Nat!" she called. "Better feed the calves again."

Nat's voice came from the living room: "Already did. Now I am listening to the radio. 'Suspense' is on."

"Oh boy," said Sydney. "Suspense! I love Suspense." He stood and strode into the living room where Nat and Prielle were floor-flopped. Near them, from an oval-topped wooden radio crackled a metallic voice. Sydney plopped beside them. Nat peeped lazily with one eye. As the radio voice graveled the program's introduction through the ack-ack of static, Nat suddenly forgot the radio and jumped to his feet. He landed on Sydney and began tickling and shouting: "Phony! Phony baloney!"

Sydney pealed with laughter and tried to escape but Nat held him all the tighter.

"Phony!" yelled Nat. "He's phony – he didn't limp at all. He's been acting! His ankle is better. Confess," he yelled at Sydney. "Confession is good for the soul!" His fingers continued to assault Sydney's skinny ribs. Sydney roared and flipped around like a fish out of water. Mom stepped in to look and began laughing.

"Stop it," gasped Sydney. "Stop it."

"Say phony," ordered Nat.

"Phony," shouted Sydney. The tickling continued. "Phony baloney," yelled Sydney.

"Say 'Phony, phony baloney," ordered Nat as his fingers continued to dance on Sydney's ribs beneath his arms.

"Phony, phony baloney," shrieked Sydney. "Stop!"

Nat eased back. "Your ankle isn't hurt at all, you big phony baloney. What were you trying to pull?"

"You didn't want me to strain it, did you?" said Sydney.

Sydney hunkered closer to hear the metallic radio words. "But the best suspense is over," he said.

The next morning, only a pale gold disc of a sun peered through morning grayness, barely showing the high barn's gray walls that extended downward almost as a foundation of the sky. From the barn's side stretched out a log fence of a lighter color. Sydney crawled through the log fence, his breath billowing and sinking, disappearing slowly in the chilly air. On a near post, the calf bucket hung upended. Sydney lifted it sideways, trickling milky water down his arm to his elbow.

"Ick," he said, blotting the dribble with his shirt. "That's what happens when someone else does your work. They never get it right."

He splashed across the pungent, mucky corral. His boots sank to his ankles in places as he came to the stable where Dad milked. Deep cracks spiraled slightly across the wooden cheeks of the stable's logs. Inside, one large cat, with fleshly ornaments stringing the underside of her belly, lapped from a milk bowl. Her herd of summer kittens circled the bowl, vigorously lapping with her.

A row of tail-end first cows steamed in the wooden room. Sydney could hear the ping-pinging of milk squirting against a steel bucket. It gradually changed to chup-chupping of milk into milk as the bucket filled. Occasionally the chup-chupping stopped and a stream of white jetted out toward the shadows; the yellow cat reared expertly up and swiveled its pink mouth into the milk-stream.

"That Inca isn't giving half of what she should," Dad complained, stepping from behind that cow. He sloshed

most of his milk into Sydney's calf pail. "That's about all
she's good for – feeding the calves. Give her some oats
after you turn the others out."

"Yeah," said Sydney. "Then she'll give more."

"Doubt it," said Dad.

"She's our favorite," said Sydney. "Ummm. What
does Inca mean? I've always wondered."

"Dunno," said Dad. "Nat named the cows from his
school books. He named Aida, and Penelope the same way.
I named Meg and Jill and Betty Lou. I knew girls with
those names."

"I always wondered," said Sydney. "Were they really
ugly like Nat says?"

"Not that bad," said Dad.

Soon Dad sat back hunched against the steaming flank
of the next cow, Aida. Black hair covered Aida except for a
South-American-shaped patch of white across her
hindquarters. She kicked at Dad.

"Soooo, you old bird bait," he soothed. "What's gotten
into you? Ever since the accident, she won't hold still."

Sydney carried his milk to the calves. As he returned to
the stable, he heard Dad's voice almost crooning.

"Easy, t-bone, rib roast, sirloin. Easy, rump roast, pot
roast, hamburgerrrr." Sydney heard a clang, followed by
"Judas priest! I'd sell you for a steel penny right now!"

Sydney entered, scattering the cats again. "Thought I
heard something," he said.

"Your imagination, again," said Dad. Steady pulses of
milk sounded in the bucket. "I don't know why such good
givers always come in such grouchy packages," he crooned

to himself. "But honey comes from bees, so I guess that is how nature ordains things."

"Mr. Speng! Mr. Speng!" faltered a high-pitched voice from outside. "It's me – H. Beesley from the Federal Land Bank."

"What?" said Dad, abruptly stopping. "Well, come on in. There's no door to open."

"Mr. Speng," repeated the voice. "Uh… I can't. This is as far as I can get."

Sydney ran to the doorway. There, attired in spotless gray clung a man to the side of the milking barn. Over his shoulder hung a strap from which dangled a heavy, calf-hide brief case. His fingers wedged in the cracks of the logs. His feet jammed between logs into a crack that ended where he stood, clinging. His shiny boots held on about a foot above the sea of muck that covered the corral.

"Oh, oh," said Sydney. "Better come quick. It's some man. He's hanging on to the wall for dear life."

"What?" exclaimed Dad. He dodged a kick from Aida and came to the door carrying his nearly full bucket.

"What! Dad bellowed. "Was you getting ready to look for me on the roof?"

"I called," said a man with a tiny head and shrill voice. "But you were hollering at your kids."

"At my durn cow," said Dad. "I don't holler like that at my kids. Well – not that much. Only at Sydney here."

"Truth," said Sydney.

The man lifted one hand from the crack and wiggled his fingers. "I tried to call one of your neighbors on the telephone, but the lines are bad, and kept cutting out. So I drove over and I thought I would pick up your late payment. Get it squared away, you know. My supervisor is after me to get your place fixed, squared away, you know."

Dad stopped talking. He let the silence build. Then he spoke as a funeral speech, with an explanation to clear everything.

"We've had a farming wreck," he said softly. "I've got a kid in the hospital. Lost half my wheat out on 89."

"Oh, that's too bad," said Beesley, knuckles growing whiter, fingers still clinging. He looked down and squeezed tighter.

"We'll get by," said Dad, just as he said to the men on the night of the accident. "Somehow."

"No," said Beesley, seeing Dad didn't understand. "No, that's really bad because my supervisor wants me to foreclose on your place. We used your contingency clause two years ago. We went into the warning language last year. We can't wait forever. The government no longer supports small farms with a negative cash flow."

"We had an accident, insisted Dad. "But we are thrashing today. I will have a check for you next week. Might not be a full payment, though." Dad started swinging the milk bucket back and forth to emphasize his point. "We'll get by somehow."

"You have not paid a full payment for five years," said Beesley. He removed his other hand from the crack and wriggled his fingers. "We need you to catch up on your payments." He stopped to make an emphasis: "You are years in arrears."

He paused for a breath. "The government, frankly, is leaning on small, negative cash-flow farms."

His high-pitched voice became shrill: "I need a large payment. You are fast running out of time." Beesley looked down and shifted his feet slightly.

"We had an accident. An accident," Dad yelled loudly, as though Beesley couldn't hear. "We will have the calf money – though most of that has to go for bills. And we have the grain money – that's most of the profit – but we do have to pay the hospital now."

Beesley shifted the strap of his weighty calf-hair briefcase.

In an intense voice, he shrilled back: "Bring things current! We are ready to start foreclosure proceedings!"

Dad stood looking at him, and stopped swinging his milk bucket back and forth. When he didn't answer, Beesley began inching his way back. His fingers creeping, his toes groping. Sydney and Dad watched like they'd been quick-frozen solid.

Sydney couldn't exactly tell when it started, but a little spot of gloom started to swell out from Beesley's words. A speck, nothing in words, just a speck of fear. He couldn't put it in words, but it didn't go away. It just hung there, like a ghost that walked into a party and stood in the air, in the corner, by itself. He felt growing fear. He wanted to do something about it, but what? What did it mean? Something bad, that's for sure. The speck of fear flickered and hid and Sydney tried to forget it.

He watched as H. Beesley toed a log. His shiny boot slipped, etching a dark scar downward over the wooden cheek as he plunked into the muck. But his fingers held, stretching him out like a basketball player in mid-jump.

"Ukhh!" he said, looking at his shiny boots descending into greenish brownish cow manure. Spatters dotted his creased pants. "Eeeuukh!" He disgustedly looked down, then back at Dad and Sydney, blaming them entirely. They watched as he waded through the muck out of the corral.

"This is unnecessary!" he exploded.

"When you come to a corral, expect manure," replied Dad.

"They've got to get those telephones fixed," H. Beesley said without looking back. "And you need to clean things up."

Dad reached inside the stable and tossed Beesley an old gunny sack. "Now you know more about real farming than all the rest of them people in suits at your bank."

After cleaning, Beesley climbed into his Chevy and drove to the highway and sped away down the road.

Dad's expression remained unchanged. Even after Beesley had gone, Dad stood there, still holding the milk bucket, still looking down the highway, expression unchanged. Then, as from a bad dream, he awakened and hurried to finish milking Aida. As in a ritual, Aida clanged a hoof on the bucket.

"Judas Priest!" shouted Dad. "Judas Priest!"

Sydney unchained the cows – listening to the shiny, worn chains rattle against wood of the stalls – then Dad shouted, "Here they come!"

Sydney followed the last cow out and looked down highway 89 at a tractor pulling a thrashing machine into view.

"Whoa," he said. "Two hours early."

The thrashing machine, a truck-sized grasshopper of
green tin, inched along the highway. As it slowly
proceeded toward them, he could see the lettering on its
side: "Randall's Thrashing Co." Mafe's grain truck
followed. Next in the parade came Klaybill's pickup
hauling a load of men in the back, content to follow slowly.
At the far end, Brid Neeter's battered cattle truck swung
wide and billowed black smoke, roaring past the entire line.
The truck bounced into the pasture and parked near where
Dad and Nat pulled at a fence post to make way for the
wide threshing contraption. As Sydney drew near, Nat bent
over. Instantly a dried, brown cow pie sailed toward
Sydney. It crumbled upon impact. Sydney returned the
biggest chunk. Neeter arrived to help just as the cow pie
floated low over his low head. Neeter paid no attention to
it.

"No monkey business," bellowed Dad without looking
up.

Nat laughed.

"You get to stack the straw," Nat said to Sydney.

"How do you stack straw? asked Sydney.

"It's a joke," said Dad. "Straw doesn't stack. It's too
slippery."

"You ruined the joke," complained Nat. "Now I will
have to think of a new one."

"I am sure you will," said Dad.

The unhurried thrasher finally entered the yard and
crept toward them at a snail's pace. Nearby lay a tarp
heaped with wheat and straw from the wreck. Beyond them
rose the round stack of wheat bundles, the thresher's
destination. Neeter's dark eyes snapped, fierce as a

rooster's. His voice cracked often as he asked and answered his questions.

"Klaybills early for once? The end must be near."

"Yeah," said Nat. "The hind end."

"Would you look at that load of Klaybills," said Dad. "He's got every cousin in the family. Probably even Carn."

A cloud of raucous blackbirds flew over them, wheeling and crying. Nat looked up. "A flock of birds," he said. He looked at the corral: "A herd of cows," he said. He looked at the procession entering the yard. "A calamity of Klaybills."

"Knock it off," said Dad. "They're good people."

"A calamity of Klaybills," repeated Neeter. No hint of a smile crossed his weathered face.

The metallic grasshopper moved in a wide arc toward the grain stack. Soon the pickup pulled into the pasture, stopped, and out hopped Arsle on his good leg.

"Wonder if you can use an extra man," he called from the distance.

"Who's that?" asked Dad.

"Cornell, there," said Arsle. He waved to the pickup. No one moved. "Carn!" he yelled. "Get over here."

Carn slumped from the pickup and tripped over a piece of wood. He sauntered toward them, demolishing dried cowpies as he came.

"Want me to work for you, huh?" he asked loudly. "What do you pay for a day's wages?"

"Half a day," said Dad. He looked like someone reaching out to shake hands instead handed him a dead sucker fish.

"Put Carn in the grain truck," said Neeter quietly. "We'll see how long he lasts there."

"Okay," said Dad to Carn. "We'll see how you do. But we don't need anyone else. Send them on out to get your place ready."

"Thought so," said Arsle. He waved to the men in the pickup and it circled unhurriedly away. Arsle walked a little closer and stood talking to Dad and Neeter. Behind them, Rindell adjusted a long rubber belt that looped blackly between tractor and threshing machine. He worked half an hour perfecting his adjustments and greasing an infinity of Zerk fittings before engaging the thresher into a trial frenzy of whirling and shaking and chomping and roaring. Then Rindell stopped the grasshopper to make final adjustments.

"There's talk about your crash," said Arsle in the new stillness. "I suppose you've heard it?"

"What talk?" asked Dad.

"Talk that Mister could have helped by staying. Maybe prevented the whole thing."

"It is news to me," said Dad. "I sent him away. He didn't leave till I told him to go. He said there was talk, you know. He has to prepare, you know."

"Huh!" said Arsle. "I could have swore he left early. Anyway, some say he hurried too much to leave. His hurrying caused the whole thing."

"No," said Dad, firmly. "I never said any of that. In fact, he offered to drive us. He warned us not to drive home in the dark."

Neeter joined in. He sounded angry. "Mister caused the whole thing! You Klaybills are jawing again. It gets around town all wrong when you do that."

Arsle jerked slightly but didn't answer.

"You know what that will lead to," said Neeter.

As they climbed the stack, Arsle said, "There's plenty more to it."

"Whatever it is, it will be all around town as truth before the sun sets."

Their voices paused and bits of straw floated down. Sydney guessed Arsle chewed some wheat. A wad of spit flew off the stack. That would be the hulls.

Hidden from view of the men by the thresher, Nat ran around the pasture and gathered a stack of dried cow pies in his gloved hands.

When the thresher thundered again, shaking the ground, its roar drowning all conversation, Nat swiveled the chaff exhaust pipe toward the men on the stack.

As chaff and straw began to rain on the men, Dad yelled first.

"Hey! I said no monkey business!"

Nat fed the cow pies into the powerfully blowing air of the chaff pipe. Cow pies began pelting the three men.

"Hey!" yelled Arsle.

"Hey!" yelled Neeter.

Sydney saw the three hold their hands up to shield their faces.

"Hey!" they yelled unison. "Stop it!"

Nat quickly swiveled the chaff pipe back to its original position and climbed, laughing, into the grain truck's bed.

"Ruin my joke, will you," he said. Then he yelled, "I am waiting and waiting. "Will you three get to work!"

"We'll work you out," shouted Neeter. "Just wait."

"Okay," yelled Rindell, sounding harried. "We're starting!"

Immediately Dad and Neeter and Arsle hurled bundles down into the machine's hopper. Sydney watched as within seconds, hulled wheat kernels began streaming into the grain truck where Nat and Carn waited.

And at the end of the thrasher, pointed toward the barn, the long chaff spout flamed a stream of straw and chaff that gilded a spot on the ground. The spot gradually swelled in the center. It rose to a mound, then a pillar, then slid over and a new pillar started.

When the straw stack rose to about Sydney's head, the grasshopper's roaring stopped. Rindell's voice sounded tiny in the sudden tranquility.

"Catch up time," he said.

"They can't keep up," growled Neeter. "Of course not. We showed 'em."

Carn's voice piped up. "Send that kid over here. I dropped my shovel."

Neeter and Dad exploded in laughter. Arsle's face reddened.

"There's more is there?" asked Neeter. "Sounds to me like there is less."

"See!" said Arsle. "See what I mean!"

Sydney ran around the tin grasshopper and fetched up the scoop. He saw Nat's face glistening with sweat. A huge heap of wheat rose in the truck. Carn rested in the corner.

"Here, Carn," said Sydney, reaching up the long-handled scoop. "You can do it."

Carn shook his head. "I doubt it," he said.

From the other side of the thrasher, they heard Arsle. "What's more is this: Mister ruined Carn by flunking him so much. Every time Carn has problems, I think of Mister."

"Some people need more time to learn," said Neeter.

"Nonsense!" said Arsle. "Flunking is always wrong."

As angry voices shouted and the machine stood idle, Sydney raced to the house and rummaged through a pantry shelf where he brought a large plastic bag smelling of dampness to the truck, climbed in and filled the bag with wheat. He knotted its top and dropped it over the edge to one side.

"It's for LaMar," he explained to Nat's look. "I promised him. He's going to be all right."

Carn maneuvered his shovel in the pile.

Nat nodded as he dug at the pile of wheat.

"He likes to chew it and make wheat gum," said Sydney.

Nat nodded and savagely continued to lower his side of the pile.

"He likes a lot of it," said Sydney.

"I don't care if you take a whole gunny sack," said Nat, sweat beading on his forehead.

With his shovel half full, Carn pulled it back toward a corner. He pulled a few more shovelfuls then stopped. "This is too hard," he said. "I quit." He climbed over the truck's side.

"You can do it," protested Sydney.

"Yeah," said Nat. "Stay here. You don't want to get into trouble."

"It's too hard," said Carn, teetering over the truck bed. "So's I quit."

Sydney and Nat watched as Carn hefted himself laboriously over the side of the truck, lowering to the bed, toeing to the wheels, and dropping to the ground. He silently opened the truck door, mounted up and quietly pulled the door closed.

"Come on," said Nat to Sydney.

Sydney scaled the truck and hopped into the wheat. Nat took Carn's pile while Sydney grabbed the long-handled scoop and began shoving it into the pile, tilting the handle down, pulling it back and dumping it, then repeating. As they shoveled, the grasshopper roared to life; wheat again streamed from the spout. Its incessant dribble covered Sydney's feet to the knees. On and on flowed wheat. Sydney shoved and shoveled with the heavy scoop. Both shoveled more and wheat flowed yet. Nat jumped over and traded Sydney places and they shoveled desperately.

Behind them, the witch's golden cap of thrashed straw and chaff rose up and up until it touched the spout. Then it tipped over, spreading out as if melting gold, thickened at the bottom and rose up again. Sydney hardly noticed the grain in the truck rising higher and higher. He felt so exhausted it seemed like death would be a likely result and welcome change.

Sydney wanted a drink more than air. His armpits felt about to break off. Still flowed wheat, kernels of bulky water that stood in swells. Sydney jerked his feet up, surprised to stand over the top of the truck where paddled his shovel in a thick creek of grain.

The grain trickled to a stop. The grasshopper roaring ceased, but the ringing continued. Wheat trickled to a drip and Nat and Sydney collapsed, exhausted at the top of the full load, heads hanging and puffing.

"What's wrong now?" called Dad.

"Got a load," said Rindell.

"Mighty quick load," said Dad.

"It's a good, big load," said Arsle.

"Mighty quick load," repeated Dad. "The thrasher bin came empty, didn't it? I forgot to check."

"Did it come empty?" asked Neeter. "Course it did. No one gives away wheat."

"Who thrashed last?" called Dad to Rindell.

"Perkins," he shouted back. "So what?"

"I might have known," muttered Dad.

"Can you do anything about it now?" asked Neeter, grinning for the first time. "Not one thing."

"Just two boys kept up with the thrasher," said Rindell in the new silence.

"That's better," said Arsle, walking around to the truck and cleaning one ear of chaff with his forefinger. "Good for you, Carn," he said with sincerity and some affection.

Arsle looked into the truck and saw Sydney and Nat with faces sweating, breathing hard. His affection vanished.

"Carn!" he bellowed.

The cab door opened and a sluggish-faced Carn leaned out. "This work is too hard," he said. "So's I quit."

Arsle looked at Sydney and Nat, still gasping to catch their breath. He looked at Carn's sleepy expression. He looked back at Sydney sweating and Nat gasping. Thick veins popped out on his neck. His face compressed in anger. Carn yipped and hopped down from the truck.

"You goofus," yelled Arsle. He aimed a kick at Carn, first with his good leg while on his bad leg. Then with his bad leg while on his good leg. Carn cowered backwards against the truck. His mouth started to twitch. Arsle stopped hopping and unhooked his belt.

"Let him stack the straw," called Neeter, walking around to look. "He's too big to lick."

"In my house I decide who is too big," Arsle shouted.

"Carn's too big," repeated Neeter in a lower voice. "And this isn't your house."

Swinging his belt up and down, Arsle glared at him.

"I'll stack the straw," pleaded Carn.

"Jump up on top, then," Arsle ordered, pointing to the thrasher ladder. Dad brought a pitchfork from the fence and solemnly handed it to Carn. Carn took the pitchfork and jabbed it into the ground. He clambered up an iron ladder to the top of the thrashing machine.

"Stay in the walkway, in the center," yelled Rindell. "Don't bend the tin."

Below, the men gathered in a semi-circle. Sydney and Nat climbed to the ground.

"This is what I am talking about," shouted Arsle. "Mister flunked Carn so many times he's quit on life, he has. Carn's always in trouble, but it's Mister that's to blame."

"Why don't you go thrash Mister then?" asked Neeter. He grinned for only the second time. "He might probably whup you."

"Too many flunkings in this town," exclaimed Arsle. "We've a whole crop of boys ruined by Mister."

Carn reached the top, away from Arsle, and relaxed. His hurry ceased. He studied the heap of soft straw as the men talked. Dad handed up the pitchfork.

"Jump in," shouted Arsle, waving his fist.

"We've done well by our school," said Dad. "Don't know how much longer we will keep it open, anyway."

"We need to close the school so we won't waste another crop of boys," shouted Arsle, turning on Dad. "Including yours. Close it right down."

"Oh no!" said Neeter.

Dad shook his head. "That would be a mistake," he said. "This town needs the school."

"Do we want to keep the school open?" asked Neeter. "The school is our childhood; we built that school. We cried in first grade, we played recess, we learned the alphabet, we added numbers, we gave dandelions to our teachers, we had peanut busts, we wet our pants, broke bones on the tricky bars. Do we want to keep the school open? That old school is our childhood."

"It will close soon enough without any help from us," said Dad

Carn tossed the pitchfork into the straw stack. It landed at the base of the witch's cap and the peak shifted slightly. Carn bent at the knees. Then at the waist. He unbent and started to turn away. "I don't like being this high," he called.

"Then jump down!" shouted Arsle, trembling, veins on his neck standing out like small ropes.

Carn looked at Arsle. He looked back at the stack. He looked at Arsle again, then back at the stack. "Send that kid up here to jump with me," he said.

"I'm not that stupid," said Sydney, still sweating.

Neeter looked at him. "Will it hurt you to be a friend? Nope," he said quietly.

Sydney shrugged. Inside he thought this must be what that speck of fear meant. "It will be worth a jump in straw to get rid of it," he thought. He wearily climbed the green grasshopper's steel ladder to the top, feeling the sheet metal buckle slightly beneath his feet.

"Stay in the center, stay in the center," called Rindell. "Don't bend the tin."

Sydney felt himself breathing hard again as he stood next to Carn.

"You go first," said Carn.

Sydney shrugged. The fear hadn't jumped at him and tied him up; it just hung quietly below, radiating. He looked at the unstable peak and decided to jump away from that. He liked jumping on hay, anyway. This could be fun.

"Whoooeee!" he yelled, plunging down. But as he fell, the sense of being in the wreck returned with out-of-mind panic and for an instant, he felt terrified, curling into a pellet and landing as a cannonball in the mound of glitter. He bounced, and as he So's, slid down the fear vanished into itchy chaff collecting down his neck. The now-tall peak shuddered as he stepped out. Straw covered his clothes. He began brushing himself off. With each brush, the memory of fear dissolved.

"Maybe I am past all of that," he thought. Then he called to Carn, "Jump. It's a whole lot more fun than a licking."

He watched Carn, who bent at the waist and leaped, sticking one leg out in front, trying to reach the far bank of the straw stack. He plunged straight down into the soft straw near the straw peak. He sank to his shoulders. Floundering in the slippery bits, he grasped the handle of the pitchfork as a drowning man would a floating log. He pulled the pitchfork toward him pulling the peak of straw toward him. The peak toppled and began to slide. It reached Carn. It hesitated. It tilted. It collapsed over him. No one spoke but the straw stack, which yelled something unclear. Straw shook and slid. No Carn could be seen anywhere.

"There!" shouted Arsle. "There! That'll learn you!"

The straw stack's side heaved. It heaved again and this time belched out Carn, feathered with straw from head to foot.

"I'll tell Aunt Mona," he blubbered.

"Go to the house," said Dad. "Nelda will sweep you off."

"One of those straws went clear up my nose," blubbered Carn. He jammed the pitchfork into the ground. He spit and blew and brushed his face. He bent far over and brushed straw from the back of his neck. "I'll tell Aunt Mona," he bawled again. Then he stormed to the house, pulling at his nose, brushing his clothes, leaving a trail of straw.

"That'll learn you," yelled Arsle. "That will learn you to quit before the job's done!"

71

Dad plucked the pitchfork from its chaffy place and cleaned up the spot where the stack of bundles had stood. He tossed remnants on the straw stack, covering all evidence of Carn being swallowed by quickstraw.

"This school needs to close," said Arsle. "I'm going to see to it personally that the school closes down."

Chapter 6

Like a perfect beetle, of the type seen at these seasons
scuttling for deeper cover, bug-shaped but for a lack of
legs, the Speng's dark blue 1946 Plymouth buzzed along
the dark ribbon of Highway 89 northward through drab
countryside. Overhead, bright but impotent, the sun
splashed its light everywhere, shimmering across pastures
of dull grass. Despite its best efforts, the sun could muster
no warmth and its rays sheened on telltale signs of the
absence of its heat: frost crystals that glistened on the
undersides of lighted surfaces.

Where fall's shades of fire recently burned in vibrant
reds and vivid yellows upon trees leaves and foliage of
shrubs, light fell among only black-barked stems and twigs
now barren of adornment. Nature's transitional tone of tan
faded into steel gray as trees stood chilled in withered
nakedness, fully prepared and fully accepting the icy
whitery soon to fall.

Inside the Plymouth, art deco chrome reflected colors
of the Speng family. Loaded into the car and filling every
seat, they dressed opposite of the dullness outside. Dad
wore denims whitish of edge, and a red and blue plaid shirt.
A cowboy tie cinched tightly at his neck. Mom wore
Sunday gingham, also a plaid, of brown and darker brown,
colors of powder and liquid cocoa. She'd drawn her hair
tidily behind in a bun. Between them sat Prielle, scrubbed
and brushed, in linty yellow. Bartholomew reclined on
Mom's lap like a full-bellied puppy after feeding. He
clutched a taped-together box of Crayolas.

As the Plymouth hit a bump, Mom leaned forward. "Be careful how you sit, Bartholomew," she said. "I'm having another feeling."

Dad jerked forward. "A what?"

"What is the matter, Dallern?" asked Mom. "Are you all right?"

"What did you say?" he asked.

In the back seat, where she sat at the passenger window, dressed as for school, Madge perked up. "Did you say you are going to have another baby?" she asked.

"Just a feeling," said Mom.

"This car is full of her feelings," said Dad. "She delivered every one of them." He rubbed his hand over his head down the back of his neck. He leaned forward. He looked Mom over. He rubbed his neck again.

"A baby!" said Prielle, her eyes growing bigger.

"Another baby will be wonderful," said Madge, her voice without expression.

"Just a feeling," said Mom. "Let's not speak of it until we are certain."

"Mom's having a baby! Mom's having a baby!" chanted Prielle.

"We'll have to put another leaf in the table," said Dad, his voice without expression.

"Mom's having a baby!" chanted Prielle.

Sydney, seated in the badlands between Madge and Nat, piped up, "Prielle will have to sit in the back seat where we can tickle her." He carried a workbook butcher-taped up its spine. Out of sight, at his feet, rested the large plastic bag of soft, newly thrashed wheat.

"No," said Prielle. "I can sit by you, Mommy, can't I?"

"Everyone moves up a seat when a baby is born," said Mom. "It is all part of growing up. Soon you will be a young lady."

"Will I look like a lady?"

"Yes," said Mom. "That's also part of growing up."

"Will I have two tummies?"

Mom deftly changed the subject. "Let me tell you about threshing day. I heard a knock at the door. I opened the back door, and there stood a scarecrow, a strawman. Carn, the strawcrow, stood there, covered in straw head to foot."

"He scares me," said Madge.

"He kept saying a straw stuck all the way up his nose." The family laughed.

"What did you do?" asked Prielle.

"I told him, 'Pull it out!' " said Mom.

"You pulled it out for him, didn't you, Mom," said Sydney.

"I helped a little with the tweezers, then he pulled it out," she replied. "He shuddered a full minute after."

The family laughed again.

"I hope you threw away the tweezers," said Nat.

"I washed them off."

"Throw them out," said Madge. "I will never use them again."

"The tweezers are clean," insisted Mom. "I washed them."

"I will throw them out," said Madge. "They have been in Carn's nose."

"We are not throwing away perfectly good tweezers," Mom said. She again changed the subject. "That put me quite out that Arsle could be so mean. Why didn't you stop him, Dallern?"

Dad, still back at the baby part of the conversation, worked at loosening his cowboy tie. "How long have you had this feeling?" he asked.

"A few weeks," she said. "Why didn't you stop him, Dallern?"

Dad fumbled again with the tightness of his tie.

"Why didn't you tell me?" he asked.

"Why didn't you stop him?" Mom asked, changing the subject again.

"He's got a mean streak, that old boy. I never saw him so mad. He didn't know whether to land a bad kick with his good leg, or a good kick with his bad leg. Either way, he'd a dumped flat."

Prielle laughed. She thought about it for a minute, finally understood and laughed again.

"I did speak to Mona about it," said Mom. "I imagine Carn also said plenty. She may send Carn to live with her brother in Utah."

"The renegade boxer?" asked Dad. "I hope he don't start on him next."

"Let's hope not," said Mom. "We're fast running out of uncles."

Dad slowed the Plymouth to negotiate a curve and then accelerated forward over low hills and concrete walled waterways. The beetle of a Plymouth motored past swamp shallows covered with cattails and wiregrass, now collapsed into a jumbled tangle of rust. Broad fields stretched beyond, bounded distantly by mountains on every side.

"Is LaMar going to die?" asked Prielle, suddenly interrupting the short silence.

"Of course not," said Mom. "You are saying your prayers, aren't you?"

"I say my prayers," said Prielle. "But what if he doesn't live anyway?"

"We have to believe that he'll live," said Madge. Her voice grew tight. "That's where faith comes in."

"That's right," said Mom. "That is where faith comes in. In that blessing, Mister promised LaMar would live, remember?"

"Sometimes things turn bad anyway," said Sydney. "Not always do things stay happy."

"What are you saying?" asked Nat. "Don't you think he is going to make it?"

"I hope so," said Sydney. "But calves sometimes don't make it. Kittens more often. Puppies, too. Once in a while, people, even when everyone loves them and prays for them. Sometimes things grow very sick, you know." He paused. "I have seen things die."

He swallowed hard. He'd waited a long time to say this, so he continued: "Sometimes I have bad feelings about a thing that is going to happen, like the wreck. It's like Prielle says; what if something happens and he doesn't make it, anyway?"

Madge burst into tears. "I'm sorry," she said. "I'm sorry. I can't help it." She sobbed, turning her head toward the window. "I'm afraid of the same thing."

"Now, now," said Mom. "We can be honest about how we feel, but we don't want LaMar to see us with cry faces.

77

"What's the matter?" said Prielle. She, too, slowly began to sob.

"He's going to make it," said Dad. "Doc Mooley will make sure of that."

"The doctors do their best, but it is up to the Lord to heal," said Mom. "This is a test of our faith. And whether we accept the Lord's will. Remember Mister's blessing that he would make it."

"Yes," said Madge.

Dad reached up and loosed his string tie until it hung out beneath his collar, catching on a button. "The doc is more dependable than faith. Seems to be rather picky where it works. Some places, sometimes, yes. Other places, other times, no. I'll stick with believing in the doc."

Mom looked sharply at him. He didn't notice. "Faith is the motor driving the universe," she said. "The sun is dependable, isn't it?"

"Yep," said Dad. "Doesn't need my faith to come up."

Nat spoke from the back seat. "I hear we are in for a hard winter this year. The spiders are heading for higher ground."

"Faith means believing the seeds you plant will sprout," said Mom. "You must nurture faith as you nurture plants."

"I don't have to believe anything," said Dad. "I plant. They grow. It is as simple as that."

"I hear they are buying a new school bus," said Madge. "A really long one. Why do you think they are getting a long one? The old one wasn't half full."

"They must have worked out a deal with another district," said Nat. "Buying in volume. A busload of buses."

Mom brushed back a loose wisp of hair and looked at Dad. "With your son in the hospital, alive only because of a miracle, I'd think you'd learn to exercise a little faith. You're not getting any younger. A man needs to make his peace with God."

"You sound like it is me that is going ..." Dad hesitated, "...to die." His voice grew a little huskier.

"No one is going to die," replied Mom. "Speaking of death, it wouldn't kill you to take a little help from the church."

Dad snapped back: "What does that have to do with death? I will provide for my family while there is an able bone in my body. I won't be obliged to them righteous souls. Not now, not ever."

"The new bus must have new snow tires," said Madge. "That will be good. The old bus always got stuck."

"Sydney," said Mom, "You need to pray with real intent. Your faith will increase as you exercise it."

"I'm just a kid," he answered. "I said my prayers and we wrecked."

"Prayer is more than just saying a string of words to yourself," said Mom.

Dad spoke up again. "You shouldn't talk about help in front of the children. You are not respecting your husband."

Before Mom could answer, Sydney leaned forward and poked Prielle. "You can't go see LaMar," he said. "That's because little kids are chock full of germs."

Prielle squealed. "Am not. Am not. Am I, Mommy?"

79

"Chock full," said Sydney.

Mom took a deep breath. She looked at Dad and then looked back over her shoulder to glare at Sydney. She bent to Prielle. "Hospitals have rules. You have to be twelve to visit. It's not because you have any more germs than Sydney."

"Speaking of germs," said Nat. "There's a big one in the back seat."

"Between us," said Madge. "We better squish it." They slid together and began tickling Sydney, who struggled to get free. He still held to the workbook.

"Ouch," he hollered, writhing in painful ecstasy, trying to brush away their hands with his workbook. "You're hurting my ankle."

The family grew silent as the old Plymouth motored forward over the narrow, empty highway. A few farm houses standing on knolls interrupted the marsh fields. At Montpelier, the largest town in the Idaho valley, the auto slowed to rattle over train rails and passed the train yard populated here and there by shabby, abandoned box cars. In town, a traffic light overhead blinked from green to red and Dad ignored it. Stores with large windows now lined the road. A handful of people walked sidewalks.

"Look at those bikes in Western Auto," said Sydney.

"See those windows," Prielle explained to Bartholomew. "Those aren't real people. Just big dolls."

Bartholomew's eyes grew wider and he flattened his face against the window. A few blocks later, the Plymouth veered to the right and parked at a new red brick building. Mom pointed out LaMar's room on the corner. Dad cinched his tie up like a clamp to hold his head on firmly while visiting strange places.

"No monkeying around in this building," he said, looking at Nat.

The family quickly exited the car and climbed the few steps. Sydney followed last, holding the workbook over the bag of wheat so Dad would not notice it. Inside the hospital, the lobby smelled of faintly of rubbing alcohol. Blue and white tiles checkered its floor. Near the end of the hallway, in a wheelchair decorated with paper pumpkins and ghosts – someone even put fake tinfoil cobwebs on the wheels – rested an unkempt, unmoving patient, bent over in lack of strength. Madge and the two youngest sat on a bench against the wall, never taking their eyes off the old man.

"This is worse than being in church," muttered Dad.

"Hospitals are nervous business," said Nat.

The children stared at the old, unmoving man. "Is he deaded?" asked Prielle.

"No," said Madge. "At least, I don't think so. Maybe they decorate Halloween to prepare for that coming event."

A door opened and a nurse stepped out. An apron girdled her white dress, bulging with a ball of teal-colored yarn and sprouting gold knitting needles. "That's Roscoe," she said, a practiced tour guide with nowhere to take people. "He's very old with no home."

"Hello, Venna," said Dad.

"Hello, Bloomington-ites," she said. "LaMar is so excited to see you." Salt and pepper hair wreathed her face. Her lips exaggerated her words, making the most of each by over-pronouncing it. As she arrived reluctantly at the end of a sentence, she added a few more words and waited impatiently for her turn to start again. "We're so glad to see you, so nice of you to come, to see the whole family, to see everyone. That's all he has talked about all week – your visit. He will be so delighted to see you, especially all of you, the whole family together." She smiled at everyone individually.

"Did they take the needles out of 'Mar's tummy yet?" asked Prielle.

"The needles? Oh, the stitches. Yes, honey, they took the stitches out last week – last Friday. His tummy is much better now – almost healed." She turned to Dad. "Doc Mooley thinks he might be out in a week – about a week or so."

"That is good news," said Dad.

"Don't forget the 'or so,' because it may be 'or so,' or even 'more so or so.' "

Venna walked to the desk and waved to Dad to come over. She began whispering, loudly, "You asked to see the bill." Sydney heard her say "Two hundred-eighty-five," probably over three hundred by the time he gets out. That doesn't count the doctor's fees – doctors have to be paid as well."

She whispered again, so low that only Sydney heard.

"Doc wants to talk to you privately about LaMar's condition," she whispered, looking intently at him. Dad looked intently back and nodded.

"It's hard," said Venna, returning to the original subject. "That's why Roscoe has given up trying to get better. Every day he tries to die – to roll on out. He sold his place to pay medical bills and now he has nowhere to go –

he lived alone, no family." She put one hand on her hip. "Not that he could go home anyway. He's just too old and weak, he's lost his independence, his freedom to live alone. I have to change him."

Sydney shuddered at the idea.

The family began walking away toward LaMar's room and she added: "I have to do everything for him. Absolutely everything." She acted like a carney watching her audience escape. "He's just too old and weak, and has lost his liberty, has nowhere to go."

Dad glanced between Venna and Roscoe. He looked like he wanted a bale of hay to stack or a cow to milk so he would know what to do.

"But you've got a place," said Venna louder but to their backs. Sydney wondered if she wanted them to take Roscoe home with them. He wasn't about to help change him.

"For now," interrupted Dad, muttering to himself. "But we've got a lot of fencing to do." The idea of fencing comforted him. He walked faster to LaMar's room and Nat walked with him. Sydney followed behind, lugging the bag of wheat, smelling hospital smell everywhere. He looked at the floor and wondered how many people died on this blue tile or that white tile. Their steps echoed as they entered a room.

Rubbing alcohol smelled stronger in this room. LaMar sat up in bed, his middle swathed in bandages. A sheet draped him. When he saw them, he grinned. His now-pale freckles almost leaped around on his face.

"Hi," he almost shouted, "Hi, everybody."

They swarmed to his bed. Nat rustled his hair and Dad patted his arm. Sydney shook hands with his big toe and waggled LaMar's foot over and over. He wanted to wrestle right there and lift LaMar around for an hour. But, of course, he couldn't. He put the bag of wheat on the corner of the bed, out of Dad's view.

"So, how you doing, old boy?" asked Nat.

"Fine," said LaMar. "Really fine. I'm ready to go home. Right now."

"You get to come home in a week," said Nat brightly.

LaMar's face flashed from joy to bleak. "A week!" he wailed. "A week? A whole week? A week here is like forever."

"We'll get you out as soon as we can," said Dad. "That's a promise."

LaMar's face brightened.

Talk floated among them about home and school, and LaMar leaned forward and began itching his middle.

"Venna! Venna!" he called. "I need my salve."

"We can get it," said Dad quickly, trying to save on hospital expenses. But her footsteps soon sounded and she entered and handed LaMar a nearly flattened tube of salve. She stayed in the room, beaming like a lamp post, waiting for a chance to begin speaking.

Nat slipped away without saying a word. Sydney watched him, knowing that Nat's silence meant he was up to something. Dad also watched him leave, also knowing he was up to something.

LaMar squeezed a little out salve and began applying it to his middle beneath the gauze.

"Does it hurt?" Sydney asked.

"Itches," said LaMar. "At first it felt like the wagon rested on it, but not anymore."

"What do you do all day?" asked Sydney.

"I don't have anything to do all day but Mister's lessons. I read my reader. And I listen to footsteps. Venna sounds like little hammers." He smiled at Venna. She smiled back and started to speak. LaMar interrupted: "Doc sounds like falling wooden pancakes. Here comes someone now. It is Mom and Madge."

Mom and Madge entered, depriving Venna of her next sentence. Madge carefully hugged him and then Mom hugged him again. As they did, a thumping came from the window.

"Look," cried Sydney. "The window!"

Through the window, Prielle's face flattened against the glass. Her hands cupped over her eyes and her small fingers waved and waved. Nat's big hands showed around her waist. LaMar waved back. Then Prielle began to sink and only her small, waving hand could be seen. Next Bartholomew sprouted into view. Hunched over with his hands binocularing his eyes, he looked sideways. Nat's hands rotated him toward the window. He peered into the window, at the directions of the voices calling to him. A delighted expression lit his face. He unhunched and waved. Everyone waved back. Then he, too, shrunk away.

"I saw Bartholomew, too," exclaimed LaMar. "I saw everybody."

"We'll get you home soon," said Dad. "When you get that gauze underwear off."

"I brought you a surprise," said Sydney. He opened the large plastic bag of wheat. He set it on the bed next to LaMar.

"Oh boy!" said LaMar. He opened it and took out a handful, scattering kernels on the sheets. He began chewing.

"Thunderation!" said Dad, looking hard at the bag. "So that's where the rest of my wheat went to. You're not leaving that whole bag here."

"Mmm," said LaMar. "Thank you, Sydney. Wheat gum. It tastes like the plastic bag."

"I guess we can spare that much," said Dad. "Bring home all you don't eat. That's good feed."

Doc Mooley's wooden pancake steps sounded in the hallway and he walked into the room. His Roman nose stood out like a handle on his red, round teacup of a face.

"The Speng babies," Doc Mooley boomed, looking around the room. He ran a critical eye over Sydney's skinny body, glanced at Nat and spent more time looking at Madge.

"Howdy," said Dad. "You've done a good job healing our boy."

"Few stitches and a brace. He's healing himself. But he's not out of the bushes yet. Another ten days or so. I will need to speak to you parents in private."

"Venna said a week."

"A week," boomed Doc Mooley into his imaginary megaphone. "She never lets me tell any news."

Madge left to take care of the children.

Dad sort of coughed and lowered his voice. "I'd appreciate it if you'd get him out as quick as you can. Those prices are a bit steep for us."

Doc shook his teacup of a face. He lowered his voice to speak confidentially, about normal volume for everyone else. "If we release him too soon, he might get an infection, maybe a staphylococcus infection, and he'll be right back in here. Those don't come cheap, staph infections don't."

Dad said he didn't want that, either. Doc reminded Dad that he'd take his fee in beef, like he'd said earlier.

"Good," said Dad. "We're doing a little fattening."

Doc rubbed his hands together.

"I didn't know we had a beef we're fattening up," chirped Sydney. It sounded odd to him, somehow.

"A couple more weeks," said Dad, who acted like he hadn't heard Sydney.

Doc beckoned Dad and Mom to follow him into another room.

LaMar began playing with an array of old medical instruments – kept in a worn bedpan. Cups, strange bent scissors, lots of long, stainless steel toothpicks and tweezer-looking things. He explained to Sydney that he made a barn that needed pitchforks. His fingers walked from barn to field harvesting wheat.

"But we never drive after dark," he said firmly.

Sydney slipped a hug with LaMar. LaMar still hugged good, and it lasted longer than it ever had. Sydney didn't mind. Just as Sydney pulled away, Venna returned. Her needles blurred, teal-colored yarn unwound from her pocket and made the knitted square more toward a slipper. She sat on the edge of the bed and looked at LaMar's stomach and hips. Her needles moved rapidly. Drawing more yarn from the ball bulging in her apron, her needles never stopped. Needles clicking as though she did her part by willing the knitting of LaMar's hip bones, leaving nothing to chance. She looked like she wanted to continue the tour. Sydney walked out and the needles continued to click softly but rapidly behind him.

As he passed, he heard Doc Mooley's voice. Sydney bent over a heat register on the floor of the hall to hear the voice more clearly. He bent further to listen more closely. He could almost hear, so he lay on the floor with his ear to the register.

"His intestine may be perforated," faintly boomed Doc Mooley's whispering voice. "He could be fine for a while, but it is an open invitation for infection. A hole in the gut is hard to heal. There are some infections we still can't stop, even with penicillin."

Dad said something Sydney couldn't hear, and Doc replied, "I'd hate to lose him after all this."

Mom said something Sydney couldn't hear, but it sounded like a prayer-and-faith tone.

"We have to keep a positive attitude," came Doc Mooley's voice. "The intestines are very subject to mood. Keeping the little guy happy is just as important as giving him shots."

Dad said so, and Sydney realized he'd felt something again, something he couldn't put his finger on – that old, odd sense of foreboding, a low sort of soft and sad message that spread across him as he lay on the floor. Fear clutched at his innards.

Suddenly Venna shrieked behind him:

"There's another one passed out on the floor! Someone call a doctor!"

Sydney whirled around to see who lay passed out on the floor. Venna looked at him, so he sprang to his feet just as Doc Mooley erupted from the private room.

"I tripped but I am all right," lied Sydney.

"Are you sure?" asked Venna. "You were very still."

"I'm fine," said Sydney. "I am mostly all better now."

"Could be a heart problem," said Venna. "Better check his heart."

"You're right," said Doc Mooley. He grabbed Sydney and held a stethoscope to his heart, listening here and there.

"Sorry," he said. "No beat. Guess this one doesn't have a heart."

He turned to Prielle, waiting the lobby. "Is this boy ever mean to you?"

Prielle nodded slowly. "He tickles me."

"That's because he doesn't have a heart." He turned to Sydney. "You better be nice to your sister so your heart will grow back."

"I do so have a heart," said Sydney. "I can feel it in there." He turned to walk, slowly puzzling over what his feeling was, and what it meant. He couldn't decipher it at all. Mom headed straight to the car to care for the children.

Dad stopped at the desk. He bent over and began writing. Sydney came closer and saw Dad scrawling in his check book. He meticulously tore a check from the pad and set it on the desk.

"That should take care of them for a while," he said. He held his head up high and sort of swaggered as he and Sydney walked to the car together. They climbed in and slammed the doors. Dad put the check book back in his pocket and carefully replaced the pen. He reached up and pulled his cowboy tie off. He backed out in a large circle and headed home. "LaMar will be good as new in a few days," said Dad. "I can feel it in my bones."

"You are putting away your checkbook," said Mom. "How much did you pay them?"

Dad didn't answer.

"We have a right to know," said Mom. "This isn't Russia, and you are not Nikita Khrushchev."

"Do we need any groceries?" Dad asked.

Mom shook her head. "What are we going to do about the farm?" she asked, on the verge of tears.

"I'll bring the calves in early," said Dad by way of answer to both questions. He paused as the car swung into Main Street. "May have to sell a couple of cows, though that may hurt us later," he said. "But we will pull out of this slump and things will be lots better next year."

"I've got a cow or two I'd like to donate," said Nat.

"Can't," said Dad. "Aida is the best giver in the herd. The other has the biggest calves. When you are a farmer, Nat, you will have to make decisions based on money, not on convenience."

"Never be a farmer," said Nat. "Never have so much as a chicken clucking on my place."

"Me neither," said Sydney. If one comes by, I'll have it for dinner. "Cluck, cluck, squa—awk!"

Dad steered with one arm and put the other across the seat toward Mom. She shifted away.

He began to sing without notes the familiar fantasy song of the farmer: "We'll get some new equipment after next year's harvest and maybe plow more ground into wheat. We could use a larger wheat check, you know. Might buy another pasture. If we could just figure out how to get another check, we might even grow prosperous."

"Straw dreams," said Mom, now shaking her head as she shook silently. "Always dreaming."

"LaMar looked really good," said Madge. "That is all that is important."

"He looked ready to come home," said Nat. Sydney didn't speak, nor did Bartholomew, who looked at Mom and also began crying, laying his head on her chest.

Before they reached their home, Mom mentioned that the mail hadn't been picked up for a few days and it might be handy to get it now.

"We could use a tank of gas," said Dad. He drove past the house and stopped next to the gas pump at the Bloomington small-town store.

"Fill 'er," he told Nat. Dad climbed out and went into the store. He came back carrying frozen milk nickels treats in one hand, and a wad of envelopes in the other. He checked the pump, and paid two dollars and four cents for gas. He handed the envelopes to Mom. He started the car and U-turned onto highway 89.

"From the Federal Land Bank," said Mom. She reached over to Dad's pocket and pulled out his pen to rip the end of the letter open.

Dad's hands tightened on the steering wheel.

"It's a foreclosure notice," said Mom. She read further. "They're giving us 30 days to come up with a plan to pay them."

"It's just a formality," said Dad. "We'll give them a plan. I'm sure they'll wait another year."

"Then they will take over our property and have a trustee sale," she said, gasping.

"It's a formality," said Dad. "This nation needs its farms."

"Thirty days is about Thanksgiving time," she whispered. Mom laid the rest of the letters on her lap unopened.

"It's just a formality," repeated Dad. "This nation needs its farms. They'll wait. They always have. The important thing is that LaMar is getting better." He looked over at Mom. "Eat your ice cream before it melts."

"I 'spose it is too late to take it back," said Mom, looking suspiciously at the paper covering the treat.

"Enjoy your ice cream," said Dad. "We may not have it again for some time."

Chapter 7

One ear up, the other drooping helplessly and matted with burrs, the Hereford cow backed into the slab fence of the village corral. More mountain burrs entangled her belly and legs. Mud stained her feet to the hocks. The cow, called Lopp, swung her head slightly as she lowered it to charge. She looked with suspicious, untamed eyes.

Lopp's calf, tall as other two-year-olds, cowered behind her, wild as an antelope. This pair came last from the summer mountain range.

"Stupid, stupid, stupid," said Sydney, looking between poles at the unruly creatures.

Neeter sagged on the pole gate, worn out from range riding, searching for the last of the town's cattle. His two horses idled nearby. One, a bay mare named Donna, rested after galloping madly over the mountains and through brush for these stragglers. His second horse pawed at the corral floor in badly controlled energy. This, his cutting horse, a magnificent palomino stallion aptly named Blade, knew arenas rather than mountains, famous in these parts as a rodeo competition champion.

"Dad is in a hurry to get these calves sold," Sydney said climbing over the pole gate into the corral. "Come on, Lopp," he bellowed, flailing his arms at her. She lowered her head and bounded past him, as if he were suddenly a cougar or brown bear. Her tall calf jumped after her. Cow and calf milled into the cluster of burgundy Herefords that next broke into a hard trot along the slab fence, circling the corral.

The range rider looked narrowly at the cow as Sydney yelled again.

"Come on, Lopp!"

Cow and calf galloped to the rear and swung around to eye Sydney.

"Obstinate old cuss?" Neeter shouted from his seat on the pole fence. "Wildest, most hog-headed on the whole range. Nothing but trouble all the day long."

"I can get her," said Sydney. He plunged into the herd again, stampeding the entire pack to the opposite side.

"Were they easy to bring down?" asked Neeter. "Up one hill and down the other. Wore me out."

"I can get her," said Sydney. "If you will just open the gate."

Sydney walked again toward the herd. Neeter interrupted, "Who's got the gate?" he suddenly shouted. "You do." He jumped angrily from the fence, dashing toward his tawny, brawny palomino. To elevate from his low vantage point, he grabbed the saddle by the horn, wormed aloft to the stirrup and swung on. His eyes flashed as the horse lunged into the herd.

"Open the gate, Nat!" shouted Neeter. Around him, cattle scattered.

Sydney slid open the gate latch and cattle moved toward the opening. Sydney waved them off and stepped back. Instantly Neeter's palomino slashed into the herd at the errant cow. With his muscular chest, the palomino bashed her against the fence. The horse backed off. The cow swung her head. Blade bashed her again, then pressed

her out of the gate. Her calf dashed helplessly back and
forth. Then it jumped frantically after her. Sydney followed
the pair until Neeter called him back.

"Can you take her on foot?" he asked. "Not unless you
butcher her and take her roast by roast."

"I think I can get her," said Sydney, certain he could
not.

"Nat," said Neeter. "Get on my mare. She'll take her
out. She's no cutter, and she's tired, but you can make it if
you hang on for dear life."

Sydney walked warily past the palomino. Its coat
darkened with sweat around the saddle. Its tousled mane
lay in white, contrasting with the deep yellow. Its eyes
surveyed the cattle as it pranced in place. Sydney glanced
again at Neeter. Neeter nodded. "Do I want to leave this
gate? Not a chance. Took me half an hour to get them all in
here, thanks to that wild goat-cow of yours."

Sydney reached the saddled mare with its rear leg
lifted in weary repose.

"Easy lady, easy." He touched the horse's neck. The
horse jerked suddenly back, flaring its nostrils, jumping,
jerking, stretching its reins.

"Just keep going," said Neeter.

"Easy," said Sydney, patting and stroking the horse's
bay neck. "Easy there, easy."

The horse took two short jumps. It stood and lowered
its head. Sydney held its reins, grasped the saddle canter.
With great effort he lifted himself but missed inserting his
foot into the short stirrup and fell back.

"I forgot to ask," said Neeter. "You do ride?"

"Sure," said Sydney, hopping off balance as the horse backed up. "Sorta. But usually not with a saddle. We don't have a good one."

"Give me a leg," said Neeter. "You need to learn saddles."

Sydney lifted up his foot and Neeter hefted him, by his extended foot, to the horse's back.

"Watch which way she's going to jump, then move with her," continued Neeter. "Give'r her head. She knows what to do. Hang on."

Sydney nodded. His stomach felt numb and the bottom of the earth seemed to drop farther down.

"You'd better knot the reins," said Neeter. "Just in case."

Fright from every bad experience he'd ever had laced his awareness. Fear from intuitions exploded within. "This is the scariest thing I have ever done," he said to himself. He remembered the wreck, and added to himself, "At least, on purpose." He clumsily tied the reins together. Only Neeter watched, but it felt to Sydney the whole earth inspected every detail as the quick mare stepped beneath him and began walking. Neeter nodded with just a hint of a smile.

"If you stay close, will you have any trouble?" asked Neeter. "Naw. Just don't fall off. Whatever you do, don't fall off."

Sydney guided the horse out of the corral and along the back street toward the lop-eared cow and calf, now nibbling at a stand of oat grass.

"Come on," encouraged Sydney in his friendliest voice. He pointed the mare toward the cow. Old Lopp

swung her head as to try this horse yet again. The mare
jumped at her, almost tossing Sydney backwards. The cow
dropped her head in submission, bad ear dangling
helplessly. Followed by her large calf, the cow walked
toward the field, beaten and out-muscled. Once along the
highway, she turned her head toward the Speng field and
began to trot. Her calf trotted behind her.

Neeter's mare stayed right at the cow's hindquarters as
they jounced along highway 89 toward the same field
cleared of wheat bundles just weeks ago. The Speng's
modest herd of red cattle dotted the field like spilled red
checkers. Heads down grazing, none of them moved. Half-
grown calves roamed among the cows, eating a bite of
grass here and there. Sometimes one of them would
suddenly plunge its nose beneath a cow and begin sucking.
Sometimes the cow stood still for a Moment, but more
often it walked away, leaving the calf standing with its
head pointed out with nothing to suck.

As they approached a lane flowing with sawdust, the
cow jerked her head up.

"Heeeyah!" shouted Sydney.

In response, the cow began to gallop, followed by its
calf. Its half-dry udder began swinging back and forth and
it leaped through a slow-moving, moss-filled creek. The
mare splashed in pursuit with Sydney clenching his knees
on the mare's crusty, sweat-dried back. They arrived at the
Speng gate to the Speng's field. He pulled the horse up at
the gate. As the horse stopped, Old Lopp and her calf
obstinately continued trotting.

"I am a little afraid about this," he said to the horse.
Without dismounting, he unlooped the stick lever, dropping

the wire gate that fell heavily open. Sydney considered tying the horse to the fence and chasing the cow on foot. But cow and calf were now well along the road. He fearfully turned the horse toward the fleeing red hides.

Without any prodding, Neeter's mare rocketed forward, leaping from standstill into a full gallop, its legs tattooing the earthen path. Sydney's confidence grew as he held his place with knees tightly clenched. But he had never ridden this fast before. Wind blew in his face and the ground blurred beneath him. He could feel the grit of tiny bugs peppering his face. Gravel flew from the hooves of the mare. As the pounding horse drew even with the cattle, the runaways stopped, beaten again. They whirled and trotted obediently toward the gate. The mare wheeled exactly where they stopped and slowed instantly to a walk behind them. Sydney felt the horse stop, turn and move in the opposite direction.

But the one short motion also plucked the horse neatly from beneath him. Sydney flew on, riding only the air, his senses in panic in this second wreck. Everything flooded back in this tiny instant, including the sense of almost dying, of upcoming pain and the broad thud of impending disaster. His return to earth jerked him to a stop. He landed sprawling in the grass on his hip and side. Still lying numbly in shock on his side, he wondered how bad was his injury this time. He wondered if he would ever walk again. Shocked, frightened, he watched the riderless mare dutifully drive Old Lopp and her calf back to the gate, her head jerking up and down. He watched the pony stop, stand still, head held up by the reins still knotted at the neck. The mare stood still only for a minute, then again began jerking her head up and down. Sydney writhed in emotional shock, being in the same wreck a second time. The mare continued to jerk her head, so he struggled through his trauma and, pain throbbing from his leg to his shoulder, painfully stood.

"Someday," he said aloud to steady himself, "I am going to learn how to stop being stupid."

Limping toward the mare, he yelled: "Whoa, there. Whoa, whoa." He paid no attention to Old Lopp, who with her big calf, settled down to snuff and then nibble on meadow grass.

Sydney limped to the mare, caught her reins, and carefully closed the gate. He untied the reins. Instead of climbing on, he looked at her stamping hooves, swishing tail, and tossing head. Fear saturated his thoughts; the memory of rushing through grit and bugs and flailing out of control in the air became so powerful that he could not climb on. He hurriedly walked past where the wreck happened, and where a deep rut yet cut into the flank of the highway.

The wreck and falling to the highway happened again in his head made him feel the exact same jolting of his body and mind. In trauma, he led the mare while walking laboriously, his side hammering sharply with each step. He looked back and forth to see if anyone saw him limping. He knew what they would think: leading a horse meant injury, either to him or the horse. He continued past the wreck site overwhelmed by fear that lessened only by looking directly toward town. Step by step reduced his fear and he realized that he'd seen no picture of this accident, or felt any hint of seeing it before, or sensed any access to the future.

"I am just scared," he admitted to himself.

Understanding that did not help. His memory of flying through the air, of the jarring earth coming up to smash into him remained in his eyes and side and hips.

Sydney glanced back at the field and noticed Old Lopp circling the fence line. Some other cattle stopped eating and followed her.

"You magpie bait," angrily shouted Sydney from the highway. The cow looked at him. She turned back to the field and renewed her grazing.

With juddering steps on the asphalt, feeling cool air in the utter quietness, he decided not to ride horses any more. The more he considered it, the more he didn't plan on ever mounting back on another horse. Lots of people didn't ride. He would be one of them; he didn't have to ride, either.

Pain in his hip and side palpitated step by step.

"Hey Speng, why don't you climb on?" yelled a voice from a passing car. Bleu's unruly hair tousled wildly in the wind as the car passed.

"He saw me, too scared to get on," thought Sydney waving. "I will hear about that for the rest of my life."

No other car approached. Alone on the highway, he took step after step, careful to avoid Donna's hooves. He became aware of the constant, perfectly equal pressure of the wind against him. He felt its swirl and thought about wind and time. He could feel tiny billows of air in the palms of his hands and he opened his fingers to more full sense the wind's edges. He felts its eddies and vortexes and wondered if any of the air stayed, or if a wind meant it all had to move forward. Where did it go? Did air move across the ocean? Or does it stay in the valley and merely shift from here to there? He remained still and from nowhere

into somewhere, his familiar disquiet returned. It grew
stronger in the steady breeze and ripped a small hole in the
very Moment of the present, opening a hollow so that he
could just peek through at the future and see an odd, flitting
image glance across his mind, like a blowing leaf. He
didn't have to pay attention to it, so he didn't. He didn't
want to pay attention to it either, it being so commonplace
and ordinary that he let it fly past and disappear, like a leaf
pitching and tumbling in the wind. The image he glimpsed
for an instant showed a Holstein, butchered and hanging by
her hind quarters, half skinned.

"We aren't going to butcher a milk cow," he thought.
"I wonder why I thought that?"

He quickly dismissed it.

Half an hour later, after leading the mare along the
highway and then back streets, he arrived at Neeter's barn
and pasture. He walked behind the horse, pretending he'd
just dismounted, and started to pull down the saddle.

"Hold it," yelled Neeter's voice from the barn. "Don't
put her with the stud. She's already with colt."

Sydney replaced the bridle over the mare's ears and led
her to the corral. Neeter walked out from the barn.

"Give you any trouble?" he asked. "She's well-trained
but very quick."

"Very quick," said Sydney. "Thanks for letting me
take her."

"Turns real sharp? She does."

"Real sharp," said Sydney.

"Didn't dump you off, did she?" This time Neeter
waited for Sydney to answer.

"Naw," said Sydney. "Not really."

Sydney felt Neeter studying his face. "Didn't scare you to get back on, did she?" Neeter asked.

"Naw. Not sort of," said Sydney. He looked at Neeter with meek eyes and ducked head.

Neeter looked hard back at Sydney. Sydney looked down. He turned away to walk home.

"Every cowboy falls off. The better they are, the oftener they tumble. At first. But a true cowboy gets right back on."

"He does?" asked Sydney. "I guess he does. Never was a cowboy, myself."

Neeter talked more about something else.

"Now if you get a chance, you talk your Pappy to take help from the bishop. I done it once, a long time ago, when I was out of work. No one ever knew. Helped me feed my kids one winter, before they all went off to college. Will you do that?" he asked.

Sydney looked at him.

"Will you?" asked Neeter. When Neeter didn't answer, Sydney replied, "I can try, but I doubt he will take anything."

"Just try, but not till the time is right," said Neeter.

Sydney nodded and walked tiredly home in the dimming day. Lights on the porch awaited his return. Glass in the kitchen door rattled and he saw the family sitting around the table. Dad angrily stood up.

"Where the thunder you been?" he demanded. "Why're you so late?"

"Lopp came down from the mountain, so I took her to the field," said Sydney simply, finding his place at the table without washing his hands.

"You're kidding," said Dad, his anger changing to instant disbelief. "Lopp? By yourself?"

"Neeter asked me to," said Sydney. "He was too tired, after chasing her all over the mountains." Sydney reached for the bowl of mashed potatoes. "He let me ride his mare."

"Old Lopp is in the field?" repeated Dad. "With her calf? How does the calf look?"

"Big," said Sydney. "Why didn't you save me some gravy?"

Dad took the gravy spoon and scooped brown sauce from his potatoes and reached across the table and dripped it across Sydney's potatoes.

"Anybody who can handle Old Lopp deserves gravy," Nat intervened. "May the next gravy come from Old Lopp herself." He shared from his amply flooded plate a spoonful of gravy with Sydney.

"Thanks," said Sydney. "You didn't touch this with your mouth, did you?"

"I usually taste my food in my mouth once or twice before I put it in my mouth for the final time," said Nat, speaking matter-of-factly.

"Take it back," ordered Sydney.

"I didn't touch it," said Nat. "What do you take me for, a mother bird?" He looked at Sydney with his mouth open.

"Much worse," said Sydney. "The perfect opposite: A brother bird. Brother birds always have empty mouths, wide open."

Nat snapped his mouth shut.

Within two days, Dad and Neeter had the entire herd in the corral at home. Their idea was to move payday closer, catch the market before fall prices fell. And, for the cowboy in them, separating calves from their mothers was payday, an annual rodeo they both starred in.

"Let's cut the calves away right now," shouted Dad from the other side of the corral.

"I've got some time," replied Neeter, looking over the herd of Speng cows and calves they'd brought from the field. The Herefords crowded the corral with their auburn bodies, filling the air with bellowing.

Parked at the loading chute, Neeter's rack door hefted up like a guillotine. Neeter sat on the back of Blade; the tall and muscular horseback presence replacing his slight physical presence on ground.

Dad moved to the calf pen as Blade lunged into the herd. Neeter's supple body foresaw each turn and halt, flowing with the animal as single unit of horseflesh, never losing his seat or his calm, determined expression, calf after calf. All but one of the big calves was cut into the pen.

"This is almost over," Sydney thought.

"Nat," Neeter said. "I'm bushed. You get the last one."

Sydney stood frozen. He looked at the panting, eager horse and felt his chest flooding with the anguish of falling. He looked at the mealy, powdery surface of the corral. He looked at the herd and saw Lopp's big summer calf. The most obstinate in the herd, like its mother. He looked helplessly at Neeter.

"Go on," said Neeter. "Remember what I told you – think about what the horse is going to do, watch its head, move as it does." Neeter jumped from the horse's back and climbed to the pole fence to watch. Dad hitched the cutting gate a little tighter; he didn't expect to open it soon.

"I don't know if I can," said Sydney, looking at the palomino standing with reins down. "I might not be able to do it."

"Can you?" asked Neeter. "Only one way to know."

Sydney turned to Dad. "Thought you were going to sell Old Lopp."

"Changed my mind," said Dad. "Look how big that calf is."

"Get on," said Neeter. "No more excuses. If you don't get on now, you may never ride again."

Sydney nodded without moving. He looked around the corral for another excuse. He didn't see one. Dad and Neeter waited. Sydney knew they'd talked about him. He stood still.

"I can't," he said with a dry mouth. "I am sorry, but I just can't."

The palomino looked as tall as the barn. It tossed its head up and down, snorted and reared its front legs off the ground. Then flaring and blowing through its nostrils, it pawed deep scoops from the corral floor that darkened its rear hooves.

"I am sorry. I can't do it."

Fear overcame him and the mental images of grass and gravel of the highway rushing up to meet him and the wreck's vacant Moment of semi-consciousness and ensuing agony towered above all other thoughts. In front of him, the prospects of sweaty tack, glistening saddle leather, dropped reins formed a daunting appearance of more than he could face. Blade's muscular chest rippled with energy and eagerness. His hooves churned the corral floor.

Sydney stopped again. The big, famous, powerful and aggressive horse stood the opposite of everything about himself: he felt small, obscure, slow, weak and afraid. "Why on earth do people ride those scary creatures?" he asked himself. "It makes no sense."

"I know, I know," said Neeter, easily reading his thoughts. "I've been scared, too. But you got to do it."

Sydney's whole body froze. His head dropped. "I am sorry," he said. "I can't."

"Come on," ordered Dad. "Get on that horse!"

Sydney didn't move and Dad started toward him. He didn't know what would happen, but he couldn't mount that horse.

"Never mind," said Neeter. Interrupting Dad, he ran toward his horse and leaped to reach the saddle horn and wormed up the side of the tall horse. Though he made no sign of a command to the horse, Blade jumped at the big calf and drove it toward the calf pen. Dad unwired the gate, pulled it partly open and the calf jumped inside, just to be free of the big horse.

With all the calves bellowing in the pen, Neeter brushed his face with his sleeve. "I'll load them up in the morning," he said. "Feed them well and get a couple of pounds on them."

Dad nodded. He didn't have to be told that. "We'll feed the cows here for three days until they forget their calves," he said. "That way we won't have them breaking out and looking all over town for calves."

"Want some help taking them back out?" asked Neeter, eyeing Old Lopp. "We'll be glad to." "We" were himself and his two horses.

"Thanks," said Dad. "Sydney, put half a dozen forkfuls of alfalfa in there to keep them settled down."

"The last supper," said Sydney, resigned to the fate of the calves.

Dad looked at him strangely.

"They are beef calves, brought in the world for this only," said Dad. "No beef, no calves. No calves, no beef."

Dad and Neeter remounted the horses, looking for something to do next. They rode back to Neeter's.

Later that night as he lay in bed, Sydney listened to faint sounds of lowing cattle. At first, he put the sounds out of his mind but the cattle calling their calves, and calves answering, continued into the night. Paying close attention, he could pick out which cow answered which calf. Then the wind would grow stronger and moan without an answer. Lying in his bed, he listened as the wind blended into the chorus, adding sloped and chiseled sounds of its own, for its own reasons. Together, like oboes accented by violins, a bass and treble cleft of natural harmony, they spoke of futility, of hopelessness, as if cows seeking their calves had the same chance as the wind seeking to tear down trees, or the family keeping the farm. He knew the calves would be gone when he returned from school the next day. He knew what lay in store for them.

"How am I supposed to keep LaMar happy in all this?" he wondered as he drifted to sleep.

Chapter 8

The school bell's tiny hammer blurred as it beat against its shiny dome. As though it also emitted electric shocks, its sharp rings jolted students to jump from their seats and hurry to exit. Leading them all, Bleu and Melvin rushed from the classroom as if someone chased them with electric cattle prods. They did not wait for Sydney. He trotted to catch up with them. Well behind, he heard them talking about him.

"He never rode Neeter's mare," said Bleu. "I saw him walking."

"I know," he heard Melvin say. "He's nothing but chicken guts. I would love to ride that mare."

Sydney trotted to catch up with them and tried to change the subject. "They came visiting our house, trying to get Dad to pay more money so we could keep the school open," he said from behind. "Bishop and Larkins Perkin."

"We are so sick of this school," Bleu almost spat. "We want it closed. We want Mister driving off in his 1953 Studebaker to teach some other poor saps." They walked past younger students.

"So, we are on sides," said Melvin looking over his shoulder at Sydney. "You are for us or against us. We don't want any Benedicts."

"I thought we were friends," said Sydney.

"We are," said Bleu. "But we don't want any Benedicts."

He and Bleu glanced at each other as Voyle Perkin walked by.

"Larkins Perkin, huh?"

Melvin noiselessly pointed at Voyle. "You with us, chicken head Speng?" he asked, shaping the words noiselessly.

Sydney looked at Voyle Perkin. Voyle wore a home-made dark red shirt with a partly torn pocket. He often played alone. But this time, he walked to the side of the building, hoping to join some younger boys in a game of after-school marbles.

"Is Mister looking?" asked Bleu.

"He's doing papers at his desk," said Sydney.

The trio spread out and walked up behind Voyle. He saw them and whirled around.

"Leave me alone!" he cried.

Pupils walking past instantly sensed disturbance and stopped, eyes big and mouths closed. Voyle backed up to the wall. Melvin, Bleu and Sydney closed in.

"Your old man trying to keep the school open," said Melvin.

Voyle didn't answer.

"You are so righteous," said Bleu. "You haven't got the guts to say a swear word."

"Gutless," said Sydney. "But you do have ears."

Voyle leaped past Melvin, right to Sydney, hoping. But Sydney tackled him. As they fell to the dirt, Sydney felt smugness of his strength over Voyle. He swung in his power and stood back in triumph. Then he saw the hurt, the same pain he often felt these days, in Voyle's tear-filled eyes. He paused and stood back, his sense of triumph fled. In an instant, Melvin pushed Sydney aside and sat straddle of

Voyle. He rolled his hands viciously over Voyle's ears, up and down, over and over.

"Stop it," shouted a girl. Sydney looked over and saw Addie, shaking in anger. "Melvin, you are a savage!" she yelled.

"Shut it, Rudolph," said Melvin. But he let Voyle up. Voyle climbed to his feet. Dust powdered his face, his torn pocket draggled nearly off. Dark red ears matched his shirt.

"Come get me," Addie said angrily. "I am not afraid of you," she said to Melvin. "Or you," she said to Bleu. Addie glared at Sydney. "I am not afraid of you, either. You shouldn't be with them," she continued. "You are not like them."

"We're together," said Sydney in a thin voice.

"You'd think you'd be nicer with your brother so hurt," said Addie. "You know what it feels like."

"He's better. He's coming home tomorrow," said Sydney. But he couldn't look at her.

Cousins Melvin and Bleu swaggered slowly away. Sydney did not follow them. Pupils dispersed and Voyle forgot his game of marbles and slumped away home, as usual, by himself.

The next afternoon, waiting for the school bell to ring, Sydney's thoughts turned to LaMar, around and around in his head like the second hand. "LaMar's coming home, he thought. "Finally, finally, finally."

He couldn't look at Voyle. He didn't look at Melvin or Bleu, either, just at the clock. Hours passed and the clock's big black hand only inched a minute at a time. Sitting in the room with his work done early, Sydney pondered his feeling of power over Voyle and compared it with looking at

110

Voyle's tear-filled eyes. He could not reconcile the two feelings, or understand where they came from. He wondered a long time. He felt bad for Voyle, but he desperately wanted to stay friends with Melvin and Bleu.

About five hours after the last recess, but three minutes before school time ended, Mister raised his hand.

"You're excused," he said.

Sydney rocketed from his desk – it felt so good to move. Out of the school he ran. Past Melvin and Bleu and carefully not looking at Voyle, or Addie who made him feel like a criminal. He cornered the door so fast he felt the leather soles of his shoes slip over the oiled wood.

Mrs. Cloner, the little kids' teacher, stood in the hallway. Sydney headed for the stairs at a dead run.

"Walk, please," she said.

He glanced at her – firmly smiling with her wide jaw and slight underbite. She always been nice to him. He slowed to a hard walk, jumped down the steps and then ran out the glass doors. Over the weed-filled ball diamond he raced, cutting cross lots, his feet blasting seed clusters from dried red weeds. He came to the welded steel net fence and bent to crawl through a hole sculpted by crawling student bodies over that past half a century. He crossed the pastures and vaulted a pole fence. Soft dirt splashed into his shoes as he landed. He ignored the gritty feeling, knowing it would be absorbed by his socks.

At the house, the Plymouth parked next to the back entrance, a passenger door hanging open. He pushed the door shut and rushed inside. In the living room, LaMar reclined monarchial among the cushions on the couch. He

111

grinned his chalky face with its freckles bleached away. His shirt hung uneven from being odd-buttoned.

The whole family circled him.

"LaMar!" cried Sydney. "They set you free."

Dad made a gruff sound meant as a chuckle, but arrived as a snort. "Not half free," he said. "But he is home. And the hospital is paid off."

"I don't want to know how," said Mom. "Down to 45 days."

"We don't need to bring that up right now," said Dad.

"I am finally home," chirped LaMar. "Good old couch. Good old pillows." He looked around at the family. "Good old everybody."

"Today they wrote letters to you," said Sydney. "Mister is bringing them over."

"Oh," said LaMar in his direct way. "I hope they are different. Last time, they were all the same. 'Dear LaMar. I hope you get better soon.' "

"Guess what else?" asked Mom.

LaMar smiled back. He settled back on the cushion to rest from this slight exertion.

"Tonight, you are getting a special dinner. Your Primary teachers are bringing it over."

Prielle clapped her hands and Bartholomew galloped in a tiny circle.

"Humph," said Dad. "We aren't needy. Why don't we just have boiled spuds like we always do? Let's give it back, or take it to a needy family."

"Nope," said LaMar bluntly. "We're not taking it back. We are going to eat it ourselves."

"I'll boil some spuds for you, dear," said Mom to Dad. "The rest of us shall eat special food. It is already here. It will be our Thanksgiving feast a little early."

"Tell them we don't want any more," said Dad. "Tell them I'll carry it back with my own two hands."

Mom smiled right at him. "They haven't offered, dear. Telling them we don't want any more when they haven't offered is like asking for more, which I personally would rather not do."

Dad humphed and rose up from his floor seat. He slipped out of the room and returned with a whetstone and butcher knife. He began whisking it sharp. Dad could never sit and do nothing for very long.

"Venna said thanks to Sydney for the wheat," said LaMar. "I ate it every day. It helped me with a problem I had. I got to come home quicker."

"Does it still hurt?" Prielle asked LaMar.

"Today it did," said LaMar. "But Venna said that one day I will wake up and the prickles will be gone from my stomach and never come back. Sometimes I still feel the wagon on my tummy, though. Venna read me a story about a mother goat that sews rocks in a fox's tummy. That's the way my tummy feels, full of rocks. But every day it is lighter. Mean old mother goat."

"I am so proud of you," said Mom. "You have been so brave."

Dad stopped sharpening his knife. "Doc Mooley wants his beef. We'll get him paid off."

"Are you going to butcher for us?" asked Mom. "It will be nice to have fresh beef for a change."

"We haven't got a beef this year," said Dad. "It's sold with the calves. And two of the milk cows, tomorrow. We've got to pay the Federal Land Bank something."

"Can I see the cows?" asked LaMar. "Please, can I just see the cows?"

"Nope," said Dad. "But Sydney can. Bring them home early tomorrow."

LaMar's face fell into its dejected, hospital expression.

"Don't worry," said Sydney, quickly. "You can see the cows tomorrow. I promise. You know I keep my promises."

LaMar's face brightened. "Good old Sydney. I would like that very much. I want to see if they are thin cows or fat cows."

Dad laughed. "I doubt you will see the thin cows eat the fat cows." He paused. "That is one Bible story that is coming true."

"What?" asked Prielle. No one explained it to her. She looked around and found no answer.

Dad and Sydney left to do the milking and chores. When they returned an hour later, as Sydney entered the kitchen, all thoughts of cows were chased away by the scent of fresh rolls and an aroma of vanilla filling the air. A pot roast mixed in its flavor. Mom turned from her work to smile at them.

Sydney took a deep breath. "Mmmmm," he said. "This smells like the garden of puddin'."

"You smell a little more earthy," she said. "Corral earthy."

Sydney hurried. He changed clothes and washed and slid into his place behind the table next to Madge.

Bartholomew turned to Sydney and said in solemn tones, "Mar's better. Mar's on the couch."

Nat carried in LaMar from the couch to his usual place at the table, but with pillows supporting him. The rest of the family crowded in.

"This is the first time we've been all together for almost two months," said Madge.

Mom called for prayer. Every one kneeled beside their chairs except LaMar, who bowed his head. This time, Mom said the prayer herself, with lots of thanking, some asking, and some more thanking. During the last thankings, a door opened and Dad quietly slipped into the room. Sydney peeked and saw him sort of hunch over and stare at the coal bucket until Mom finished.

"Amen," said Mom.

"Amen," said the children.

"Came in," said Dad. "Just in time."

Chairs scraped and the children resumed their sitting positions. After Dad washed, Mom called upon Prielle and she pronounced the blessing on the food.

"Me, too," said Bartholomew. Madge helped him as he mispronounced "bweess the fooo."

After, Mom sat long enough to direct passing the roast and potatoes first to Dad. He'd wholly overcome his reluctance to eat something besides boiled spuds. He ladled mounds of whipped potatoes, a board of meat and a chunk of tuna casserole. Others began helping themselves to salads, Jell-O, rolls, peas and corn. Space on plates disappeared beneath piles of steaming food. Mom filled LaMar's plate.

"I felt the baby quicken today," said Mom.

"What does that feel like?" asked Madge.

"Like a little butterfly," said Mom.

"A boy butterfly or a girl butterfly?" asked Madge.

"Just a butterfly," said Mom.

"When will it come?" asked Madge.

"In February or March, with the calves," said Mom. "We are in farm rhythm."

"This is the best dinner I have ever eaten," said LaMar. "I ate Jell-O at the hospital. Bluak!"

"You can eat a little Jell-O salad," said Mom. She spatula-ed a small block of it on his plate. He immediately pushed it to one side.

"We're going to whip that infection," said Dad, packing up his food up as fast as he'd packed it in. Mom handed a platter of rolls to LaMar, who took one and passed the plate to Nat, who took two, and passed it to Sydney, who took two. Madge took the last one.

"Well, old man, what do you remember about the wreck?" asked Nat.

Mom frowned and wiggled her finger, to say that there are some things best left unsaid. LaMar didn't see her and said in a matter-of-fact tone, "I came to."

Dad stopped in mid-flight a spoon dripping with casserole. "What do you mean you came to?" A noodle slithered down from his spoon onto his lap. Dad dabbed at the noodle and missed.

"At the crash," said LaMar emphatically, as though rehearsed many times before to someone who didn't believe him. "I wakened up." Everyone stopped eating and stared at him.

"You didn't move," said Sydney.

"I couldn't. I couldn't talk or move, or look. But I wakened up."

Dad retrieved the noodle from his dirty trousers with his finger and popped it into his mouth.

"You were out cold," Dad said. "The whole time."

"Nope," said LaMar. He slid a block of melting, encroaching Jell-O through its pool back toward the edge of his plate so it wouldn't contaminate his potatoes. Then he went on:

"We were on the hayrack, me and Sydney, we were. Sydney said he knew this would happen. When the tractor killed, Sydney waved, real hard, but the car didn't see us, or slow down, or anything. It splattered us all over the road. I grabbed at Sydney, but I couldn't hold on to him. I sank through the straw. It felt like I lay right under the wagon and it pushed me into the road. I don't remember anything else until Dad and Sydney were hollering, and I tried to answer, I really did. The hayrack just kept pressing me. I guess I went to sleep for a bit then."

He said it very ordinarily, stopping to take a bite of potatoes and shove back the Jell-O. A corner of it broke off and plopped off the edge of his plate to the table cloth.

"What else do you remember?" asked Mom in a friendly voice. She inched a little nearer. The rest of the family remained absolutely silent.

LaMar continued: "I woke up when I heard Dad and Sydney hollering, but I couldn't move or open my eyes. It just hurt too much. I tried to answer, I did really. I just couldn't move at all. Or hardly breathe under all that straw. After a long time, Dad came and got me." Here, his eyes clouded and drops ran down his cheeks.

"Maybe we'd better leave the boy alone to eat his dinner," said Dad.

LaMar continued brashly "They cleaned the straw off me, and Dad gave me a blessing. It made me feel better. I could go to sleep then. That part I like best." LaMar smiled up at Mom, whose face froze in shock and disbelief.

Dad shot a stab of a glance at LaMar, then he looked down. He looked up again. "Aren't you going to pass the rolls, Sydney? You've ate half the plate yourself."

Sydney reluctantly replaced one of his rolls on the plate and passed it to Dad.

"I don't understand how you know this blessing story so well," said Mom, now recovered, and with an added eagerness in her voice. She spoke each word carefully and didn't look at Dad. "You sound like you've told it before."

"Yeah," said LaMar. "Venna, she made me tell it over and over until it didn't make me cry any more. My favorite part is where Dad gives me the blessing and I go to sleep. It is Venna's favorite part, too. She said that kept me alive."

Dad almost jumped.

"Venna!" he exclaimed. "The county tattletale!"

He bent as to stand, to leave before he'd eaten all his supper. Then he settled back and studied his plate for a long time in the silence. He prodded his casserole. "There here has mushrooms in it," he finally said.

"Mush-room," said Prielle, leaning far forward to look at it. "It sounds very messy."

A knock rattled the glass in the kitchen door and interrupted the moment.

Madge answered the door to find Mister, who still wore his school white shirt and tie, carrying a manila envelope under his arm.

"Hello, everyone," he said. "Don't get up. I am just dropping off some letters from LaMar's friends."

"Nat, get a chair," said Dad.

Nat stood with his mouth still full of food to find a folding chair from a back room. Mister eased into the conversation by talking to LaMar, by now resigned to make a potato dike against the still-melting Jell-O. Mister volunteered that he would be glad to come over in the evenings to help LaMar keep up with his school work, especially the arithmetic. Mom said that would be a fine thing for him to do. If he could spare the time from his home.

"I don't mind," Mister said. He untucked the manila envelope from his arm and passed it to LaMar. LaMar made a place for it on the table between a long casserole and the plate now empty of rolls. He inserted his hand and fished out the first letter. He read it slowly, word by word:

"Dear LaMar, I hope you get better quick so you can come back to school. Yours truly, Reuben."

LaMar nodded and read the next one:

"Dear LaMar, I hope you get better quick so you can come back to school. Yours truly, Voyle."

"Each letter is the same," said LaMar. "Just like the last time."

"Wait," said Mister. He reached for the envelope and pulled out the letters. From them, he pulled one and handed it to LaMar, who read: "Howdy, I hope you get better quick so you can come back to school. Yours truly, Addie."

119

LaMar looked up at Mister. "I will read the rest of them tomorrow," he said.

"I guess I shouldn't have put a sample letter on the board," said Mister.

"Would you like some dessert?" asked Mom. "It is a lovely pudding called 'Raspberry Tartish.' "

Mister's eyebrow cocked up and he said he might try a small helping. Nat slithered from behind the table. He began to whip thick cream with a hand-cranked egg beater. Mom added a little sugar and vanilla.

As everyone watched, Nat made the most of the stage. "I am not just whipping this cream. I am beating, thumping and pounding it. I am lashing, cudgeling, quirting, and trouncing it."

"Yeah," said Dad. "Probably making butter."

Nat paused. "By the way, speaking of blessings, shouldn't we bless this cream? Someone left the bottle in the fridge. Everyone knows the food in the fridge is exempt from blessing."

"We blessed the food we are going to eat," said Mom. "I am sure it is taken care of."

"How does the blessing know what food we are going to eat?" he asked. "That would be a predestinated blessing. That means we have to eat this cream, want to or not."

"Test it," said Dad. "Let me eat yours."

"Doesn't matter," said Nat. "The blessing already knew. So I will eat my share, after all."

"Excuse me," said Mister. "But the blessing is also a thanking for the great privilege of having food to eat. We often forget that part."

"That settles it," said Dad. "I am thankful to have your portion, Nat."

"Good," said Nat. "You will all be thankful to have some new butter on your raspberry tartish."

"Nat!" said Madge. "Don't you dare!"

"It is vanilla flavored," said Nat. "I can add some sugar to improve the quality of thankfulness. I am sure the blessing expected that much, at least."

Mom stood up and walked over to supervise. "Hey," objected Nat. "It has yet to be lambasted, walloped and whomped."

"So, why were you speaking of blessings?" asked Mister.

Nat pretended reluctance as he gave the egg beater to Mom who peered into the small bowl and turned the beater over to Madge.

"Nat is a genius at getting out of work," Madge said. "Somehow I knew I would end up whipping the cream."

"Can I help it if I am a genius?" said Nat. "I just have to live with it, that's all." He sat down and took another helping of potatoes and gravy. He looked regretfully at the empty roll plate.

Mister turned his head toward Mom. Mom looked at LaMar.

"I told them about Dad giving me a blessing after I got hurt, and how it made me go to sleep, and how it made me get better," LaMar said. "If we can make butter, why do we buy it?"

"Oh," said Mister. "I didn't know that."

"They put salt in store-bought butter," said Dad. "We used to always churn our own. Now we have grown to like salted butter. It is a whole lot easier to buy than make."

"That is a wonderful testimony, LaMar," said Mister. "I hope you get a chance to give it in church sometime."

"We better get him back to school before we have him talking in church," said Dad quickly. He turned to Madge. "Just whip cream," he said. "Don't have to whip up everything else in the room."

Nat eyed a half a roll on Sydney's plate. Sydney saw him and picked up the roll and took a bite. During his bite, a sliver of disquiet returned, grew stronger and he remembered the odd, flitting image glancing across his mind, like a blowing leaf. Again, he didn't have to pay attention to it, so he didn't. He let it fly past and disappear. This time, though, he recognized the image of a milk cow, butchered and hanging by her hind quarters, half skinned. He quickly dismissed it as nonsensical. "We aren't going to butcher a milk cow," he thought.

That evening, after the conversation subsided and the dishes were washed, Dad, who always had to be doing something, brought his grandfather's old square-barreled .22 into the kitchen. He took it apart and oiled each piece. Sydney and Prielle watched as he put the parts together again to form a rifle.

"Where are you going hunting?" asked Sydney. "Can I go? Other boys my age shoot a .22."

"Might next week," said Dad. He worked the pumping mechanism; it functioned smoothly. Dad held the gun and aimed for a long second at a spot on the blue tile floor before pulling the trigger. The click echoed across the kitchen.

Chapter 9

The kitchen's pale blue tile floor showed snake-like trails from the iron wheels of the wooden milk cart, trails of rocks, dirt and mud. The homemade cart making the snake-like tracks held LaMar, seated on a couch cushion and swathed in a blanket. LaMar clutched the cart's handle, grinning like a china monkey.

"Hang on!" ordered Sydney, self-appointed horse to the cart. Leaving the kitchen, they reached the sharp descent of the back steps. LaMar holding with his diminished might made a show of clamping tighter. But the weight of the cart overwhelmed Sydney as it rumbled crazily down the rough stone steps and he hung on with all his might to keep it right. Sydney's chest tightened: the cart wobbled and bounced and LaMar wavered to one side; Sydney about screamed.

"So fun!" called LaMar at the bottom. "Let's do that again!"

Sydney didn't answer.

"Boy, oh boy, oh boy, oh boy," said LaMar. "I am going to see the cows."

"I brought them home early," said Sydney.

"Look how blue the sky is," said LaMar, looking in wonder. "There's a bird; it's a fat sparrow."

Sydney looked at him. "It is not fat. It ruffles its feathers against the cold."

"It's almost winter," said LaMar, shivering in his blanket. "Guess I lost the fall."

"Where do you want to go now?" asked Sydney.

"I want to pet one of the cows," said LaMar, speaking to Sydney as would to a horse. "Please. Giddap, my good old Sydney."

Sydney pulled the cart over the grass to the pasture nearest the house. Inside, cows waiting to be milked lifted their heads toward them in unison. Sydney moved to old Inca, the tamest. She stood still with her head swung in their direction, ears cocked forward. The cart came alongside.

"Sooooo," said Sydney. He stroked her silken ribs. LaMar reached up and touched her neck and repeated, "Sooooo – oooo there. Nice Inca. Nice old Inca."

"Dad's feeding her oats so she'll give more milk," said Sydney. "Even though he says it won't do any good because it is too late."

Something caught in his mind when he said that. A low trigger, it clicked and made him remember something he didn't want to think about.

"I thought he gave oats only to a red cow," said LaMar absently as he stroked the cow's neck. "A Hereford he is going to butcher for Doc Mooley."

"Yeah," said Sydney, trying to remember what stuck in his brain. They stood close to the cow and felt the comfort if its warmth. "He keeps oats out to the field." He paused. Something wasn't right. "No," said Sydney. "He keeps oats in the cow stable." Then Sydney caught his breath as the realization hit him, along with that split-second image he'd dismissed so quickly.

"No," he said. "No. He don't. He don't have oats out to the field."

125

The boys looked at each other. Sydney's face filled with disbelief and denial. He saw LaMar's face trying to understand.

"He's not going to butcher old Inca? Is he?" asked LaMar in a thin voice.

"We better get you back into the house before Mom comes home," said Sydney. He began pulling the cart toward the house. LaMar clenched the handles for support.

"Inca is Mom's cow. She's our pet cow," said LaMar as they bumped over the pasture. "We love our old Inca."

"Dad said he hated to but he had no choice," remembered Sydney. "I thought he talked like that because he hated to waste his oats on her."

Tears began running down LaMar's pasty cheeks.

"Don't worry. I won't let him do it," said Sydney. "I won't." The cart bumped over the grass.

"The path we are on needs changing," Sydney said. He didn't expect LaMar to understand.

"We've always followed our path," said LaMar. "It is hard to change what we've always done."

Surprised that LaMar understood, Sydney pulled the cart faster.

"Uh-oh," said LaMar. Sydney looked up and saw Mom driving the dark blue Plymouth into the lot. It turned toward the pasture and skidded to a halt. Mom leaped out and began running toward them.

"What are you two pot-muffins up to now?" she shouted angrily. "Sydney Speng! You get him up here right now!" She continued to run toward them. "Don't tip him – be careful." She met the cart and searched LaMar with

angry gray eyes. "It's about to snow. He's not healed, and
here you are risking his life in this rickety old contraption!"

"I'm fine, Mom," protested LaMar. "We wanted to see
the cows, that's all."

Mom tested the cushion and found it solid.

"See?" said Sydney, rocking the milk cart and LaMar.
"We wouldn't hurt him." He rocked it again.

"Stop, stop," shouted Mom. She ran at Sydney and
swiped a cuff at him. "What is thee matter with you, boy?"
she demanded. "Why are you acting this way?"

The boys were silent as she carefully picked LaMar up
in her arms and carried him. LaMar lay his head on her
neck as they moved. She struggled at the steps, where she
weakly stopped and let him steady himself. Sydney winced
as he remembered the butterfly of a baby within her. Mom
disappeared into the house with LaMar. Sydney followed
from a distance, finally walking into the house. Prielle held
the door open, a smug look on her face.

"So!" she said. "That's what you get for not letting me
come with you."

"Good thing for you Dad's out to the field," Mom
said, breathing hard. "He'd a given you a good licking for
this. And I am not the one to say that you wouldn't deserve
it, taking this child's life in your hands like that!"

LaMar lay silently on the couch. He didn't look up.
Sydney looked at him and then quickly slipped out to put
the milk cart back. He drove the cows in the stable before
Dad came home, and, after supper, climbed to his bedroom
earlier than usual.

Fully dressed, he lay awake in the darkness thinking.
He knew what he had to do.

"Can the future be changed?" he wondered. "It must be changed or I wouldn't see it. What other reason is there for me to see it? Still, if it doesn't happen, would I see it? What would it be like to not see these things? What does it mean?" He could only ask the questions. He couldn't answer them.

Hours passed and Sydney could sense darkness growing thicker; he guessed the hour at nearly midnight. He waited, still fully dressed, beneath goose-down quilts. He could no longer see his shoes poking up, nor could he see Nat, asleep on the other side of the room. Nat's breathing whisper-sang as slow minutes passed.

Finally, Sydney pulled back the quilts. He held his breath as he rolled over creaking springs to the edge of the bed. His shoes tramped softly finding the floor. He crept out of the bedroom to the stairs, skipping the squeaky one, and stepping over the cracked board step. At the foot of the stairs, voices rang from the kitchen.

"They caught me," he thought.

Voices continued – angry voices, but not at him. He listened. Mom and Dad argued. Sydney tiptoed closer to hear. A slit of light showed through the door to the kitchen and lighted a stripe down his face. Dad's voice hit heavy like a bludgeon. Answering, Mom's voice snapped and cracked like a whip.

"I can't wring money out of a turnip," barked Dad. "What isn't there can't be got."

"Why must you always wreak your violence upon things important to me?" she snapped back. "When we need money, my things are sacrificed first."

128

"I don't have anything worth sacrificing," said Dad. "It's all long gone. Tell me, just tell me, what other choice is there?"

"Sell her. Trade her. Just don't butcher her in front of the kids. Think of LaMar. He'll blame himself. He does that. He's already feeling guilty."

"No one needs see it," said Dad. "I've got to provide for this family." He paused. "Especially if there is another mouth to feed."

"Is this the price of a baby?" asked Mom. "Do I have to choose?"

Sydney heard her cry. Sydney pressed his eye against the crack and saw Dad resting his foot on the stove and as usual, sharpening his butcher knife. Dad ground his heel on the stove. Sydney could smell burning shoe rubber. Mom stood opposite, wiping her eyes with a kitchen towel. Next they'd be arguing about faith and righteous souls.

"Babies and calves come every spring, as long as the mother is healthy," said Dad.

"As long as the bull is around," said Mom, dabbing her eyes.

"If I lose one more Hereford, I just as well sell the place," said Dad. "If it's got to be done, it ought to be done quick. And it will be."

Sydney crept back realizing the obvious – that he couldn't use the kitchen door to escape. But apple crates and old tables now piled high against the front door. He couldn't use that door, either. He stole back up the steps to his bedroom. After a long glance at his bed, he slipped his fingers beneath a window and lifted. Wood squeaked. No one stirred, so he lifted again. A rush of cool air sprinkled

129

his face with bug wings and encrusting window dust. He wedged an old yearbook of cow medicine under the window. He bent over and crawled through the narrow opening and reached up to a thick cottonwood limb. Cold air bit his face as he embraced the limb. Down to the trunk he slipped, feeling the gnarled bark roughen his stomach and arms. Once on the ground, he stopped to look around. Overhead, just a clipped fingernail of a moon peeped down. Its light edged nearby clouds in silver. Around the pasture, ancient shaggy trees stood in a line – giant, silent and gnomelike. Star holes riddled the sky and a few distant clouds floated easterly. The air felt wintery now, just without snow.

He moved stealthily through dead leaves directly away from the house. He turned toward the pasture. He felt numb and unreal, being in a fairy tale, being an offspring gnome to the trees but without their magic. He climbed the pasture fence and walked to the blots of cow-shaped shadows lying on their bed of straw. Aida stirred first, her South-America shaped patch of white stood out, but her fore-quarters were almost invisible. Aida planted her front legs and elevated South America.

"Soo-oo there," whispered Sydney. "Easy there, you skitty old glue pot. Easy there."

"Don't nobody move, he whispered softly. "Just you – old Inca." He gently smacked her rump. "Upsy daisy." Inca swung her big head around to look at Sydney. For the first time he noticed a white spot in the upper center of her forehead, a target mark. Sydney shivered and slapped her harder.

"Upsy daisy!"

Lowing in protest, Inca and several other cattle clambered to their feet. Sydney stationed himself at her rear and prodded her into a slow gait forward. Other cows followed in an obedient caravan.

"He—yahh!" scolded Sydney to the other cattle. "Get back there." He stepped in front of Aida and whooshed his arms at her. She bucked and bellowed and half the herd followed. Sydney watched helplessly as cows kicked and mooed, knobby, twisting shadows. At the house, light splashed from the kitchen door and Dad's voice barked, "Git! Durn dog!"

Sydney fell flat into the pasture on his stomach and hugged his face against the frigid earth. Clouds hid the moon; night muffled the pasture.

He turned his head slightly and saw the door still open and light streaming out. Through the corner of his eye, he saw a dark figure striding toward them. Sydney rolled into a low ditch and pressed his face against the grassy bottom. He thought he heard a faint, faint click and working mechanism.

"He's got the .22," he thought in a panic. "It's all oiled and ready."

He lay perfectly still, barely breathing. He wondered what to do. If he said anything, he would get a licking, for sure. Dad's lickings weren't soft; he used a belt and a guy would be home in bed and miss school for a couple of days – that's what happened to Melvin and Bleu. He breathed so slowly he almost began coughing.

"Dad won't shoot what he can't see," he thought. A long minute passed. He didn't dare look up; any movement would give him away with Dad this close.

131

"Heerh!" Dad shouted from feet away. "Settle down."

The cows recognized his voice, slowed and knelt back to the pasture floor. Sydney heard the .22 click again and he realized Dad put the safety on. Sydney remained motionless until he heard the back door slam. Knowing his father still watched, he remained still for another five minutes. When he saw the kitchen light darken, he waited another few minutes. His stomach chilled. His arms didn't want to move, though his whole body shivered wildly. When he raised up again, the cows had bedded down. Inca lay away from the rest of them. He walked to her. She obediently stood. He drove her from the pasture through the corral and big barn door. She plodded obediently in front of him along the back street toward the summer pasture. Sydney admitted to himself that he really didn't know where to put her. He just wanted to get her away and hidden. When they came to a long and dense stand of poplar trees, he headed her. Puzzled, the cow turned to walk home. He headed her again, and pushed her into the trees. A path worn by cows running from flies secluded the back parts of trees, invisible from the front.

"This is perfect," said Sydney, aloud to himself and the cow. He felt good to hear talk, even if from himself. Talk made the project more real. He pulled a limb across the path behind her and found a fallen strand of barbed wire to tie as a makeshift fence. He reinforced each end with dead branches and turned to go.

"Bye," he said aloud to the cow. "We'll hide you better tomorrow. Stay here tonight. Tomorrow you'll be in a barn. In somebody's barn."

He wondered what friend could to help him conceal a cow. Hiding a cow meant rustling a cow. They hang people for rustling.

He looked at the cow. A pale shaft of moonlight showed through the tree limbs across her and brightened the white spot on her forehead. For a moment Sydney felt foolish, as if a few wires and branches could stop Dad. He paused to stroke her nose a few times, and then turned for home. His fast walk turned to a trot, his feet grinding gravel that in the moonlight looked like streams of blood. When he reached the house all the rooms were dark. He slipped in through the kitchen, holding the glass in its window so it wouldn't rattle. He took off his shoes and crept each step on the stairs and soon he lay back in bed, prayers skipped. He couldn't pray. He felt a partner to the devil.

Almost immediately Mom's voice sounded in his ear.

"Get up, Sydney," she said from another continent.

It couldn't be morning, he thought. Not until Mom came upstairs and pulled at his covers did he mumble that he'd be right up. She left and he sank into the mattress again.

"Better not let Dad catch you in bed," she called from below. "He's been out all over the neighborhood searching for Inca. He's mad as a hornet."

Sydney bolted up in bed. "I'm coming," he said. He waited for Mom to leave and then pulled on his jeans and started finding socks. While he searched the floor, the kitchen door slammed downstairs.

"Where's that dang kid?" he heard his father bellow. "He better be in school or he's in for the thrashing of his life." Sydney dropped his shoes and began looking wildly

133

for a place to hide. A moment later, Dad's hard boots hit the stairs like the blows of a maul. Sydney began sobbing and ran one way and then the other. The steps pounded upward. Then Dad burst into the room and Sydney began to cry.

"Hide my cow!" thundered Dad. "I'll hide you!" He unbuckled his belt and pulled it snapping through the loops. As he drew the thick leather belt back, Sydney dived into the bed and tried to pull the covers over him.

"Stop it now, Dallern Speng!" Mom's voice sounded across the room. She'd followed him upstairs. Sydney watched his father turn slightly. Dad turned back and raised the belt. The strap fell heavily and smacked a trail of fire across Sydney's bare legs. He screamed. Just as Dad rocked back to strike across his back, Mom stepped over the room and draped herself over the top of Sydney. He felt her soft body fall heavily over his body. Her protruding stomach pressed against his back. A smack sounded and he felt his mother jerk and quiver. She burst into tears.

"Just you do it, Mr. Speng!" she said, spitting out each word by itself between sobs.

"You got in my way," shouted Dad. "I didn't hit you. I aimed at him, for taking my beef."

"You hit my children, you hit me," cried Mom. "I will tell everyone in this town that you hit me."

"Stay out of my way," shouted Dad. "He needs a licking."

"Just you try it again, Mr. Speng!" She spit the words, spreading herself across Sydney. "Go right ahead! See what happens!"

Sydney heard the hard boots stalk from the room. Descending heels crashed angrily on every step. When Dad reached downstairs, Mom climbed from the bed. Sydney's tears soaked into his pillow; from the humiliation. The pain would have been so much better; Mom taking his licking hurt more than a soul could endure.

"Are you all right?" he finally choked in broken words.

She nodded. Tears smeared her face and her mussed hair. "The belt hit my leg – the baby is all right."

"I am sorry," he said. "I am so sorry."

"Don't be," she said, shuddering and stroking her red-welted legs. "We all do our best. You tried to protect the cow. I try to protect my children. Dad tries to protect the family. We all do our best. We just have different jobs to do."

"I hate him," said Sydney. "I will always hate him."

"Don't hate him. He's butchering for LaMar," said Mom. "This is just as much for LaMar as your cart ride. Dads have the hard things to do. He loves you. I know he does."

"He hates me. He never does anything but beat me and yell at me and make me work. Now he even beat you. I hate him."

A distant shot rang out. Another followed. Neither Sydney nor Mom spoke. Nothing could be said.

"Inca is dead," he thought. He stared at Mom's red legs. "Now I will see her hanging upside down, half skinned. That picture in my mind has come true. I couldn't stop it. For trying, I got a beating for myself and Mom."

"At least she's out of her misery," said Mom.

After a few minutes, Dad's voice rang out from downstairs.

"Get that kid out here with a bucket of hot water and some rags."

The moment he spoke, Mom's mouth clenched tight.

"Do I have to?" Sydney asked. "Do I have to?"

Mom's mouth clenched tighter and her lips turned white.

"The worst is over," she said. "This part is just work. You can bear it. That's part of growing up. You are a man now."

"I will never stop hating him for this," said Sydney. He took his time getting to the barn. Hot water from the bucket sloshed through his jeans as he walked.

At the barn, Doc Mooley's beef hung suspended from an old wagon singletree. Half its hide draped the half that wasn't skinned. Just exactly as Sydney had seen in his mind.

A shaft of light filtered through the logs of the barn and shone on the carcass. An odd, translucent azure reflected upward from its glassy, dead eyes. Sydney stared, transfixed. Dad stopped what he was doing and dropped a handful of straw over the carcass head to extinguish the light.

"I need this hindquarter scrubbed down," said Dad quietly. "Doc Mooley isn't accustomed to eating manure with his beef."

About three hours later they finished. Sydney wanted to escape, even to school. His whole body smelled of cow entrails. He scrubbed at his hands with soap, but it smelled yet. He tried the homemade lye soap Mom used for laundry. He scrubbed again and again until his hands were stinging and rough. He almost wished he could use the soap on his eyes to wash out the things he had seen. Inca was no more than a memory; no remnant would be left. By the time he had come home from school, nothing would remain. Head, hide, entrails would be hauled away. The meat would be in a locker. Which part was Inca? He didn't know.

He hurried upstairs and changed into his school clothes. He didn't speak to LaMar, but noticed that LaMar's eyes were red.

Supper came early that evening, quietly. Mom fed the children before Dad came in from milking. Sydney saw LaMar's eyes remained red. Neither spoke. Sydney sat in the living room by LaMar and tried to read a library book.

Then Dad came in from milking.

"We have eaten. I will put your dinner on the table, Mr. Speng," he heard Mom say. Sydney looked into the kitchen and saw Dad looking at her. Dad did not answer. Mom put his plate by itself on the table. "Just ask me if you want anything," she said. "Anything at all and I will get it for you, Mr. Speng." Then she left the room.

The children wandered quickly from the icy kitchen into the cold living room. Before long they drifted off early to their bedrooms.

"Are you sure you're finished eating, Mr. Speng?" Mom's voice came from the kitchen. Dad grunted something in reply. Mom waited until he finished and left before she returned to the kitchen to do the dishes.

With the others gone, Sydney didn't speak to LaMar until the next evening during a quiet time. Mister stood in the kitchen with Mom.

"I'm sorry I didn't keep my promise," Sydney said quietly to LaMar.

"You tried," said LaMar. "It's my fault. If I hadn't been hurt, this wouldn't have happened." His pale face dropped and began to shake. "I should have listened to you on the wagon."

Sydney stepped over and hugged him. "Don't worry," he said. "It's 'purt near summer."

LaMar nodded without hugging him back.

"My stomach might hurt again," he said.

"You have to try harder to be happy," said Sydney. LaMar smiled with his mouth but his eyes watered.

"I know. But it is quite hard," he said.

LaMar waited in his blankets for his lessons to begin. Sydney walked out of the room but half hesitated when he saw Mister walk into the cold living room.

"Getting enough rest, Sydney?" Mister asked in his roll-calling voice. "You almost went to sleep in class yesterday."

"Naw," said Sydney. "I am all right. Dad butchered, that's all."

LaMar piped up: "Dad shot old Inca."

Sydney waved to stop LaMar from saying anything more, but LaMar always said what he wanted to. He went right on: "Nobody wanted him to, but he did anyway. Sydney tried to stop him."

Dad walked in then. He laid a hand on Sydney's shoulder. Sydney twisted free. He sat away from Dad, by LaMar, and stared at the floor.

"Yep," said Dad. "Butchered a milk cow. Had to. Doc Mooley wanted a beef. Small Hereford, large Holstein, doesn't make too much difference. More meat on the Holstein, anyway." Dad sat on the corner of the couch. Sydney started backing away toward the kitchen.

"Almost didn't," said Dad. "Sydney here almost kept me from it. Moved her—in the middle of the night – hid her in a stand of trees. Would have worked if she hadn't stuck her head out and started bellowing for breakfast." Dad looked at Sydney. "Durnedest kid I ever saw."

Mister's eyes began searching the room to guess what happened. He glanced at Sydney and back at Dad. Dad looked down, picking a burr from the cuff of his trousers.

"Don't suppose you let him off too easy on that, either, I don't suppose," Mister said. His voice spoke quietly, inviting an answer.

"Nope. He upset me." Dad studied the burr, as to guess which pasture might have burrs.

"Dad gave Sydney a licking," blurted LaMar.

"A kid that doesn't try to save an animal he loves isn't worth his salt," said Mister. "I'd think you would have been proud of him instead. Takes a man to do something that brave."

Sydney looked at Mister in surprise. Then Mister surprised him more. He reached over and gently gave Sydney a little hug. At first he twisted away, but the warmth of the hug lingered. He let Mister finish. A flash of guilt tinged him about being against Mister.

139

Dad didn't look up. He rubbed the burr between his thumb and forefinger. "Got a farm to pay for," said Dad. "There's the Federal Land Bank really pushing. I got to save my farm."

"It is my fault," said LaMar. "If I could get better by myself, we wouldn't have to kill old Inca." Tears began rolling down his pale cheeks.

"I won't have any of that," said Dad. LaMar wiped his face with the corner of a quilt. "Anyway," continued Dad, "Inca knew she would be butchered." He flipped the burr into the dark and cold fireplace.

"Oh?" said Mister. He leaned forward a little.

"I drove her in and gave her some oats. I guess I should of milked her first, but I just couldn't bring myself to. She didn't eat, just looked at me and held steady." He scuffed at the rug. "Took me two tries. I couldn't see her none too good. She just stood there, like she gave herself to me."

Mister watched Dad scuffing at the rug and gave him a few moments before speaking. He startled even Sydney by what he said next:

"That is how our Savior gave His life for us, willingly, up on the cross, like that."

"What?" said Dad. His shoulders snapped back and he glanced up and, for half an instant, his eyes met Mister's eyes. Then he looked away.

"I dunno," he said. "I dunno."

Chapter 10

A cow of wind swirled through Inca's empty stall, tugged at her hay but not eating it. The wind cow replaced the flesh and blood cow with a body of moving air. It floated upwards and roamed the earth above fences. The wind cow felt icy and her hide and tongue pressed against all parts of a guy that weren't covered. Her chill sank beneath the skin with a penetrating sorrow that lingered even in warmth. She roamed especially when manger chains held other cows to the earth in their stalls. Their steaming bodies respected Inca's empty place by leaving it cold for the draft.

The same swirling breeze drew away fall and invited winter. Earth gave up some of its sky to sinking clouds stuffed with snow gray that formed a low ceiling. Just a narrow aisle lay between earth and atmosphere. With dark clouds hanging low overhead, Dad finished his fencing at the field that now held the bull and cows. So, at home, beneath the threatening sky, Dad stowed tools in the granary, draped old canvas dams over the growing mounds of cut aspen and pine. He wrapped the tarp over the horse-drawn mowing machine no longer used, but kept workable so it could be put to service in an emergency. He daubed the shiny blades of plows with tar. He wheeled the push rake and dump rake against the back fence with teeth bared skyward in a voiceless howl against the coming cold.

Mom stuffed rags into the loosest window frames. She replaced cotton sheets with blanket sheets and, from beneath the stairs, dragged out boxes of long underwear and leggings and mittens. She stretched long underwear across the bed of each child. She pulled thick quilts from the scented cedar linen box to warm each bed. She tugged the living room door tightly shut; that room wouldn't be heated. Winter would be lived in the kitchen, warmed by the cook stove. A pullout bed for LaMar stood in the corner of the kitchen.

The single connection to the outside world, the radio, whose antenna ran outside to a high pole Nat once erected, now filled a more important role in the kitchen. Sometimes they listened to the news, or radio dramas, and talked about the war and its tommy bombs and tommy guns. Or sometimes in the evening, the family gathered around as Mom told pioneer stories, or read from old magazines, or from a school book.

A skiff of snow fell that night, just enough to color the ground and accent the barn. Frosty breath of the wind dropped in temperature and overhead clouds grew both whiter and deeper.

After that skiff of snow, Neeter hauled away the last load of calves, the black and white ones Sydney fed. Returning from school he saw truck tire tracks arced through the light snow to the loading chute. It felt odd to him to have calves in the morning but not in the evening. Sydney tried not to think about them, though he missed their calfy mee-eehs and pressing noses. With the smaller herd of milk cows and no calves, the barnyard itself grew quieter, as though the cattle grieved. But he found comfort in not having to feed calves. He walked to the stable to see if Dad wanted more chores done. The few remaining cows stood expectantly at their stalls as Dad stoked hay for them from another part of the barn.

"LaMar needs to get happied up," Sydney thought. He kicked a gunnysack to one side of the stable. "He is so sad now."

One of the mother cats slunk around the corner followed by a wary kitten. They leapt into the darkness as Sydney took another step.

"Cute kitty," he thought. "I'd like a kitty. Hey – I'll bet LaMar would like one, too. I'll catch him a kitty—that will make him a glad attitude. A glad-ittude."

He looked around for a trap but found only the gunnysack he'd kicked to one side. Dried manure stiffened the sack, wiped there from the calf-haired briefcase guy. Sydney sized up the stable for a hiding place.

"The oat bin," he thought. "That will work."

The three-foot high wooden oat bin box with leather hinges stood nearly empty in the far corner of the stable. With plans in his mind, Sydney placed the milk dish just below the bin. He picked up the gunnysack and squeezed into the narrow box. He lowered the lid into darkness. The bin smelled richly of rolled oats and shut out the cold. He waited for the kittens to come out. In a few minutes, when they circled the milk bowl, he would pop out and fling the gunny sack over them. He should be able to grab at least one kitty.

In his mind he'd already caught the cute kitty and he saw himself putting the kitty in an empty room of the barn, feeding it, taming it. He'd stroke it and it would purr at his touch.

Sydney heard Dad come into the stable. He heard hay rustling into mangers. He heard Dad crooning cuss words at Aida.

"Steady, you big ugly concoction of soup bones," said Dad.

"The cats will be out soon," Sydney said to himself, his thought bright in the darkness. "I'll wait another minute."

Then light striped into the box. Sydney looked up. The lid opened slowly. Dad's hand and a pan were coming down. Dad stared out the window.

"Dad is going to mess everything up again," thought Sydney angrily. "He messes everything up."

He stood up just as Dad's hand touched his hair.

"Awaaaaugh!" yelled Dad. "Waahuuh!"

Dad jumped back and landed on Aida, who bellowed and kicked off her hobbles. Her hoof clanged like a bell against the empty bucket. The empty bucket rolled away on the floor. Dad jumped away from Aida against the wall and his coat caught on a nail and held him in place. Aida blew at her alfalfa and kicked again. Dad twisted to the side to avoid her flailing hoof.

Sydney stood. He stared for a minute. Dad looked so funny hung on a nail, ducking from Aida. Sydney started to laugh. Dad looked angry for a flash, then Aida kicked again, and he twisted and began to laugh, too. He laughed so hard that Aida kept kicking. Dad twisted away and tried to unhook his coat. Sydney looked at him laughing and ducking from Aida, and laughed all over again. He held to the oat bin for support. Finally, Dad got free.

"What were you doing in there? gasped Dad. He reached down for the bucket. "I thought I'd grabbed a skunk!"

"Hiding from the cats," said Sydney, barely able to speak because of his laughing. "I wanted to catch a kitty."

Dad picked up the milk bucket. "Thought I grabbed a skunk," he said, laughing more. Then he added, "Those cats are too wild to catch this winter. We'll get one next summer. Quite a good plan, though." He laughed again. "And a good one on me."

Sydney reluctantly climbed from the box. "Now I'll have to come up with something else to make LaMar happy," he said.

"You will," said Dad. "For starters, you can tell him about this. It will be good for something. And easier to feed than a kitty."

Sydney hurried to the house. After dressing in his winter clothes that Mom put out for him, he climbed downstairs and sat on the couch with LaMar and told him of the kitten episode. LaMar laughed, too. A little.

"Good," Sydney thought to himself. "It is good to hear him laugh again." He thought a minute. "It felt good for me to laugh again, too."

"What's that smell?" asked Sydney as he came into the kitchen.

"We have beef liver tonight," said Mom.

"Yuk," said Sydney.

"Ewww!" said Prielle from the table.

"That better not be old Inca's liver," said Sydney.

"Hush," said Mom. "It is not old Inca any more. It is just liver."

145

"I don't like onions, either," said Sydney. "They always taste slimy. Eating cooked onions is like eating steamed angle worms."

"I don't want any," said Prielle.

"Neither do I," said LaMar.

"That's enough," snapped Mom. "Anybody who won't eat liver can just wait in the cold living room while we eat."

"I'd rather sit in the living room than the liver room," said Sydney.

Mom turned abruptly and grabbed Sydney by the shoulders and whirled him around, opened the living room door and pushed him inside. She pulled him down hard on a chair.

"Now, young man," she said. "You can just sit here until you are hungry enough to say you are sorry."

"Won't be for a while," said Sydney. "I can't eat old Inca."

Mom strode out, but left the door open so Sydney would have some warmth. He remained sitting while the family ate supper, mostly without talking.

Sydney listened to the wind moaning though the trees. He began rocking slightly, concentrating on the sounds from outdoors.

"Are you sorry yet?" Mom called when the other children finished eating.

"Nope," said Sydney. "Can't eat old Inca."

He sat for a while longer until no one paid any attention to him. They washed the dishes and prepared for bed.

"If you think hard enough, you can guess the future and be mostly right," he thought. "If I am mostly right, then when I see the future, I can figure more out."

With the dishes done, Sydney rejoined the family around the kitchen table. Wrapped in blankets, LaMar sat closest to the stove. Sydney pulled a chair up close so he could talk quietly.

"So," said Sydney to LaMar, starting casually, "How are you feeling now? Does your stomach still hurt?" He grew more pointed. "Is your stomach getting better?"

LaMar shrugged. He didn't mind the questions. "Sometimes it is better. Sometimes not. Sometimes my stomach hurts."

"Does it hurt to walk?" asked Sydney.

"Nope. Not my stomach," said LaMar. "Food hurts it sometimes. Some food hurts. But not walking. I can walk. Soon."

"Listen," said Sydney. "Listen to the wind." The boys were quiet as the growing wind howled over the roof and through the trees.

"Listen," repeated Sydney, "it's almost like I can hear old Inca calling in the wind."

LaMar shrugged. "It's going to snow soon," he said. "That's all." He turned to Mom and abruptly asked, "Do cows really have spirits? Do cows go to heaven? Do they know their calves there?"

"Cattle are our product," answered Dad. "Cows are how we make our money."

"I am sure cows have spirits," said Mom.

Sydney slid his chair back. He decided to ask. "So where do cow spirits go?" he asked in a very casual voice.

147

"Sometimes, in the wind, I almost hear old Inca calling for hay in her quiet way." He looked out the black window pretending the answer didn't matter or that he didn't care about such things. "It's like she's a long ways away, in the sky, and I can barely hear," he continued. "Then her voice splinters into the howls and whistles of the wind and she is gone before you realize she called at all."

No one answered, but they listened: in the winter you listen because that is all there is to do.

"Their spirits must go somewhere," Sydney mused. "Cow spirits must float into the sky and roam the earth in the wind."

No one answered on this nearly silent night.

Sydney thought about what Carn said and supposed that cow spirits could fly anywhere they wanted. He couldn't ask Carn. After the thrashing day, they sent him away to live in Utah with an uncle who used to be a boxer. This would be all for the best, people said. Mom hoped the uncle didn't practice his boxing on Carn. She called the uncle a family renegade, and unpredictable.

The family paid half attention to Sydney's musings. They really only thought about how to pay the Federal Land Bank. Nat and Madge sat at the table doing homework. Madge often helped Dad because she was good at math.

"This check cannot save the farm," Madge said.

Dad shook his head. "I don't know," he said. "Beef prices are down. Twenty-one cents a pound on the hoof. I hoped for $2,500, but I only sent them about two-thirds that. I'm still a few thousand short, but it may be enough to hold them over."

"No one in this family does the math but me," said Madge. "It doesn't even come close."

"I've done some math," said Mom. "I know. What shall we do?"

"I could look for work at the phosphate plant," said Dad. "I don't know if they are hiring right now."

"We could drive up there," said Mom. "It won't hurt to look."

"I've thought about looking down in Utah," said Dad. "Might come down to finding a winter job down there."

"We will do that if we have to," said Mom.

"Maybe the bankers will go away," said Dad. "Haven't heard from them for a while."

LaMar turned to Dad. "If you get a job in Utah, will you stop butchering our pets?" he asked.

Dad laughed. "We don't raise pets. It was a mistake to make pets of them. We raise cows. Cows are our product. That's how we make our money."

Dad continued: "They'd rather be born and live good for a while than never, ever be born. If we didn't raise them, these cattle would never be born. They'd never exist. Which is kinder?"

"Do cows find their calves in heaven?" asked LaMar, undeterred by Dad's logic.

"Well, all life is eternal," said Mom. "I suppose that … well, I don't know. But we do know the Lord loves all His creatures."

"Maybe now she is a spirit, maybe she can fly anywhere," said Sydney. "Maybe the ghosts of dead cows turn into the wind. Maybe after they are butchered, they become wind cows."

"Doubt it," said Dad.

"If Carn were here, I would ask him," said Sydney, returning to the subject he'd been thinking about. "Carn knows about spirits and ghosts. I wonder how he is getting along with his uncle who used to be a boxer?"

"I hope this uncle is kind to him," said Mom. "Oh! That stove is so hot!" She slid her chair back a bit farther.

"The real question is, are there bellows in heaven?" said Nat, poking into the conversation from his homework. "If bellows are allowed, they will find their calves. Mee-ee—eehs, and Haaa-aaa-ughws!" he mimicked the sounds.

"I am trying to concentrate," objected Madge. "I am reading Shakespeare and it is hard enough to concentrate without all these pretend cows bellering."

"What are you reading?" asked Mom. "I always enjoyed Shakespeare."

"Hamlet," said Madge. "Hamlet is so removed from our world I can't make it real. Ghosts and revenge and killings. It's all too ancient."

Mom slid her chair farther back from the stove and a little closer to Madge. "Carn is a Hamlet figure to me," she said. "Orphaned, raised by uncles who are not loyal to his father. Afraid to do anything, afraid not to. Carn is a local Shakespearean tragedy."

"He's a local tragedy, nothing Shakespearean about it," said Madge.

"Comedy of Errors, Much Ado about Nothing," said Nat.

"I hope this uncle doesn't practice on Carn," she repeated. Her face looked drawn and tired. Since the foreclosure notice, a line down her cheek became more pronounced and her pregnancy showed now.

"I don't feel well at all," she finally said. "I am terribly afraid something is going wrong inside me. It just doesn't feel right."

Dad leaned forward. He looked at her a long while. "Do you need to go to the doctor?" he finally asked.

"What can the doctor do?" asked Mom. "This is a time for us to practice our faith. And our prayers." She looked at the family. "It is late. Let's say family prayer and get the younger ones in bed. Nat and Madge, you can stay up later if you want to."

"I am not young," said Sydney.

"Bedtime for all those who don't have homework," said Mom to her kitchen school and family pupils. The family, excepting LaMar and Dad, slid from their chairs and knelt beside them. LaMar folded his arms and closed his eyes. Dad looked out the window. Nat said prayers, asking for LaMar to continue to heal, for help to save the farm, and to bless Mom and the baby if the Lord willed, and with studies. He asked a blessing on President Eisenhower to watch out for the Russians so they wouldn't drop tommy bombs on us.

"I got to save the farm all by myself," said Dad as they stood up. "The Lord, He's too far up there to care. You watch."

A distant knock interrupted their conversation.

"Mister's a little late tonight," said Nat.

The knock sounded louder at the kitchen door. Madge pulled the door open. "It's nobody," she said. Then a tall figure stepped from the shadows into the doorway.

"Oh," said Madge. "Excuse me. I thought you were someone."

The man's laugh came from a Bugs Bunny cartoon. "I'm not," he said in a shrill voice that came from a small head. "I'm nobody, too." He paused. "I've been waiting years to say that," he said to the family. "It's from Emily Dickinson."

"Come in," said Madge, hesitantly. "Would you like to sit down?"

Without looking up, Dad spoke from the corner furthest from the stove. "We can't afford no life insurance," he said.

The man cleared his throat and paused. His expression lost its feelings. "I'm not selling anything," he said. "I am sure you remember me from the corral. I'm H. Beesley of the Federal Land Bank office. I sent you a letter."

Dad snapped to look at him. No one else moved. No one spoke. The warm air grew thick and Sydney wondered where the .22 was.

"Don't make no appointment, let us know you were coming?" Dad asked, standing.

"Phone lines are down again," said Beesley. He looked around and didn't see a phone. "May I sit down?"

Dad pointed his hand toward the kitchen table. Beesley pulled a chair out and sat. He motioned toward another chair and Dad came over to it.

Beesley owned the kitchen now. Beesley owned the house. Beesley owned the farm. Everyone trespassed on Beesley. He lifted his calf-hair briefcase to the imitation marble table top, opened its latches and removed some papers. He leafed through them, pulled one out and spoke:

"Concerning your loan. It is three months delinquent – five years, really. We sent you a foreclosure letter."

"We got it," said Dad. His thick hand rubbed through his hair and then over his nose. "We've had a farm accident," he said. "I tried to tell you that before. Hospital took all that I planned to pay the bank."

"You didn't make a full payment for the last five years," said Beesley. "Even after this payment of $1,874 – calves, I presume – you are still behind $4,379.83. What are you going to do?"

"How long do I have?" asked Dad.

"Thirty days," said Beesley "Unless arrangements are made, the sheriff will be here to evict you one month from today. Five days later we will have a trustee auction." He pulled a calendar from his case and glanced at it. He looked at Mom. "Tell you what," he said. "We will extend it to Dec. 21st. How is that?" he said. "That should make everyone happy."

"Can't you hold off another year for the rest?" asked Dad. "We've had a farm accident. Doesn't that mean anything to the government?"

"You're not going to make a full payment. You'll have to come up with the whole amount – that's another $4,400. The accident, well, that's too bad, but a healthy account can stand an accident. An accident and a fire. And accident, a fire and low beef prices. You are not behind one year. You are behind five years. If it hadn't been an accident, it would have been a broken down tractor or an illness. These are the best of times, a most prosperous period – although these are the lowest beef prices in years. Your cash flow is negative, that's the problem. You're just not making any money here.

Times are changing. The government isn't willing to subsidize small farms any longer."

"Could I start out with a new loan?" asked Dad in a tremulous, almost begging voice.

"Not with the cash flow experience of the last five years, no."

"I grew a pretty good crop of wheat," said Dad. "If it hadn't been spread all over the highway."

"This country is sinking under wheat," said Beesley, his high-pitched voice growing exasperated. "Why can't you understand? You're trying to compete with Kansas and Iowa where they grow thousands of acres of wheat. What I am saying is that your little farm is on marginal farmland anyway. The growing season is too short. You can't do much better, and tractors are not going to cost less in the future than they do now. Your farm just isn't profitable."

He spread out his hands and put them on the table. Emphasizing each word, he said: "You're farming business does not make money."

"What do I do?" shouted Dad. "Move my family into the barrow pit? Is that what the government wants – migrants from another dust bowl?"

"I advise you to either make the payment in full or seriously consider selling out and moving to the city."

Beesley leaned back and put the papers into his calf-hair briefcase. He left one paper on the table for Dad. Then he pressed down the brass clasps that snapped metallically on his briefcase. "You have some equity in the land. You do have some liquid assets. Your inventory of cattle is easily negotiable into cash. That's one advantage a farmer has. Nobody wants a foreclosure."

"Just like that," said Dad.

"I do know a cattleman in Wyoming who is expanding. He may want to buy your cattle."

Dad nodded without speaking.

"These are the best of times," said Beesley. "Make the adjustment in the best of times. You do have that advantage."

"Some advantage," said Dad. "Get rid of the cash crop. I will have to sell every cow I own."

Then Beesley stood up. "Your crop yields too little cash," he said. "December twenty-first." He stood, picked up the briefcase.

"Shall I call the Wyoming man for you?" asked Beesley.

Dad just nodded. Mom found a piece of paper and searched for a pencil until Nat handed her the one he'd been using. Mom wrote down Mister's phone number on the page of homework, tore a corner off and handed it to Beesley. Beesley put the number into his pocket and nodded to her. He raised his eyebrows at Dad and nodded once more to him. He turned around and opened the kitchen door, rattling the glass in the windows, and walked out.

No one spoke. Mom silently waved toward the bedrooms.

Chapter 11

Later in the night, while Sydney and the family slept, air stilled and warmed. In the warmer air, Ma Nature ladled whipped cream over the world; the dark grass, rusty bike frames, bone-gray wood accented by a skiff of snow disappeared entirely beneath heaps of white. The storm smoothed and beveled sharp edges, abrupt lines, flat planes; ovals appeared over blocks and mounds and smothered anything left outdoors. Whiteness capped fence posts with fluff and topped even barbed wire with finger-thick drifts. The blanched surface absolved sins of ugliness and replaced them with universal purity. Snow covered and softened impending financial doom as well, offering a new world away from harsh reality and shortages of the olden grays. The Wyoming man would save us, Sydney believed. He would call and save us and save the farm.

LaMar's legs grew stronger as the snows grew deeper. He trembled at first and puffed lots of air with each step. Later he stopped breathing so hard. One morning, Mister came in his Studebaker to take LaMar to school. Mom worried a big fuss over him as he left.

Sydney watched. He didn't care if they offered him a ride; he could have walked. But Mister finally invited him in, so he rode with them. Even in the winter, the Studebaker smelled new. Warmth spread inside. Very warm warmth.

"You're helping the family a great deal, Sydney," said Mister. "You're becoming quite a man. I think you've grown two inches this winter."

"Thanks," said Sydney. "I feel taller these days."

LaMar, used to talking to Mister, began chattering. "Sydney said there are two sides at school—their side and your side. I'm on your side, Mister," he said.

"You don't have to be on sides. We don't want any fighting," said Mister. "They won't bother you."

LaMar continued, "Sydney used to be on their side. Whose side are you on now, Sydney?" he asked. "Will you please be on our side? Will you please?"

Sydney stared at the floor, silent.

"Please, Sydney," repeated his brother.

Sydney looked angrily at LaMar. If they had been home, he might have told him to shut up or even cuffed him one. He acted mighty spoiled these days.

"I'm not taking sides anymore," he finally said. "Nobody wins in a town fight."

"Good," said Mister. "If no one took sides, there would be no town fight. You do have a lot of ability, Sydney," he continued. "You can stay above this. You can learn not to fight. It takes a lot of ability, but you can rise to the occasion."

When they pulled up in front of the school, children lined the sidewalk, watching. A few small faces gaped from indoors. LaMar carefully steadied himself and lifted one foot, then another toward the concrete steps. Mister reached to hold him up, but again LaMar spoke up. "I can climb steps," he said.

LaMar lifted his strong left leg up and then brought his right leg up to meet it, and repeated the process. Laboriously he mounted the steps, breathing hard.

"He can so walk," a girl in a quilted orange and green coat said to a girl next to her. "You said he'd never walk, but he can so."

Mister colored at the neck. "You are doing just great," he told LaMar.

At the top step, LaMar turned around and grinned his monkey grin at the crowd. All the pupils began clapping.

"Easy, there," said Mister in a voice heavy with authority. "LaMar will sit at a special desk in my room."

LaMar shook by the time he made it into Mister's room, still wearing his coat. His face tightened and his hands trembled. He carefully sat at his special desk, cushioned with a flat pillow sewed by Mister's wife, whom everyone called Sister Mister.

Mister stepped to the hall and pulled the cotton rope and the school bell pealed across town; an extra clang also pealed for LaMar. Everyone in the village noticed. Returning to the classroom, Mister asked Sydney to lead the Pledge of Allegiance to the Flag.

Bleu and Melvin walked late into the room. They ambled between Sydney and the other students and dusted snow from their cuffs before stopping.

"I pledge . . ." began Sydney.

"I pledge," joined in Bleu, two words behind. "I pledge," argued Melvin, two words behind Bleu. Their out-of-synch voices muffled beneath the general pledging: "… with liberty and justice for all ... and justice for all ... for all." Sydney ignored them and returned to his seat to hear Melvin whisper, "Now the old man is going to bear his testimony."

Mister stood and cleared his throat. "Class, we welcome LaMar Speng back among us. He is much better and we are lucky he is able to be here."

"He's darn lucky too," whispered Melvin.

"We can all help him by not staring. Help him with doors and down the steps when he is tired."

"I can walk all by myself," insisted LaMar.

Mister rubbed his hands together. He nodded. "You do very well," he said.

"Here it comes," whispered Bleu. Melvin folded his arms and bowed his head.

"And remember him in your prayers because that has already helped a great deal."

"Amen," said Melvin loudly, unfolding his arms.

Later, when Mister excused the class for recess, he slipped out of the room. Immediately pupils surrounded LaMar's desk. By the time Sydney pushed his way through, kids from the three youngest grades peered in the doorway again.

"Does it hurt a lot?" asked Addie, "I mean, to about be busted in half and all?"

"Will you ever walk really good again?" asked Ann. She pursed her thick lips. Sydney reached LaMar's side.

"Sure," he answered venomously to Addie. "It is fun to have your hip broken. Try it sometime."

"I didn't mean that," sniffed Addie. She wiped her nose. "I'm sorry. I didn't mean to be hurtful."

Sydney's voice grew softer. "Sure. He'll be running again."

LaMar's eyebrows rose. "I'll be running by Christmas. Doc Mooley said so."

Bleu and Melvin sauntered to LaMar's desk.

"Don't let the old man worry you none," said Melvin. "When they close down the school he won't be around anymore. He won't be teaching here next year."

Neither Sydney nor LaMar answered in the sticky silence.

"We're on sides," said Bleu, his mouth curling at the tips. "Those who want the school closed and the others who don't. We've decided to let you be on our side."

"I am on Mister's side," said LaMar bluntly.

"Better not be," said Melvin. "His side is going to lose, and everybody on it. But we ain't gonna hurt you—you are already a cripple." He turned to Sydney. "At least you are still on our side against old potlicker."

"Sydney's not taking sides anymore," piped up LaMar. Sydney glared at him and motioned him to be quiet.

"What!" said Melvin. He looked at Bleu.

"Sydney told Mister that he wasn't on a side anymore," said LaMar.

"You traitor!" blurted Melvin in surprise. He ignored Sydney's gesture. "You Bene – ! We can hurt you. You're not a cripple. Not yet."

"Don't worry," protested Sydney in a voice beneath Mister's hearing. "I just said that for Mister."

"Bene-- Arnold," said Melvin. "I don't care why you said it."

"It is over," supplied Bleu. "Benedict-shun. Benedict-shun Arnold."

"The important thing is that you said it," continued Melvin. 'We won't have Benediction Arnold on our side."

Sydney considered telling them what Doc Mooley said about keeping LaMar a positive attitude. He should have told them earlier, but they didn't ever really care too much about LaMar. "I will tell them after school," he decided.

"Benediction Arnold," said Bleu. "It is over. We hang traitors."

"It is not like that," said Sydney. "Come outside. I have to tell you something right now."

"There is nothing you can say, Benediction," said Bleu. "It is over."

Sydney followed them out of the room. "I had to say that," he whispered to Melvin. "We have to make LaMar feel happy. It is the only way he'll get better. The doctor said so," he added in desperation.

"Sure, he did. Sure, traitor, sure," said Melvin angrily. "Say what you want to; you are still a traitor." His hand doubled into a fist and lifted and crashed into Sydney's side. Sydney bent double from the sharpness.

"I haven't changed sides," pleaded Sydney over his hurt. "I still want to be friends."

"Shut up," said Melvin from a distance. "We will hurt you."

Sydney watched them walk away. They laughed.

"They are glad it happened," he thought. "They didn't want me as a friend. They are out of people to hurt, so they picked me." Pain watered his eyes. He knew they would never forgive him. It had been hard enough to stay friends with them even when he stayed on their side. He watched them walking out together and knew they'd talked about him for a long time. He couldn't keep from silently weeping.

He sat very quietly by LaMar. He didn't answer when LaMar asked, "What happened?"

"Shut up," Sydney said. "Sometimes you just need to shut up."

LaMar's face darkened. LaMar's face remained dismal as school ended, all the way home, and while they sat in the kitchen. After dinner, both their faces grew more sober when they heard Mom talking. She'd slipped on the ice of the crooked flat rock step and tripped. She fell into the snow and returned to the kitchen crying and holding her front. Dad helped her sit.

Mom took a deep breath. "It feels like this feeling is going to come out prematurely," she said, breaking into a sob. "It feels like the beginning of a miscarry."

"Let's get you to the doctor," Dad said.

"I want to rest," she said, sobbing. "I want to lie down and not move."

Later, after Dad had taken Mom to the hospital, and just the older ones sat in the kitchen, Madge asked softly, "When do babies count as babies?" She continued, "Do they have to be born to be a baby, or are they babies from the first?"

"Sounds like you are reading Hamlet again," said Nat lowly, slipping out of his heavy coat as he entered. "To babee, or not to babee, that is the question."

"If you ever had a serious bone in your body – I really want to know," said Madge.

"I bone-seriously don't know," said Nat.

"Maybe it is when they start to flutter like a butterfly inside the tummy," said Sydney. "How did she feel when they rushed for the doctor?"

"What?" asked Nat becoming solemn. "What happened? Did something happen to the baby?"

"You could be serious," said Madge. "Mom fell. She started to bleed. The baby probably will not survive. We've lost our little brother or sister."

"Oh," said Sydney. "I am sorry. I didn't know."

"Oh," said Nat. His countenance dropped. "I didn't know, either."

The three of them in the kitchen were silent. A sense of infinite loss hung over them undivided by the familiar things this child would never come to know – the stove, the sink, blue tile floor, the imitation marble table, the chair with one stick glued together on the back, the rattling glass in the kitchen door. And each of the family members it would never know, or be changed by, or be held by, or teased. And they would never come to know it; tiny fingerprints never made, baby clothes never worn, baby spoon never used to feed or scoop off a tiny mouth, the baby chair left in the attic. No babbling, no smiles, no crying. No baby.

"This is a hard year," said Nat mournfully. "We're losing everything. Nothing will be the same next year at this time."

The next morning, all Dad said was: "We lost the baby."

Because there could be no funeral for a baby that tiny, heaven held its own funeral in its own color. More snow fell, white on white, draping layers of new altar cloths across virginal winter landscape.

Mom stayed in the hospital. Later, Madge whispered to Sydney that Mom wouldn't be able to have any more children. The way she said it sounded like the slamming of a steel door against the hopes of the family, against Mom, against the future. The shock of it numbed the family. It could have been any of them who wouldn't be born – LaMar, or Sydney, or Madge. No one talked about it. No one spoke of it to anyone else. It remained a family secret, because that's what Mom wanted. Mister and Sister Mister would never know. Even among family members the subject remained too painful to discuss.

Brid Neeter may have guessed something bad happened. Because within two days, Dad called him up and asked him to ship three of the final four milk cows to the Preston slaughter market.

"Nothing is going right," Sydney thought. "How can we keep LaMar happy in this sorry, sad, failing, bad luck, dismal winter? Yet, after everything else, we can't lose LaMar."

"Will you promise to tell me if you see something?"

Sydney looked at LaMar again. He shook his head. "Can't promise," he said. "It isn't like that. You don't understand."

"Just tell me, then," said LaMar.

"You remember what I told you about the wind cows?" asked Sydney.

LaMar nodded.

"It's like they are getting revenge on us," said Sydney. "Every time we sell, or butcher, bad things are happening."

"Oh, Sydney," said LaMar, sounding just like Dad. "You have such an imagination."

"Sydney!" said Dad. "Wood box is low."

164

Sydney quickly inserted himself into his coat and walked outside to collect wood that he loaded on the sleigh and began pulling it toward the house. His frozen breath billowed against the house light and he looked into the cloud, feeling he saw something important. Just at that instant, and for only that instant, the actual air itself ripped slightly open to an inner, secret picture: he saw a glimpse that quickly disappeared and the air zipped itself shut. Nothing more. No clue. No explanation. Nothing.

"No. It can't be," he thought. "It can't be. I can't do anything about it, so why should I know?"

This time, though, he paid such attention that the image etched itself in his thoughts. He knew he would see it over and over in his mind. In his glimpse, he saw a corner of the cemetery with two open graves. And a strong wind howled snow over the open tombs.

Chapter 12

A feather, frizzled by time into an almost white ball, flew up as Sydney fluffed the covers on their upstairs, sway-bellied bed. He puffed it away so that it vanished into non-existence like the long-ago chicken upon which it once grew. Returning to this sway-bellied double bed for the first time since the wreck, LaMar watched as Sydney pulled heavy covers back. They knelt quickly on the cold floor and said prayers – LaMar taking more time than Sydney – and climbed between icy sheet blankets. Their legs touched lightly before each pulled his away.

"Stay on your own side," ordered Sydney, adjusting his pillow. "I about had you trained. Now you will have to be trained all over again."

"Don't kick me," said LaMar. "You might hurt my tummy."

"You haven't slept here since the wreck," said Sydney. "I will have to train you somehow."

"Just don't kick me in the tummy."

"I will kick your legs."

"But not too hard. It might hurt my tummy."

"Maybe I will try poking you."

"Not in my tummy."

"I have to train you somehow."

"I like not getting kicked when I am asleep."

Sydney looked around at the old bed frame. "I could put a board between us," he said.

"That might hurt my tummy," said LaMar. "I might roll over on it."

"Think of this," said Sydney. "If you cross over this line, a pretend giant knife will cut you in half and sew you back together again so fast you won't even feel it."

From his side of the bed, Sydney could feel LaMar shudder.

"We will call it the, the – he paused, thinking of the most outlandish, terrible name he could imagine – "the grumptious," said Sydney, drawing the word out.

"The grumptious," repeated LaMar. He remained silent for a minute, then asked, "Is that something like you knowing the wreck would happen?"

"No," said Sydney. "They are different."

Sydney saw him looking across the sway-bellied bed.

"How did you know it would happen? I know you knew because you said so."

"Dunno," replied Sydney, looking away. "You need to forget about that – it will hurt your tummy." He waited for LaMar to change talking to something else.

"How?" repeated LaMar. He looked at Sydney again.

Sydney shrugged. "I don't know how. I just do."

"That's no answer," said LaMar, in his usual blunt manner. "How is what I asked."

Sydney shrugged again. "It just comes to me, that's all. I don't do anything special."

"What else is going to happen? What else do you know about? Do you know if I will get well?"

"Never mind," said Sydney. "But I did know about old Inca. That's why I tried so hard to stop it. To see if I could change what would happen. But I can't."

"Does that mean we are stuck with what is going to happen? That we can't change anything?"

"I don't know," said Sydney.

"Do you promise to tell me when you know something else is going to happen?" asked LaMar. "Promise, promise?"

"Depends," said Sydney. "I can't promise. It just depends."

Sydney's mind filled with the picture that had come to him of two windswept graves. He wondered long who the graves were for. What two people would die? When would they pass away on across? Over and over, he wondered.

"Please?" asked LaMar after a pause.

"I am going to sleep. Go to sleep or I will send the grumptious after you."

"Don't be silly," said LaMar. "It can't get me on my side of the bed."

When Sydney could hear LaMar sleeping, wind sighing in the cottonwood trees bent over the house just above his window kept him from sleep. Trees swayed in the wind sometimes rattling their leafless branches against the roof. Moaning through the branches, the spirits of cows shrilled, howled. Some bayed in the distance, some were close. Some of their calves answered in high-pitched calf mehhs. Sydney felt like he lay in a world of graves and phantoms, of those gone and of those going. In his half-sleep, he couldn't tell which were which.

"Who will it be?" he wondered. "LaMar almost died, but he didn't." He thought about each member of his family – Bartholomew, Prielle, LaMar, Marge, Nat, himself and even the baby we lost. "But they don't bury babies that small."

Yet he thought more, and wondered about Arsle, and how he limped everywhere he went.

"Who?" he wondered. "Who will it be?"

Then he thought about the school, and whether it would really close and what it would look like empty. He didn't want to think about that either – its sidewalks covered with snow, its playground weeded over, wind constantly sculpting new drifts. The school wasn't a living thing unless people walked in it. So they would never put the school in a grave and bury it. Its body would just linger on without its spirit.

Then he thought about the farm. Dad would never let them take the farm. A long shudder trembled over his frame in the dark. Dad would never let them. Would he? The graves – the image of the graves flared open in his mind laced with the pain of losing something very dear and close. What? Nothing. Only something dear, something very close.

LaMar slept deeply now. Sydney shut his eyes and pulled the heavy covers up to his nose. He took a deep breath and wondered how they could ever live through the next month.

There would be a party, certainly a party, some kind of party. And the school operetta. Always an operetta, and the cattle would be sold. And maybe . . . a funeral, he thought as he drifted off to sleep.

The next morning led into the next week somehow, though no one forgot anything for one second, and the week passed normally enough until Saturday when Dad

announced at breakfast that he would use a sleigh to feed
the cattle in the field. He could never sit still and do
nothing, so he'd put heavy sleigh runners under the rack.
The hay wagon looked the same, only it rested on runners
instead of wheels.

"Can we go?" asked LaMar.

"I reckon I will bring back a jag of willows," said Dad.

"Jag of willows?" asked Mom.

"Jag of willows," said Sydney, matter-of-factly.

"What is a jag of willows?" asked LaMar.

"Make the fire a little hotter," said Dad.

"Oh," said LaMar. "Please?" he asked. "Venna said I
needed to get some sun. And fresh air. Is it windy?"

"No," said Dad. "It's clear and warm. A beautiful
day."

"My bones are all better," said LaMar. "They've
knitted." He looked at Sydney. "It will make me happy," he
said.

"I will help," said Sydney. "May we go?"

Dad didn't answer. He looked at Mom, sitting in a
rocker Dad brought from the living room.

"Mom," called LaMar. "Is it okay if I go out to the
field with Dad?"

She didn't answer.

"I'll pull up with the sleigh and the team of
horses," said Dad. "You two be ready." Dad left to harness
the team.

"Listen Buster," said Mom. "One bad bump and
you are home for the rest of the year. Do you understand?"
She didn't get up but watched LaMar and Sydney dress for
the outdoors. LaMar began adding snow gear. He put on

leggings over overalls and two pair of socks, shoes and somebody's old boots very large for his feet. In a few minutes, Prielle called that the sleigh and horses were outside by the swing that hung from a limb near the house.

"The horses are smoking," she said. Bartholomew rushed to see. One draught horse, black with a stripe down its head and the other draught horse bronze colored with a splash of white on its forehead – Old Strip and Old Dot – the team stomped and steamed.

Sydney pulled on his boots and buckled them to the top.

"Sleigh is smooth as rooster feathers," called Dad from the sleigh. "It's the warmest day left of the year."

LaMar stood, so thickly dressed he moved like a doll without joints. Mom made to help him but remained weakly slow. She handed him the cushion from her overstuffed rocker to sit on. Sydney carried the cushion to the sleigh, and, as they climbed on, they saw Mom at the window, bent over, watching anxiously. As Mom watched, Dad insisted on helping LaMar get situated. Sydney climbed next to him. Then Dad pulled one rein and his cheek "squicked." The team started at a trot and the sleigh glided from the yard to the barrow pit of the highway, soundless but for the melody of the team's clopping hooves. So quietly traveled the sleigh that it seemed to stand still while the world turned slowly beneath its runners. Vastness of the white framed the world in every direction. Icicles hung in upside-down crowns on roofs and snow-capped chimneys released winding columns of coal smoke that looked the blacker against the stark background. Highlights of snow traced tree limbs, now appearing more

171

crested and elegant, standing aloof; regal sentries over royal families who pathed through whiteness wearing bulky coats of arms.

On the team trotted, finding the thickest snow, runners leaving perfect toy truck roads through the drifts. Sydney and LaMar huddled close and watched the houses slip by.

As homes fell behind, the boys could look across the fields at other outfits feeding other herds cattle.

"They looked like a curving red zipper on white cloth," said Sydney.

"They look like cattle eating," said LaMar.

Arriving at their field, clopping of hooves stopped with Dad's "Whoa there!" He vaulted down and opened the gate. From the ground, he squicked in his cheek. The horses tossed their heads swiveled their ears forward and waited. Dad squicked in his cheek a second time and the team walked uncertainly through the gate.

"Whoa," called Dad. The horses stopped and he climbed on.

"Giddap" he called without touching the reins; the team's massive hindquarters flexed as they confidently jumped forward, deepening the road to the haystack.

Sydney could see frost bristling on the backs of the cattle. Their noses turned expectantly toward the coming hay; a few of them lowed. Closest to the hay, Old Lopp pushed against the stackyard fence. The cow next to her dropped her nose to the ground as if grass would magically appear. A cow with red and white dividing her face to her nostrils, lifted her duotone head and lowed impatiently. Another cow with a split ear craned her head almost in a half circle without taking a step to watch the wagon. The bull, rounded shoulders, drooping horns and keen sense of kingship, battered his way through the herd. Other cattle waited impatiently; their heads followed the sleigh's every move.

After Dad filled the rack with hay, the team guided itself as Dad and Sydney kicked or pitched hay off into the snow where cattle quickly bunched, seeking and eating along the windrow. Some settled into first hay while others followed along without eating, hoping for a thicker spot to come. Noses inserted into piles of hay came out whiskered in green.

When they finished pitching hay off, Dad guided the sleigh toward the willow pasture.

"What are we doing?" asked LaMar.

"Kindling," Dad explained. "Willows burn hot. Willows extend the wood we have so we don't have to buy coal." He added, "Willow burns cleaner and hotter than fir."

"Oh," said Sydney.

"Giddap!" Dad shouted, and the team walked then trotted slowly over the field. Dad pulled them to a halt near the willow-lined creek.

"Syd," ordered Dad. "Carry the willows after I bust them out."

Sydney and LaMar looked at each other. Dad walked to willows along the creek bank and began breaking off dead, barkless branches. Sounds like gunfire burst from the limbs as Dad bent them to the ground where they snapped. Sydney dragged them to the sleigh and heaped them loosely on its bed. When dead willows heaped the entire bed, he climbed on the rack and Dad also returned to the sleigh, squicked the team and again they pulled the sleigh over their newly broken road.

"Heeaaw! yelled Dad as they pulled to a drift. Strip lunged forward, followed by Dot. Halfway into the drift, the sleigh bogged down, horses' bellies swimming and hooves pawing. Strip surged forward in her tugs while Dot bucked ineffectively.

"I'm cold," said LaMar. "I am starting to shiver and my leg feels like the rock is there again. Can't we go home?"

"Never should have brought you," said Dad. "Try standing. You'll get warm."

LaMar dropped his head and hugged his body for warmth. Sydney slid next to him to help with his warmth.

"Hee-yupp," cried Dad.

Sydney held to the front and put one arm around grumpy LaMar, who hugged closer only for warmth. The sleigh pitched ahead as Strip churned forward, the muscles in her haunches standing out like flatirons. Dot reared in her harness. Dad picked up the pitchfork by its tines and whacked Dot across the back with its handle.

"Giddap, you potlicker," shouted Dad. The sleigh lurched forward. They passed the windrow of hay where cattle champed, heads down, noses thrust forward. Dad looked over the herd and suddenly pulled the sleigh to a halt.

"Whoooo, there," he said quietly.

He hopped down and walked slowly among the cattle. The natural distance between man and cattle vanished between provider and provender. He reached out and patted one here and there. Cattle continued to chew and Dad

174

moved along inspecting each one. Here and there, he lifted
a tail to see that each cow appeared to be swelling with
calf. After walking the entire line, he looked at Old Lopp.
She jumped back and watched him warily. He bent over
and formed a snowball. He threw it at her, pocking her tall
side with a pimple of snow; she jumped like a deer. Dad
didn't even chuckle.

Sitting on the wagon now surrounded by broken
willows, LaMar and Sydney waited as Dad hurried back to
the sleigh, wiping what must have been some hay dust from
his eyes. He climbed on the wagon, briefly sloping the
corner toward his weight, and squicked the team forward
toward home.

"They all look to be with calf," he said. "Some are
already making bag."

Soon the sleigh traveled silkily along the road edge.

'I wanted you to see the cattle, and remember them,"
said Dad. "Things are about to change forever."

The boys nodded. A white cottontail erupted from a
ball of weeds, the team shying briefly, jerking their heads
up, as it bounced away through the fence. The boys
watched it vanish away into the whiteness as though it had
never been there, as though the bounding rabbit leaped
directly into the past, an instant memory.

Dad pulled over at the town store. Between projects,
with nothing to do in so much snow, cold-weather loafers
Arsle, Neeter and Mafe sat on the steps of the town store
cooling off after soaking inside heat most of the morning.
The loafers looked glad to announce news. Arsle began.

"Tough-chewing hay you got there," he said to Dad by
way of greeting.

"He's got tough-chewing cows," added Neeter. "One of them is a tough kicker, too."

"The school notice came," said Arsle, to be the first to say it, and with a slight sense of victory. "You will want to read it. It is posted inside."

"They are going to do it?" said Dad, as much a statement as question.

"All done," said Mafe, echoing Arsle's victory. "All done."

"Just a matter of time?" asked Neeter. "We knew they would."

"Everything changes," said Dad. "The whole world is changing. Nothing will be the same."

He hopped down from the sleigh and half-cantered into the store. In a moment he walked out again. He shook his head. "The only part of change that doesn't change with change is pain," he muttered, almost to himself.

"What does it say?" called Sydney to the men. "The notice."

"They are closing the school Jan. 1, 1958," said Arsle. "Christmas vacation for Edison Elementary will extend forever."

"Darn shame," said Neeter. "Has it been a good school? Been best in the valley." Arsle and Mafe smiled at each other.

Dad carried in his hand a letter crossed by blue pencil lines over it. He unbuttoned his coat and put the letter inside without showing it to the others.

"Just some kindling," said Dad shortly to answer the first question, and nodded a quick good-by. He turned away, disinclined to talk more.

176

Chapter 13

People lamented the new silence coming to the school. The quieting of its bell that hung over the town, the bell that would no longer clang its presence four times a school day. The coal-heated hot-water-radiators would remain unheated, boards would cover windows, sagebrush once so vigorously grubbed would reclaim the softball diamond, the swings and even cracks in sidewalks. The school's oil-smelling floors, its chalk dust, its glue, its filmstrip projectors, its scissors, its old encyclopedias – all would become part of its own history of mostly forgotten characters of the invisible, inert, untouchable past.

And the lifeblood of the community – its exuberant youth – would be loaded daily in a bus and whisked away, injecting their vivacity and loyalty into another town's school.

On Monday, gray-faced and distracted, Mister came back to himself in the classroom. But the school closing made of Christmas a new portal that would shut on the past and open to a suddenly changed life.

"I know you are expecting us to do the Christmas operetta, this year as always," said Mister. The pupils waited expectantly. "But," he said, "with the school closing and all, we just won't have the time and budget to put on the operetta."

The pupils looked at each other in surprise. Addie shrugged and Melvin laughed.

"I wasn't up to being Santa this year," he said, confident the cancellation came as a courtesy for him, automatically the role of the oldest male student.

Mister rubbed the wrinkles in his neck. "One other thing," he said, stepping into the middle of the room to address all the classes. "I know this is very unusual. However, my wife, Alicia, felt devastated with the school closing on January 1. She felt more disappointed in not having Valentine's Day party than in the closing. I propose we have a blended party, a Valentine's party along with the Christmas party, on the last day of school, a Monday. That will be on Christmas Eve, December twenty-fourth."

The pupils looked around and shrugged.

"A party is a party," said Addie. "I don't care."

"Thank you," said Mister. "It will be very important to Alicia. We will furnish the refreshments."

"That settles it," perked Ann, smiling widely.

"Wonderful," said Onga, clapping her thin hands.

"Now," said Mister, "We shall begin arithmetic with the eighth-grade boys. "Bleuford, eight times seven, please."

The look of triumph fled from Bleu's face and shifted to fear, then pain, then sullen hatred. "What?" he asked, "What did you say?"

"Eight times seven," said Mister. "Fourth grade arithmetic. I owe it to you to prepare you for graduation this spring. I've talked to the school board – we will not hold children back grades anymore."

The class spontaneously burst into applause. They looked around at each other with pleased smiles. Mister startled at this response. He turned to Melvin and Bleu.

178

"You two must graduate, so you must learn. Anyone else who wants to refresh math skills can join Melvin and Bleuford in a special class. Soon you will learn algebra. Melvin, Bleuford, Mrs. Clonerson's younger sister, Ingrid, has agreed to tutor you for the next week and a half."

Melvin and Bleu looked at each other. Mrs. Clonerson's younger sister softened the blow.

"Now, if you will excuse me." Mister left the room.

"Now he stops flunking people," said Melvin. "He should have stopped last year."

"Algebra," said Bleu the way someone would about measles, mumps, and chicken pox. "He has already made arrangements. He planned it all along. Pot belly doesn't know what he's starting."

For a split second Sydney felt oddly at home on the other side of this war. He sank lower in the desk, rested back on his neck and launched an attack. "Too bad you couldn't be Santa," he shot back to Melvin. "You are so jolly!"

He smiled at Addie and she smiled back at him.

"We've been nice to you Speng," he hissed. "That's over now. You are going to get killed, smart-mouth twerp." Melvin paused while Mister came back with math workbooks in his hands. Then Melvin whispered, "Along with your precious friend, Mister."

"Don't worry," said Addie, still holding her formless, damp handkerchief. Her happy eyes lingered on Sydney. "Their breath is worse than their bite."

Pupils in the back tittered, and Melvin's eyes grew angry.

Addie laughed and this time Sydney grinned back at her.

That Monday evening as the family huddled around the kitchen stove and its willow-enhanced heat, Dad read his letter from the Post Office. From the Federal Land Bank. That came Saturday: Everyone knew what it was. The letter's envelope had blue lines over it and important words rubber stamped on it. Dad said he signed a paper to take the letter. He hadn't opened it until this morning, and now he felt to read it to the family

"This is another 30-day notice to pay up or get out," he said. "Except now we are down to eleven days. The deadline is on December 21st – a week from this Friday. If we are not out before then, they will bring a U.S. marshal to evict us on that very day."

"We must sell the herd to Preston," said Mom. "We can't take a chance on losing everything. We never did hear from that man in Wyoming."

"Prices dropped to 18 cents a pound," said Dad. "Lowest prices in memory. I'll have to sell the whole herd." Dad paused and put more willows in the kitchen stove. "Even that may not quite make it. Even if I send those heifers."

"Just how close are we?" asked Nat.

"Close, but not certain," said Madge.

"I really hate to have all those mothers and unborn calves butchered one by one in Preston," said Dad.

Mom shuddered.

"Even then I may not quite make it," he said. "It will be very, very close. We may have to find something else to sell. Maybe the team, too."

"Will they come and take away our house?" asked Prielle. "How will they move it?"

"No," said Mom. "But if we sell the herd, we will have to move ourselves. Without our cattle, we can't make a living."

"We will sell the herd to save the farm and house, and then we will move to the city," said Dad. "Like H. Beesley says. It is all very simple."

A knock sounded at the kitchen door. Sydney opened it for Mister to hurry inside into the narrow circle of warmth radiating from the cook stove. Mister pressed closer to the stove. Then Mister pressed even closer to the stove, extending his hands above its burners. Noticing the awkward silence, he turned to LaMar.

"And how is LaMar this evening?" he asked to lighten the subject.

"My tummy hurts again," said LaMar. "I get tired so easy."

"Maybe it is the cold," said Mister, frowning at Dad. Dad handed him the letter, which he read carefully and shook his head. He read the letter a second time and shook his head again.

"I didn't realize things were this bad."

"Any news?" asked Dad.

"As a matter of fact, I did get a call tonight from a certain Garth Orr of Evanston. He is interested in your herd. But he said he couldn't possibly get here before the 24th."

"That's three days after the marshal kicks us out," said Dad. "And takes over the farm."

"The phone line went bad then," said Mister.

"Did he say what he would pay us?"

Mister shook his head. "Bad lines," he said. "Couldn't call back. But I am sure it will be a fair price."

"I hope so," said Dad. "We need every red cent from every red cow."

No one smiled.

"What will we do?" asked Mom. "Can we delay it a few days?"

Mister shook his head. "This is legal, judge stuff. A trustee sale is not flexible. After that date everything you own will belong to the Federal Land Bank. They hold an auction five days later. They will auction everything – cows and drill and rake and plows, even the egg beater. Everything – off to the highest bidder."

Dad straightened up and glared around the family. "I don't want a word of this to get out," he said. "Not one single word. No one must know. Do you understand me?"

"The Pocatello newspaper published it," said Mister. "The buzzards know. They will buy, pennies on the dollar."

"No one here reads that," said Dad. "I prefer to keep it quiet for now."

"We must practice our faith," said Mom. "After winter comes summer. Somehow we will get through this."

"Sometimes I don't think it will ever be summer for me," said LaMar. "I just feel too sad and tired to make it to summer."

"You've got to get better," said Mister. "When summer comes you can run and play. There's lots of fun things to do in the summer."

Dad joined in. "Picnics, and Fourth of July, and campouts."

"But I know how you feel," said Mister. "Sometimes, I don't feel like I will make summer, either."

"That is enough," said Mom. "I won't have that kind of talk."

"What is it like to die?" asked LaMar. "Do you know, Mister?"

Mom made a sign to Mister to change the subject, but he shook his head.

"That's a good question," he said. "It deserves an answer. Obviously, I don't know by experience, but by teachings. When we die, we stay who we are and as we are, except we lose our body. We are awake and we will know everything that happens.

"When we die, our spirits – our minds and our thoughts and our awareness – will continue to go on. We will still be us. We will just leave behind our mortal husk and this world. It will be as if we walk into another room where different people are standing, and we will communicate with them, much the same as we talk to each other now."

"Dying sounds about the same as moving to the city," said Dad.

"Who are they?" asked LaMar. "Will I know any of them?"

"Your Grandpa and Grandma Speng, aunts and uncles who have died. Each generation eventually gathers over there, some go sooner, some go later. But finally, everyone goes, and all gather there."

"Humm," said LaMar. "I didn't know that. That doesn't sound any more scary than a family reunion."

"Reunions are much more scary," piped up Nat. "The relatives are undead."

"But don't worry – I will cross the veil before you do," said Mister.

"Well I never!" said Mom. "This is quite enough of this talk. Instead of death, we should be talking about how to fix things so we won't be so worried. It is time to exercise some faith."

"The way I see it, faith is like voting," said Dad, quick to change subjects. "My no vote cancels your yes vote."

"No," said Mom. "Your no vote only cancels you. It does not affect me. Salvation is an individual proposition."

"Faith is not just a blind leap hoping you land safely," said Mister. "True faith is much, much more."

"Faith looks blind to me," said Dad. "Blind and more."

"True faith is a two-way conversation, just not with words."

"That's where I check out," said Dad.

"That's where it becomes meaningful to me," said Mister.

"Yes," said Mom. "The feelings that come guide us."

"Can't rely on feelings," said Dad. "Feelings depend on mood. A mood can be anything."

"These feelings are different. They come from above."

By way of an answer, Dad just shook his head.

"How do you feel about the future, about what you should do?" asked Mister.

"Me being without faith, I see nothing but out," said Dad. "I've no choice."

"And me being with faith, I still see no exit but an exit," said Mister. "The school will close."

"I guess you could just up and retire," said Dad to Mister.

"I guess you could just up and sell," said Mister to Dad.

Dad and Mister looked at each other.

"'Spose I will," said Dad. "I have always had the confidence that I can provide for my family one way or another."

"'Spose I will, too," said Mister. "But for me, this is the end of the line. The job is too much of me, and I am too old. What would be left of me without the job wouldn't be worth anything. If Alicia and I had children, that would be very different. But I have too little else in my life."

"My land is my life," said Dad. "I am a slave to a thankless master – thankless miser, I should say. It is the land that holds me, not the cattle, not the grain."

"You two either have faith or you don't," said Sydney. "I am somewhere between. I only have a tiny faith, just enough for it to give me a licking – I am afraid all the time."

"Oh?" asked Mister.

"I see things," said Sydney. "Things from the future. I can't say what. But every time we sell a cow or butcher, something bad happens. Now at night I hear the spirits of cattle dead moaning and lowing in the trees.

"My prayers aren't answered so I don't know what to think. I guess I have only part-faith."

Like he just woke up to the fact that Mister remained standing, Dad pulled a chair from the table and dragged it to Mister. Mister joined the closely seated family circle.

"That sounds more mental that spiritual," Mister said.
"But if you are seeing things from the future, then it is for a
reason. You can't change the future, but you can prepare
for it."

"When we wrecked," said Sydney slowly, looking
around at his family watching him closely, "I knew
something bad awaited. I didn't know what, but something.
And later on, I knew Old Inca would be butchered. That I
knew, but I wish I hadn't. It did no one any good."

"That so," said Dad with a curious edge to his voice.

"It is your special gift," said Mom. "You must nurture
it."

"I hate it," said Sydney. "It hurts me and others."

"In a way, I understand," said Mister. "I've seen the
school closure coming for years, but I haven't enjoyed it."

"I am so unhappy," said LaMar. "I feel like this is all
my fault. My tummy hurts all the time."

"You can't feel that way," said Mom. She stopped to
put a pan of water on the stove for a hot water bottle.

"You've got to feel happy. Look, LaMar, see how
happy Dad and Mister are?"

"I'm happy," said Dad. Dad made his mouth go into a
smile. He looked at Mister. Mister tried to move his mouth
into a smile, but it didn't go up. Mister tried more, and
managed to stretch his mouth up slightly. LaMar looked at
one, then the other. He started to laugh. "You look so funny
when you do that," he said to them. "Like clowns with big
smiles and sad eyes."

Sydney started to laugh also. Then Mom, and the
children. Finally, Dad and Mister started laughing, too.
Their shoulders shook a little even after they stopped

laughing and they turned their faces down. Mister excused himself then, and left.

LaMar stopped laughing and began to cry softly and held his side.

"Rocks are back in my stomach," he said. Mom poured hot water from the pan into a hot water bottle and LaMar winced at its heat. He clutched the rubber bottle to his side. Mom took it from him, put it in a pillow case and gave it back. Dad picked up LaMar and carried him gently to the fold-away bed now back in the kitchen. Nat and Sydney climbed up the stairs to bed.

LaMar's stomach hurt again the next evening, and he held his side again. He cried quietly with his face turned away when Mom started to examine him.

"You're going to the doctor," she said firmly. "Tomorrow night."

"Guess I will go to Montpelier and arrange trucks to haul my herd to Preston," said Dad. "I can't take a chance on that guy from Evanston. What's got to be done ought to be done quick." He shook his head slowly. "I certainly don't enjoy this."

The next afternoon, after school let out, after he'd finished his work, Sydney hurried home. When he came into the yard, he stopped in surprise. Cutting through the backyard were tracks of a heavy dual-wheel truck with chains.

"Wow," said Sydney. "Look who's been here." He studied the deep tracks as he followed them toward the coal shed where they ended at a mountainous heap of lump coal that showed extra black against the snow.

"Dad finally decided to get some coal," said Sydney. "Oh boy." But near the porch, the old oil can coal bucket with its top cut out stood empty. He stopped long enough to use the back of an ax to break a few big lumps into smaller lumps. Dust blasted his face and hands as the ax smacked the big lumps. He filled bucket with fist-sized chunks and carried it inside. He entered the kitchen, the glass in the door rattled again. Where he expected rich coal heat to greet him came only chilliness, though. The living room door remained closed and the family gathered around the stove. Bartholomew and Prielle sat on a single chair next to the oven. Next to them, LaMar swathed by a quilt, rested on a pillow from the rocker.

"Here's some coal," said Sydney as he entered. "Let's heat this place up."

"Oh!" said Mom. "What are you doing with that coal? It isn't ours, you know."

"It isn't? What is it doing in our coal bin, then?"

"Don't take a lump of that," said Mom. "Someone brought it by accident. Dad has gone to find out why. We won't burn any of it; not a piece."

Sydney reluctantly hefted the bucket back to the porch and returned inside. Later, he leaned over the cook stove with a slice of bread when glass in the kitchen door rattled and in strode Dad.

"Thunderation! What an outfit!" he stormed. "I am surprised they stay in business, the way they operate."

Mom stopped darning a lapful of stockings. The children quieted and Sydney set his bread on the stove to toast it nice and brown while Dad talked.

"Nobody knows anything over there," Dad said. "First I talked to the girl. Then I talked to the old man. All they'd say is that I paid for it this fall. Out of my grain money. They swore I did it. Old man Sleig even told me I'd taken leave of my senses." Dad writhed out of his coat and unsnapped his boot buckles like he blamed them for the whole thing. "The old man said he wasn't about to come and get the coal. He said if someone made a mistake, he'd take the entire personal responsibility. What a way to run a business!"

"What shall we do?" asked Mom quietly. She began darning another sock.

"Nothing!" thundered Dad. "There is nothing we can do."

"Well, it wasn't the church," said Mom. "We know that much. Sister Klaybill came by again this morning, trying some more."

"Maybe the bishop done it," said Dad.

"No," said Mom. "He promised he would talk to you first. He is an honest man."

"Thunderation!" Dad exclaimed, "Thunderation!"

Holding to Dad's leg, Bartholomew repeated, "Thu-shun! Thun-shun!" He stamped his foot.

Dad strode into the bedroom to change into his chore clothes and returned to the kitchen. "I have arranged to truck the entire herd to the Preston stockyards," he said. "I can't take a chance on that Evanston fellow. We can't lose the land, too."

Mom stopped her darning. She stood up and walked in front of Dad. She looked at him directly into his face.

189

"What?" asked Dad. "They won't be here till next week, next Tuesday."

"No," she said very quietly. "That's a mistake. Now I know. We must wait."

"We can't wait," he said. "It is one week away. We'll be out of our house. "Where are you going? Go camp in the mountains?"

"Wait," she said. "It is wrong to slaughter that whole herd. We must wait."

"We can't wait," said Dad.

"We must," said Mom. "I have a special feeling we should wait."

"One of those faith feelings!" said Dad. "Well, this time it is wrong and we can't wait. We will lose everything if we wait."

Mom didn't answer. She stood in front of Dad and looked him in the eyes.

"We can wait a couple more days," said Dad, relenting. "See if that fellow from Evanston calls again. Maybe we can move him up."

"Don't sell them to the stockyards," said Mom.

"If we have to, we certainly will. What we've got to do, we ought to do quick!" said Dad.

Mom looked him in the eyes and shook her head.

He stormed out of the house and rattled the milk bucket on the porch on his way to Aida, muttering, "That woman!"

Just Aida remained in the stable. "Is if it weren't hard enough!" He stuck his head back in and yelled, "Syd! Come down in a few minutes and give me a hand with bringing the extra milk cans back to the house."

"In a minute," said Sydney. When Dad didn't answer, he pulled a chair up by the kitchen stove next to LaMar. He pulled out his pocketknife and began to whittle again on a piece of willow. He began to make a cow's head. He made the forehead flat and the nose long. It ears were pressed back, to fly like an airplane.

"What were you talking about, moaning in the trees?" LaMar asked. "What is it you are making?"

"A wind cow," said Sydney. "You can hear them in the trees in the wind. They kick right through you. And they are bitter. Very, very bitter."

"You told me that before, but I still don't believe you."

"Spirits of the cattle dead, roaming the earth."

"Are there really such things?" asked LaMar.

"Listen," whispered Sydney. "Especially when the wind blows."

LaMar bent forward to listen. They could hear the wind racing over the old house and howling through bare trees.

"Syd!" scolded Mom. "Dad wanted some help, I recall." She turned to LaMar. "And you, young man, are going to the doctor just as soon as Dad finishes."

LaMar looked sadly at Mom. "Can you come with me?" he asked.

"I'm sorry," said Mom. "I'm not up to going anywhere tonight."

"Can Nat go?" asked LaMar.

"He's at a basketball game at Soda Springs," said Mom. "So is Madge."

"Who will go with me?" asked LaMar.

"Sydney can go." Mom looked at Sydney.

"Sydney hates that place," said LaMar.

"I hate that place," said Sydney. He saw LaMar's troubled face. "I guess I could go."

He hurriedly pulled on his chore clothes and trotted to the barn. As Sydney neared the milking stable, he heard Dad talking to Aida.

"Easy, pot roast," said Dad. "Settle down, you sack of soup bones." Sydney heard a clang, followed by, "Judas Priest! To think I'd end up with you! I have died and gone to the devil, milking only you morning and night."

When Sydney poked his head into the stable, he saw only the one cow and Dad milking with one leg out, ready to stand and rescue the nearly full bucket.

"What do you want?" asked Sydney. "Maybe you need to repent."

Dad ignored him. "You must be happy, no matter what happens to the farm."

"Yes," said Sydney. "Is that all?"

"For LaMar's sake," said Dad. "That is all. Drag a couple of empty milk cans to the house, please."

Sydney turned back to the house. He heard Dad talking to Aida in a soothing voice:

"Easy, you manure spreader, you collection of kicking, you torrent of tantrums. . .."

Sydney heard a clank.

"Jupiter!"

A short time later, after they bundled up, Dad carried LaMar to the car, which spewed smoke as it warmed. Dad had wiped a cloth sack filled with salt over the inside windows to melt the ice. Sydney followed, carrying a quilt for LaMar, and soon they were driving. Chains on the

Plymouth's tires clanked over the icy road. The radio
sputtered loud in static, on and off, with news about Ike and
DeGaulle and John Foster Dulles and that Russian guy,
Khrushchev, news that Dad thought important, so the boys
talked very quietly in the back.

"Dad can save the farm," said Sydney. "I know that.
That is what Dads do. You don't have to worry about that."

"But what about Mister?" said LaMar. "Nobody will
save him. Who can save him?"

"I don't know," said Sydney. "Things are not the way
they should be. Everything that is supposed to be the same
is coming loose. It's like swampy ground that sinks
wherever you step on it. You feel like any minute you
could go down on in up over your head."

"I heard the wind cows last night," said LaMar. "Just
like you said. They were moaning and bellering through the
trees. It was our milk cows that we sold, bellering through
the trees."

"Don't think about that today," said Sydney. "Try to
think of happy things."

"I can't feel happy when everything is so sad. What if
Mom and Dad get divorced?"

"They won't," said Sydney. "I've heard them argue
worse than that."

"That's the worst one I have ever heard," said LaMar.

"Nah," said Sydney. "A real, real bad one is worse.
But why can't you stay happy longer? I'd think you'd be a
little happy. But oh no, you grumpify way too fast. I can't
keep up with your mouth going down.

"And," said Sydney, "there's more to it. If you want to
be happy, you are happy. If I want you to be happy, I have

to try day long. I can't do it. Your happiness has to come from inside you, not inside me."

That said, they rode in silence.

At the hospital, Dad knew just what to do with Sydney. He left Sydney on his familiar bench in the front hallway, looking at the blue and white tiles, and the old statue man, Roscoe Sloan, at the end of the hall. Metallic red tinsel fringed his wheelchair. Sydney tried to imagine Roscoe Sloan's girlfriend – she must 99 years old, at least.

Darkened stores filled the town around him placing everyone else outside the hospital a million miles away. He stared at Roscoe Sloan for a long time, until interrupted by a car pulling up in front. Its lights gleamed briefly through the glass doors. Sydney wondered what part of the valley they were from, and what they would look like.

"Pull the door shut, Addie," said someone.

"Huh," thought Sydney. "Someone else is named Addie." He recognized their coats in the muffled darkness. "It is the Luttys. What are they doing here?"

Soon they pushed open the door and a pocket blizzard from the outdoors – snowing started – swept them inside. Addie spied Sydney on the bench and smiled. Her father walked up the hallway looking for Venna.

"I'm so scared," she said. She flounced her ringlets and smiled at him. At his eyes. "I am going to have my tonsils out."

Sydney managed a half-smile. "Oh," he said. He couldn't help noticing that Addie looked more and more grown up and womanish every day. She looked into his eyes and smiled. He felt himself grow huge and his mouth would hardly work. Addie looked up the hall and turned back to Sydney. "Doc Mooley says my tonsils are swollen twice their size. He says my cold will go away forever after they are out. What do you think?"

Addie had such a way of looking into eyes. Sydney felt inflated, more huge. He tried to think of something to say. He remembered an old joke from *Boys Life* that also described Addie.

"I guess your tonsils are finally big enough to date."

"What?" asked Addie.

"Yeah," said Sydney. "Doc Mooley is taking them out tonight."

Addie smiled. She giggled. Sydney smiled back, but he when he looked into her eyes, he felt as helpless as a cow in a tournament of tiddlywinks.

"Bye," said Addie. "Got to get my tonsils ready for their date." She left when her father returned. As they were walking down the hall, Sydney heard Bishop Lutty asking, "What are you talking about, Addie? Tonsils don't have dates."

"Mine do," said Addie. The Luttys disappeared into a room. Her father's patronizing laughter crackled faintly through a closed door. After they disappeared, Dad came back with LaMar. He sat LaMar on the bench next to Sydney and rumpled his fine hair. LaMar slumped against the wall.

"I got another shot," complained LaMar. "I can't stay happy if they keep giving me shots."

"Stay here," said Dad. "I've got to go talk money with the hospital people. All I ever do is talk money – actually talk no money – anymore."

After Dad left, they were quiet. Footfalls sounded down the hall. "It's Doc Mooley," said LaMar. "His steps, they sound like falling wooden pancakes."

"I know," said Sydney. "You told me that already."

Doc Mooley walked up to the boys and he stopped. A serious expression showed on his face. "This little guy has a tough fight ahead," he said solemnly. "The perforation in his intestine has opened up again. It dumps terrible germs into his body. He's too weak to operate. We hope he'll continue to respond to penicillin. What I am afraid of is that some staph germs will come into his body that the penicillin can't kill. We are going to let you go home tonight, but you have to come back tomorrow."

"Oh, no!" said LaMar. "Not back here!" He started to cry. Sydney reached over and hugged him. He felt LaMar's sobbings lessen and stop within his arms. LaMar is such a good hugger.

"Sorry," said Doc Mooley. "That is the way it has to be. I have called the Primary Children's Hospital in Salt Lake City. They are calling specialists in Denver and Los Angeles to see if they have medicine that has worked on intestinal perforations."

He stopped to emphasize the next point: "We may even call New York and Chicago. We are going to get this problem fixed for good." He waited again. "But we can only hope."

"Is that kind of hope like faith?" asked Sydney.

"Informed faith, I suppose," said Doc Mooley. He paused. "If there is such a thing. Sounds like an oxymoron to me."

The boys looked at him without understanding. Venna came by and took LaMar, carrying her now red knitting under one arm and putting LaMar under her other one.

"I hope you are trying to make your brother happy," said Venna, turning back to Sydney.

"Oh, he is," sobbed LaMar as he walked off.

As they entered another room, Sydney heard her tell LaMar, "We are going to give you an enema."

"No!" shouted LaMar. "Not one of those things!"

"Sorry."

The door closed.

Sydney sat alone when Doc Mooley came back.

"Your brother is sure sad," he said. "Are you doing everything you can to cheer him up?"

"It isn't easy with Dad losing the farm and the school closing so Mister doesn't have a job. And you know Mom lost the baby."

Doc nodded. "Things are that bad?"

"Yeah," said Sydney. "Real bad."

"I am on the school board, you know," said Doc Mooley. "We've tried and tried to find a solution. But we came up with no other choice."

Dad walked up, putting his checkbook into his pocket. "Now you got my milk cows. You get Sydney next."

"I don't want Sydney," said Doc Mooley. "I have a date with a lovely pair of tonsils."

Dad looked at him.

"I'm going to take them out," Doc explained, and left chuckling.

Dad shook his head. "That man's sense of humor is about as dry as Dingle. You wouldn't think he'd read *Boys Life* at his age."

Chapter 14

On Monday evening, Dad announced: "I am shipping the cattle tomorrow. I can't wait any longer. Just our luck that beef prices are the lowest for years – 18 cents a pound on the hoof. It will be very close if we can get enough out of the whole herd to meet the $4,400."

"You must wait," said Mom. "Please don't ship our mothering cows to the slaughter yards."

"Trucks are lined up to do the job. We'll round the cattle up in the field and load them right there. By Wednesday, we will have our money and be done with the problem."

"You must wait," said Mom firmly. "Cancel the trucks."

"I am the farmer here," said Dad. "What do you know about beef sales?"

"I don't know about beef sales," said Mom. "I just know we should wait."

"I can't make such an important decision on a feeling, not this time. It is just too big. I can't gamble the family's future on what time of the month it is."

Mom colored and drew back her hair. "Never has one of these feelings been wrong," she said angrily. "But I always regret if I don't follow them. It is exactly for this family's future that we must wait."

Dad turned to walk out of the house.

"If you walk out of this house and ship those cattle, there won't be a family to save, Mr. Speng," she said in measured quietness.

Dad turned and looked at her. She started to cry.

"Can't you understand?" he snapped. "I can't change my decision based on whims and superstition."

"Fine," said Mom, drying her eyes on her apron. "If I am wrong, we will walk away from everything without a whimper. You will lose the family or the farm. It is your choice to gamble. But either way, the children and I will move."

"You wouldn't," said Dad.

"I haven't forgotten, Mr. Speng," snapped Mom. She folded her arms and squared her shoulders. Her lips pressed so tightly they were almost white.

He glared at her and stormed out of the house.

That evening, Dad set a tall, full pine spruce on the porch to dry.

The boys walked inside.

"Did he say what he would do?" demanded Mom, as they entered, only glancing at the tree.

"Nope," said LaMar. He walked slowly to a chair near the stove to rest.

"Did he say anything?" asked Mom. Her voice trembled.

"Nope," said Sydney, deciding not to share the part about pig-headed. Dad could share that himself, if he wanted. Knowing Dad, he probably would. Mom stooped at the dirt she'd swept up to brush it into the flattened tin that served as a dust pan.

"It is a hard thing you are asking," added Sydney. "Most people would side with Dad."

"It is hard for me, even," said Mom. "If I didn't have faith, I am sure I couldn't do it. I understand why he is struggling." She emptied the dirt into the wood tub behind the stove.

"But I have learned that the most difficult times are the most important times to follow the whispers of the Spirit."

"That's what Sister Pourgette said," relayed LaMar.

"Bless her," said Mom.

Sydney shook his head. "I don't know." He levered the nearest round stove top open to see if it needed more wood. "Yet," he said, looking in at the chamber that always seemed empty, glowing at the bottom with red embers and white wood ashes. "Yet." He started again. "After seeing what I have seen, I can see how you could see that."

Mom looked at Sydney. She walked over and hugged him. She started to cry. "I needed that," she said. "I so needed that. Bless you."

"Huh?" asked Sydney. "What did I say?"

"Your gift," said Mom.

Dad took a long time to unharness the team and rub them down with burlap sacks. He fed them the alfalfa from the barn he'd saved for the milk cows.

"He's feeding them alfalfa," said Sydney, peering through the kitchen window. He stretched his lips out with his fingers to imitate the greedy, fleshy, nibbling lips of the work horses seizing into dried hay.

LaMar laughed slightly.

Through the kitchen window, Sydney watched Dad clamber up on the tractor where it rested next to the

201

chicken coop. Sputtering and stopping, sputtering again, sending black against the crisp blue sky, the tractor expired and resurrected a dozen times. Sometimes it lurched forward, spinning its worn tires in the frozen snow before dying. Sometimes it died just as Dad revved up its motor. Puffs of exhaust issued from its pipe like smoke signals of distress. Finally Dad turned it off and walked slowly to the house. Sydney returned to the table and pulled up his homework sheets and pretended to read them. Glass in the kitchen door rattled and Dad came into the kitchen. He carried a load of wood and clattered it noisily into its tub behind the stove.

"Guess I will go to town tonight, make sure my trucks are lined up for tomorrow," said Dad.

Mom did not speak.

Dad didn't look at Mom, but peeked a tiny glance. He leaned over the stove and opened the flue windows at the side to allow the fire to burn hotter.

"The trucks," said Mom.

Dad didn't answer. He scraped a chair up closer to the stove and sat. Mom remained standing.

"What about the trucks?" asked Mom in half a voice, dreading the answer.

Dad half twisted in his chair, and slumped to one side.

"Guess we'll lose the farm," he said in a very tense voice. "Canceled them. I can't lose my wife and kids."

"Oh, Dallern!" cried Mom. She stepped to him, threw her arms around his shoulders and embraced him. She began sobbing helplessly. "Thank you. I have prayed so hard. I love you so much," she said. "So very much." Dad

held on to her until she stopped. She must have gotten her
tears on his face, because his face grew wet, too.

"That don't mean I have to like it," he snapped through
her affection. "I do not."

"This is right. It is so right," she said. "You will see."
She insisted on kneeling in family prayer right there and
saying it herself. As usual, during the prayer, Dad walked
over and looked out the window at the barn.

"By the way," he said. "I have some boxes to put under
the tree. Nothing in them. I picked them from the dumpster
behind Western Auto."

Dad brought in the empty cardboard boxes, one for
each of the family: a radio box for Madge, a .410 shotgun
box for Nat, toy boxes for Prielle and Bartholomew, a toy
truck box for LaMar, a bb gun box for Sydney. All he gave
Mom and himself was an empty lamp box.

Now will be a good time to work on my Christmas
valentine for Addie, thought Sydney. He carefully cut an
ordinary sized thing. Next, he cut and glued together smaller
and smaller valentines on its center, from white to pink to red
to purple. All the time he cut, he thought about moving away
and never seeing Addie again. Across the front he wrote in
twirly letters, "Addie Lutty." Then in smaller letters, "Heart
of my heart."

The thought of never seeing her again rushed across his
whole body. In tiny, meaningful letters he wrote, "with love
from Sydney."

The next night, Mom and the children, including
LaMar, decorated the Christmas tree. Well-used tinfoil
icicles draped its boughs. Bubble and painted bulbs strung
around, with long-flattened tinsel strung in opposing

directions formed bright X's over the breadth of the tree. Homemade children's ornaments from years past dangled here and there. Sydney re-made Dad's boxes and placed them unwrapped under its long, ornamented boughs.

A knock sounded on the kitchen door. Sister Klaybill, carrying a plate of cookies mostly covered by wax paper, came in. She set the cookies on the table and reached inside her coat.

"Carn sent a Christmas card to Sydney," she said. "I'll leave it on the table." She walked near to Mom. Sydney listened more carefully. He heard Sister Klaybill saying that Carn wouldn't come home for Christmas and she hoped he would have a good Christmas in Utah.

"I hope so, too," replied Mom.

"Now Norda," she whispered to Mom – quietly, but Sydney could still hear: "Shan't we help a little with your family Christmas?"

Mom smiled. "Our tree is beautiful. We don't need any help at all. Please come see our tree."

In the living room, a fire burned in the fireplace as LaMar slept on the couch. Sydney sat on the floor with his back against the couch and lights twinkled on the thick tree that sent its scent throughout the room. Sister Klaybill poked her head in. "My laws!" she exclaimed. "It looks just like the window of ZCMI."

"Yeah," said Sydney. "It's pretty."

Sydney could hear her and Mom talking about how pretty the tree was. Then Sister Klaybill left.

When she'd safely gone, Mom began to snicker quietly. Later, when Dad came in from dueling with Aida, she smiled still. She told Dad what happened and he started to laugh, too. It sounded so good to hear Mom and Dad laughing together.

"Thanks," said Mom. "You've made us all happy. We are ready for Christmas morning."

"If we have a Christmas morning," said Dad. "I am sure Santa wouldn't mind if you put your most important stuff in boxes so we can carry it in a hurry to the car, come Friday."

Mom nodded. "We don't know what will happen on Friday," she said.

The family went to bedrooms and returned with arms full of dresser clothing, and opened Sydney's delicately re-hooked boxes and stuffed them full. Sydney came and again carefully re-hooked the boxes closed.

As the family gathered around the Christmas tree, Sydney read his card from Carn.

"Dear Sid,

How are you doing? I hope LaMar is better.

I am a school custodian. I make lots of money working for Uncle Ross. I like it here. I am not coming back, ever. Maybe someday I will see you again.

Your family is always nice to me.

Your Friend,

Cornell

P.S. Uncle Ross is hiring head custodians. He pays $400 a month.

Dad whistled. "Four hundred a month. Every month. Huh!"

205

Later than night, another knock sounded on the door and Mister came in, peering toward the living room and showing a surprised expression as he stared at the huge tree there.

"My land!" exclaimed Mister. "Look at that, would you!"

He turned to Dad and spoke importantly. "The phone lines are fixed again. Garth Orr just called. He definitely wants your herd. He's going to pay extra to get the whole herd, but he can't come until next Monday."

"What does he propose?" asked Dad.

"He'll bring trucks and some men and haul the whole concern away, including your hay to feed them with," said Mister. "But he absolutely cannot come until Monday."

Dad didn't speak. He turned, as in agony. "Won't help us. They will lock everything up on Friday."

"Have faith," said Mom. "We've come this far. Let's give the Lord a chance to answer our prayer of faith."

Dad looked at her like she'd declared herself a Martian or a communist. He just shook his head.

Sydney waited until Mister left, then he said: "I know exactly what we can do."

Everyone looked at him. "Let's have Christmas early, just in case," he said.

"That's one of Sydney's ideas that makes sense," said Madge.

"Why not?" asked Nat. "We'll all skip school."

Dad spoke directly to Mom: "We celebrate Christmas on Saturday morning," he said to her. 'If we have anything to celebrate by then."

"This is in the Lord's hands now," she said.

Wednesday morning Mom made an announcement of her own. "LaMar is staying home from school for the rest of the year," she said. "He is just not well."

Dad banged the milk strainer on the porch and a gust of wind and snow accompanied him as he came inside the kitchen carrying a stainless-steel bucket filled with milk. Mom carried four two-quart bottles and a pint for the cream that would rise later, and set the large bottles next to the bucket. Dad carefully poured milk from the bucket into the bottles. As each bottle filled, Mom held a small funnel with a filter of gauze over it. Whenever a speck showed on the filter, she looked at Dad.

"Didn't sleep a wink last night," he said, ignoring Mom. "Standing by and giving away my land doesn't suit me."

"Faith helps me sleep at night," said Mom. "I saturate in the love of the Lord."

Dad finished pouring milk and went to pour the last dribble into the bottle.

"We don't need the settlings," said Mom, interrupting her reverie.

Dad picked up the bucket, held it to his mouth and drank the last dribble. "See if I get sick," he said, as the bucket handle banged metallically against the side. "Just see."

He continued. "This is absolutely crazy. We don't have a single shred of hope. We are lying down and letting the truck run over us. Makes no sense."

"You made the choice last fall. Things could have been different," said Mom. "With all the people around who believe, I'd think now, at last, you would at least try to exercise a particle of faith."

Nat spoke up from the table. "Dad filters out particles of faith like Mom filters out particles from the milk."

Madge laughed. "That is so accurate," she said. "You do have filters in common; you just use them for different reasons."

Mom and Dad looked at each other and at their teens.

"This is serious," said Mom. The teens nodded, smiling.

"We know," said Madge.

Dad shook his head and clanked the milk bucket in the sink to be washed. "All night long I mulled it over. I admit that Mom does have faith. And she probably has reasons for her faith. Of that I have to admit. And Sydney probably did see the crash before it happened. I will admit to that."

"So what does that mean to you?" asked Mom.

"The human mind is an incredible thing," said Dad. "It could be the mind's subconscious is much more powerful than we ever realize."

"The subconscious mind can gaze into the future?" asked Mom. "Don't be ridiculous. Don't put man where God ought to be."

Dad took off his chore coat and hung it on the porch. He returned angry. "And here we are, unmoving as sitting ducks. Just waiting for pot shots to pick us off."

"This sitting duck is still quacking for breakfast," said Nat. "I refute it thus: Qua-ack!"

Mom and Dad each frowned and waited to continue their discussion until after breakfast. Nat and Madge left for the bus stop together.

"Quack," said Nat as he walked out.

"Quack-quack," said Madge, behind him.

"I am trying to raise a family of faith, and you undermine everything I say," said Mom after the door closed.

"I am trying to save the farm, and you block me at every turn," said Dad.

They squared off, Mom on one side of the stove and Dad on the other.

"I don't see why you couldn't at least be quiet on some things," said Mom.

"Did I get any consideration at all from you?" demanded Dad. "Not one jot or tittle."

"Faith needs growing space, like seeds," said Mom. "Some sunshine, and some water."

"Children need to understand that to succeed, they must do things well," said Dad. "The better they do things, the better off they will be. Can't you understand that?"

"When they develop faith, they will be able to negotiate the blind spots, like this one," said Mom. "You can't understand that."

"No," said Dad. "I can't."

"You could try," said Mom. "With just a smidgen of faith."

"No," said Dad. "I can't."

"With just a smidgen of faith, it will flourish and grow and you can feel it, if you would just try," said Mom, desperately.

"Losing the farm will be a great confirmation of faith," said Dad.

"Let's not argue in front of the children," said Mom. "If we are to have Christmas on Saturday, we will need to have some peace on earth."

Dad sat down and ate his wheat mush with thick cream and brown sugar, spoonful by spoonful, carefully, like setting a post or straightening a crooked bale. Sydney left for school, while Dad dug at the old trailer. That evening, a tarp covered the old trailer, now filling with boxes.

Inside, Mom and Dad didn't argue, or even speak to each other. Instead, Dad built a fire in the fireplace. Mom and Madge washed dishes and packed them in more boxes.

The house looked empty even with the Christmas tree. The family sat on the couch in the living room. Madge came into the living room wiping her hands with a dish towel. She switched off the room lights, and the family looked at the Christmas tree also lit with fireplace flames' buttery lights flickering over its green boughs with colored and blinking illuminations.

Dad and Mom sat on opposite ends of the couch and the children surrounded the fire, each with a bit of its heat.

"I never realized things here were so perfect," said Dad. "If only things could go on this way."

"Yeah," said Sydney. "Too bad we have school."

No one spoke.

"When I grow up, I am going to be rich," said Sydney.

"You can be," said Dad. "You can get whatever you want. Just depends on what you want to trade your life off for."

"Money," said Sydney. "Lots of it."

"Then you trade your time for money."

"Time?" asked Sydney. "Just time? That's all you have to trade to get money?"

"That's plenty," said Dad. "Time, it's what your life is made up of."

Nat sort of rolled over. "Me, I'm going to travel," he said. "I'm going to see what a big city is like."

"I saw one once," said Dad. "It scrunched all the people so tight together they didn't have a chance to be themselves. They were all too busy being each other."

"I want to get married," said Madge. "Just so he is cute. And goes to church. And to college. And is rich."

"You might get what you want," said Dad. "But it might not be worth it when you get it."

"Seek ye first the kingdom of God," said Mom. "All else shall be added unto you."

Dad stood, tossed another log on the fire. The log flowered sparks in every direction.

"You will be happy now," Sydney told LaMar. "We will have a fun winter. I will make sure of that."

"What will you do?" asked LaMar. His voice sounded sleepy, like he spoke only to please Sydney.

"I will think of something," said Sydney.

"You will have to do more than that to make me really happy," said LaMar.

Sydney watched logs burning and dreamed of living in a house warm in every room, no matter how cold the outdoors, a house where everyone stayed happy all by themselves, and where the police were not coming to take it away. A place without open graves, where nobody would die.

Mom let them stay up a little later than usual before unplugging the Christmas tree lights and sending all into their rooms, extra cold because of the whining wind.

On Thursday, a fine, dry snow fell all day, adding one more layer of coldness to the coming doom.

Chapter 15

On Foreclosure Friday, Dad opened the door and a bluster of air whirled inside, ruffling towels and giving wing to papers. Its icy edge cut through warmth, and when Dad finally shut the door, half a second later, the stove started over on the long project of half-heating the room.

A fine snow covered Dad's coat and hat and even his mittens.

"I'm going out to the field to feed," said Dad. His words slurred from exhaustion and his face showed lack of sleep. "Blizzard is coming. I can feel it in my bones."

"In this wind?" asked Mom. "Can't you wait till afternoon? It may stop."

Her eyes showed redness and similar lack of sleep. "What if the sheriff comes while you are gone?"

"Tell him I have gone to feed the Federal Land Bank's cattle," said Dad bitterly. "I doubt they will feed them in this wind. I will only be away for a couple of hours. The bank can wait that long."

Mom didn't answer; she brought a frying pan from the stove and filled his plate. "Not quite cooked," she said. Dad looked up. Before he could say anything, Mom continued, "I have been cooking nearly an hour. That stove doesn't want to heat up in this wind."

Dad began eating. While he ate, Mom took his sheepskin coat from the hall, and a padded hat and thick sheepskin mittens and put them on a chair near the stove. Dad finished eating and stood; for a Moment he rested with his hands over the stove. Then he slipped into the coat.

Mom came over to Dad and buttoned his sheepskin up around his neck. She hugged him. He finally returned her hug but turned away quickly. He pulled on a sheepskin hat and fastened the ear flaps together beneath his chin. He slid his hands into huge mittens but pulled them off. "Can't work in these," he said. He pulled on a pair of cloth gloves and over them his leather gloves.

"If I'm not back in three hours, I'm in trouble," he said. "Not that anyone can do anything about that."

"We'll pray for you," said Mom.

"There's consolation," said Dad. "Would that cattle could eat prayers."

He walked out, and when he opened the door, again wind charged the kitchen, emptying it of warmth and comfort. The force of the wind was such that it continued even after the door closed. Mom pushed it tighter though it didn't move after Dad's pull.

No sooner had Nat and Madge caught the bus in a cloud of swirling whiteness than Dad drove out of the lot with the team.

Mom put more wood in the stove and drew the children around her. Everyone knelt in prayer:

"Help us be able to sell the cattle on Monday, and help Dallern to return home safely," she prayed. The children climbed into chairs next to the stove. As Sydney dressed for school, the wind picked up. Through the windows, nothing could be seen but the howling, snow-colored wind. Sydney walked toward the door, but Mom announced:

"No school for you, young man. We're in a blizzard, a regular 'Bear Laker'. You are not going out in that." She paused a minute. "Neither is H. Beasley, nor is the sheriff. I just hope the school bus makes it to school through this."

Sydney gratefully retired to the stove. He pulled a chair up next to LaMar, who was wrapped in a quilt, as usual these days.

"Hear that?" asked Sydney over the wind growing louder. Its whine deepened into a dull roar that banged tree limbs against the roof.

"The wind cows are angry," said Sydney. "They are angry at being sold."

LaMar shuddered within his quilt as the morning slowly passed. "It is the milk cows," he finally said. "The others haven't been sold yet."

"Well," said Mom. "So. The sheriff won't be coming today in this. He won't be here till Monday, and we can sell our cattle to the man in Wyoming after all." She stood near the boys. "The Lord works in mysterious ways."

Outside the wind thundered and even when it slowed, howled louder than Sydney could remember. Through the kitchen window, they could see tree branches whipping back and forth. A pine rocked to one side and then the other, fluttering its limbs like so many loose, waving hands.

"I want you to bundle up and bring in half a dozen loads of wood," Mom ordered. "Bring anything left of the coal, even if it's just dust."

Sydney waited half an hour before he slowly bundled up and headed for the door.

"Put it on the porch and stay out till you're done," said Mom. "If you open the door with every load, we'll get colder and colder instead of warmer and warmer."

Sydney opened the door and pulled it quickly shut. He felt Mom push it from the other side. Outside, the wind hit like a wall of ice, sucking his inner heat away.

The vast body of billowing air let nothing weak stand before it. The snow flew horizontally like a field of tiny white bullets no longer susceptible to gravity, and whirled along trying to return to the sky from whence they came. Blowing snow covered the land like a fog, obscuring objects at any distance. Sydney could see but a dark shadow where the barn stood. He could see none of the nearby houses.

He felt himself being savagely pushed without reason or mercy or lull. He hurried to tug the sled from where it usually leaned against the side of the house. The wind had blown it over. He kicked through the snow till he found it and lifted it out.

Wind cleaned it instantly and, at the same time, blasted his side; hunched over, he pulled the sled to the woodpile. As he gathered wood, wind flapped his coat. He grabbed wood and stacked it on the sled, its shredded bark quickly claimed by the wind. He dragged the sled load of wood through buffeting air to the porch where he quickly unloaded it. He returned for another load. The wind pinched his ears and nose with its cold and pressed him forward with every step.

He loaded quickly; he put his shoulder down and, against its force, made his way back to unload. He stacked another load. As he returned, small pieces of wood flew off. The gale caught the corner of his hat and, before he could catch it, lifted it up off his head and carried it away. He watched as the hat danced over the snow, caught momentarily on the fence, then bounced away on the other side to who knows where.

His ears froze; his nose felt like ice and wind found ways to thrust its icy hands on his neck and back.

He left the sled where it stopped and from the heap of coal loaded the bucket with lumps that they didn't own, but which Sydney knew would never be hauled away. He carried the bucket as he opened the door and burst inside.

"Where's your hat?" demanded Mom.

"Probably in Dingle by now," said Sydney.

"You look frozen. Bring in a load of wood to the kitchen before you unpack yourself."

He brought an armload of wood from the porch. After he dumped the wood into its box, he felt Mom's hands on his ears.

"Your ears are like icicles," she said. She held her hands on them. Sydney pulled off his mittens and put a hand over his nose. His whole head felt as if it were encased in ice. Mom let go of his ears to put wood into the stove. She reluctantly also put a few lumps of coal into the stove.

"This frozen country!" she exclaimed. "I don't know why we put up with it!"

The children playing by the stove moved to let Sydney closer. Mom opened the oven door to let its heat into the room. Sydney uncoated himself and sat in silence next to them.

Dad still hadn't returned.

Half an hour passed before he felt his ears and nose lose the pinch of cold in the deepening wealth of coal-fired heat.

As afternoon approached, Mom looked nervously at the clock. "Dad is supposed to be home by now," she said.

"He'll be home soon," said Sydney. "There's nothing we can do, anyway, if he is late."

"You better go check on Dad," she said. "It's been five hours."

"I can't go out in that," said Sydney. "I'm just a kid. He probably stopped to fix a fence or cut some wood."

"I don't know where on earth your father could be," said Mom.

"Maybe he stopped to get another jag of willows," said LaMar.

Coal heated the house warmer than it had been all winter, though the wind outside continued its roaring.

"You have to go get Dad," said Mom. "I have a very bad feeling." She paced at the stove. She picked up a dish cloth, smoothed it across her arm and set it folded on the counter. She walked back to the stove and moved pans. Then she walked back to the counter and stared out the window. She looked down at the folded dish cloth and snatched it up and draped it over the oven to dry.

"He'll be home any minute," said Sydney, watching her. "He always comes home late."

"Not this late, not in this weather," snapped Mom, like it was Sydney's fault he hadn't returned. "You know what it is like out there."

"I can't go after him," said Sydney. "I don't have a way."

"You must," said Mom. "If it's got to be done, it ought to be done now."

Sydney looked at her in disbelief. "I don't have a way," he repeated.

Mom bowed her head in silence. Then she looked up. "Go get Bridley Neeter. Maybe he has a tractor or something. He will know what to do!"

"Can't we wait a few more minutes?" asked Sydney.

"No!" snapped Mom. "Right this minute." As if in concert with her point, the wind's roar increased, sweeping over the house in near-hurricane force. "He's in trouble," she said. "I know he is. I can feel it."

Into Sydney's mind inserted a picture now very near: he saw the pair of graves opening the snow-covered ground. He thought for a long minute. He stood up. "I will go," he said. "What do I have to do?"

"We're going to bundle you like an Eskimo," said Mom. She pulled out sweat shirts for him to pull on, one after another. He pulled on a second pair of overalls. He buckled his boots on, and Mom pulled one of Dad's hats over most of his face.

"I can't see," Sydney protested. Mom helped him into his coat, taking time to pull the sleeves of the sweatshirts bunched on his arms forward to his wrists. She looked at his hat. "That won't do," she said. She opened the hall door and closed it behind her. She returned with one of her head scarves, a red wool one.

"I will not wear that," said Sydney. "I'd rather freeze to death."

"Not your choice," said Mom. She put the cloth over his head and knotted it tightly under his chin. "No one will

see you," said Mom. "Maybe only Neeters." She pulled the
hat over the headscarf, and tied another scarf over the hat.

He pulled his mittens on and Mom pulled the sleeves
over mitten cuffs. "I should tie your mittens on, like we do
with babies, to make sure you don't take off those scarves,"
she said.

"Very funny," said Sydney.

Prielle laughed. "You do look funny," she said.

"Yes," said LaMar. "You do." He laughed.

"Shut up," said Sydney.

"Go," said Mom. "I'll be praying for both of you."

"Good," said Sydney. He felt strangely for a moment,
strangely insulated. For the first time in his life, he almost
understood what prayer meant, that praying could be more
than just saying a string of words. He looked at his mother.
Then he opened the kitchen door and walked into the wind
that erupted over his face and body.

Outside everywhere showed white; the sky showed
white, the earth showed white, and everything in between
showed white. Wind roared and pelted with snowflakes that
stung when they hit, like being in a gravel storm.

"I can't do this," Sydney yelled but the wind yelled
louder. He walked off the porch into the vast ocean of
constantly exploding, freezing wind. Wind cows kept
pressing their clammy tongues against his face. They
pushed against him as though he walked into an entire herd
of them. They jumped and bellowed and kicked him with
hooves of air. He felt alone among them.

The path he'd made to gather wood already filled with
loose snow. The outline of his footprints remained with
whiter snow inside. A low drift lined the path to the

highway. Walking hunched into the wind, Sydney reached
the highway and followed it. He kicked at the drift,
disturbing settled snow back into flight.

Away from the house, he felt the full force of the wind.
Instead of the cold that pinched his face while gathering
wood, now he felt pressure from the tight air like a kind of
huge ball being constantly batted into him. No traffic
showed on the highway; its surface concealed with a foot of
snow that was textured with occasional two-foot high
drifts. Sydney tromped along the road, listening to the
roaring and watching it swaying trees and fences and
hurling snow before its face. Once, he glanced backward
and saw his steps filling with snow. He felt the bottoms of
his boots build higher with snow at each footstep. After a
few more steps, the snow fell off. Then it would build up
again. One boot never gained evenly with the other boot, so
he walked into the wind lopsided as well as bent.

Wind shoved him from behind so hard he almost felt
like running so he wouldn't fall on his face. When he
reached the back streets where Neeters lived, more snow
heaped roads than on the highway.

Neeter's house came dimly into view, small behind the
tree-high mounds of snow built up along its driveway.

Staring at the door, he wondered if he really should
knock. He thought about Mom. "She's praying for me," he
thought. He reached up and knocked on the door. Nothing
happened. He pounded again. Nothing happened. "Maybe
no one is home," he thought. He pounded again and when
no one came, he turned and started to walk away. Then he
turned back, pulled off his mitten, and knocked as hard as

221

he could, bruising his cold knuckles against the frigid door. This time, a voice called, "Is someone out there?"

"Yeah, someone is. Me, Sydney," he shouted above the wind. The door scraped open and Neeter's wife, Robin, looked out. "Come in," she said quickly. Sydney came inside to overpowering heat. She quickly shut the door behind him.

"Sit down," she said.

Sydney stood at the door. "Where's Mr. Neeter?" he asked. "My Dad's in trouble. We need your help again."

"Why, he's gone overnight," she replied. "He can't return in this blizzard. What's the matter?"

"My Dad went out to the field to feed the cattle and he hasn't come back. We think maybe he got hurt."

He paused, feeling emotion sweep over him.

"Otherwise, he would have ridden the team home," said Robin Neeter. "How are the roads out there?"

"Up to my knees," said Sydney, pointing to the snow on his trousers. Robin Neeter looked at him a long time. "Brid says you need to ride a horse," she said. "He says you could ride like you were born in a saddle."

Sydney shrugged.

"I'm going to send you out on the palomino," she said. "It's the best horse we have."

"The palomino," said Sydney. "Oh. I don't know. Maybe I'd better take the mare. She's is not worth as much."

"No, you take the palomino. It's more likely to make it through this wind."

"It is worth a lot of money," said Sydney. "It is a very valuable horse."

"Not worth as much as your Daddy," said Robin Neeter. "I'll get Blade saddled for you."

She slipped into long boots, a yellow storm coat and a stocking cap. "Just a minute," she said. She walked out the door into the wind and returned with the bridle. She ran hot water over the bit until it warmed.

"Let's go," she said. "I am sorry we don't have time to give you a cup of hot Postum first." She stepped into the wind, protecting the warmth of the bit by holding it in both hands. Sydney followed.

"You can borrow my saddle," she said. "Stirrups are longer." She turned to Sydney. "Stay in here till I have him caught."

Sydney watched her walk from the tack room into the horse barn, her yellow coat standing sideways in the continuing gusts. He heard prancing hooves, and a nicker. He heard more prancing hooves. Then he heard Robin Neeter's voice talking to the palomino.

"Easy. Easy. Easy. There, there." Then she called through the door: "I've got him. Bring me the blanket and the saddle." Sydney picked up the blanket and heaved the saddle, almost too heavy to carry with both hands, and dragged it to her. She surprised him with how easily she lifted it over the tall, shifting stallion. She quickly tightened the cinch. "

"Take this," she said, tying a lariat near the saddle's pommel. "Don't fall off, whatever you do," she said. "It will be the early end of the both of you."

"Are you sure you want to do this?" he asked.

"Are you sure you want to do this?" she asked.

"What's got to be done ought to be done quickly," Sydney shouted over the wind.

"Get on," she said. "And don't get off until you are back here. And don't let him run." She led the palomino outside where the wind flared its mane and swung saddle stirrups. With its long hair blazing like a low fountain in the torrential air, the golden horse ducked its head and pawed snow. It reared up a foot or two on his hind legs like some creature the blizzard couldn't tame – any minute Blade would tear away from the earth and mount into the sky.

"I'll help you on," she said. "God bless you."

"My Mom is praying for me," said Sydney.

"I'll be praying for you, and your Daddy, too," she said. "It is all we can do."

Sydney walked to the side of the horse. It stood higher than he remembered. Over him swept a wave of re-living the wreck, of falling from the mare. Terror touched his whole body and he froze from more than the Arctic blast surrounding him.

"You climb on the box," said Robin.

"I can't do this," said Sydney. "I just can't."

"You can be as afraid as you want to be, but this time you have to climb on the box," repeated Robin.

Again, the image of two graves flashed into his mind, and remained as he climbed up onto the wooden box. Blade pranced away, and Robin Neeter pushed him back. As he came close, she yelled "Now!"

He lifted his foot toward the stirrup but with his thick padding, couldn't reach it.

Sydney stretched his leg across the saddle, but the horse jumped away and Sydney tumbled to the ground.

"You all right?" she asked. "You've got to be quicker with this old boy."

Sydney climbed the box again and waited for her to push the horse near enough to climb on. This time when the horse came near, Sydney stretched his leg up and jumped. He landed just as the horse sprang away. He held on, his feet searching for the stirrups.

"Good boy!" said Robin Neeter, nodding. "You had me worried for a minute."

Sydney waved to her.

"This is insane," she said.

Chapter 16

Leaving Robin Neeter watching anxiously and waving, Sydney wheeled the horse toward what part of the vast frozen landscape he guessed to be the street – without even waving goodbye.

Sydney clenched both mittened hands on the reins, facing into the storm. The palomino pranced beneath him, tossing his head, blowing raggedly through his nostrils, his mane flowing like visible air. Sydney felt he rode a keg of dynamite that could explode any moment and leave him scattered in pieces across the snow. He clutched tightly with his legs and watched the horse's ears for any hint of a jump. The palomino lunged forward, covering ground against the wind much faster than Sydney walked with the wind. But up on his back, Sydney felt the wind and cold worse; it ripped at his whole body and tried to tear him off. He grew colder sitting that walking. He hunched over and held tight to the saddle horn. He noticed his old walking tracks, icy outlines filled with a whiter snow.

Snow obscured the world in such a way that, at times, Sydney realized he couldn't see exactly where he was. Houses looked strange in the murky white air, mountains totally disappeared and the land looked a prairie without ridges or edges. He pulled up the palomino, which pranced, eager to move. He looked back and saw, by studying fences, that he'd crossed the highway without seeing any trace of it. He wheeled again and began following fence tops.

The wind now buffeted their sides, whipping at the loose reins and stinging Sydney's face. They moved forward slowly and at great effort. Cold that surrounded him while walking now penetrated his wrappings; he felt his body chilling. Through the whitened wind, he saw a vague shadow of what he recognized to be the last house in town. A mile to go.

Sydney rode along the posts, hoping he would know when he'd arrived at his field. They plodded on, and on, and on. Sydney could feel the palomino stop prancing and begin walking as he waded through snow up to his belly. Wind and snow bit and shoved with greater intensity and Sydney began shaking uncontrollably.

He clutched more tightly on the reins and hugged his knees against the horse, not just to hang on, not just for warmth, but in an embrace as the horse became his companion, his only way of dealing with the wind and the snow. He realized with a shock that the palomino stallion's wild, turbulent spirit that terrified him was the only force strong enough to battle this storm; his only link to survival. He began to love the horse he once hated. He stroked its neck, thick with frosty yellow hair.

His shivering warmed him and he felt more alert. Watching each fence post top that came and fell behind, he felt like they stood as frozen sentries against the marauding day. He oddly thought that soon the snow must stop blowing, for it must have all blown away by now. Post after post came and dropped behind.

Sydney knew where they were now – at the gate into the field. As the snow grew ever deeper, the big horse wallowed through snow to his chest. The palomino hesitated. Sydney remembered that action. He gripped his legs and grasped the saddle horn with numb fingers. The palomino began bucking and jumping through drifts.

Sydney repeated aloud what Robin Neeter said: "If you fall off, it will be the end of both of you."

"Easy, boy. Easy boy," he shouted in a rasping voice.

He could see tracks on the other side of the fence. Dad left the gate open. But no sign of Dad or the team or the wagon showed through the blizzard.

"This is our place," he said to the palomino. Immediately the snow grew shallower, though now they again faced the roaring wind head on. Broad pastureland stretched around with no visible landmarks, no cattle, no team, no wagon. Snow in a never-ending lake raced over the surface to nowhere. With each step, the horse broke through heavy crust and sharp, art-deco drifts. The palomino stopped prancing and showed signs of weariness.

"Come on, old boy," said Sydney, leaning forward and patting his neck. "We can do it."

The wind now felt thick, like they moved against a mass of some congealed, invisible white mud. The sense of frozenness in his face, hands and feet deepened from shooting pains into numbness. Flexing his toes and fingers did no good, but he continued anyway just because he thought he should.

"I am sure they are in the willow pasture," said Sydney, now used to talking to the palomino. He paused, feeling it important to speak the whole truth. "I just have to find the willow pasture." Missing the willow pasture meant going over the nearby steep mounds drop-off and falling into deep drifted snow over both their heads.

"That would be the end of both of us," he explained slowly and carefully because, although the horse spoke a different language, it seemed to understand.

Sydney ducked his head. He guided the pony toward the fence line leading to the willow pasture, and, after a long time, saw a distant outline of the gray brush.

At a slight ridge of snow, the palomino stumbled and nearly fell, jerking unexpectedly. Sydney instantly saw they'd crossed a ditch. He jolted to a side, losing the stirrup and felt himself crashing off.

"No!" he shouted. He held to the saddle back with a mittened hand; with great effort and a powerful jerk the horse righted itself. Sydney felt himself hanging and swinging. He'd lost his center of balance; now nothing could keep him on. He knew the horse would gallop away the minute he fell. As he dropped, he hooked his mitten over the reins and held on with all his strength. He saw the snow rush to meet him at alarming speed. The horse bucked over the ditch and Sydney landed deep in the snow; surprisingly the snow cushioned and stopped his fall. The palomino jerked at the reins and tried to run. He dragged Sydney through the snow.

"No!" cried Sydney. He thought again of the two open graves, windblown in the snow, and wondered if one were for Dad and the other for him. "Whoa!" he yelled. The obedient palomino stopped still.

He held to the reins with his frozen hand curled. Gradually the horse calmed, fatigued. Sydney managed to stand up. Walking as on wooden legs, he led the pony back into the ditch. The tired pony stood motionless for an instant. Sydney found it hard to stand straight up. He grabbed the saddle horn and quickly, without waiting to put his foot into the stirrup, pulled himself across the saddle. The palomino began to walk with him stretched over it sideways.

"Whoa," he said.

Again, the horse stopped. He pulled himself up and managed to straddle the horse. His feet kicked into the stirrups and he reined the horse toward the nearing gray willows. The vague shape of willows emerged with more clarity and he turned to walk to them. Wind lessened as they approached on shallow snow. In lower wind, the view opened. He felt like his eyes began to work better. His shaking returned, but the burst of effort warmed him.

"I feel better," he thought with surprise. Then, even more surprised, he thought, "The Lord works in mysterious ways."

He hunched over farther. Horse and boy came to an open gate and, in the shelter of the willows, found the trail easier to follow. Here the wind's roaring slowed to a whine as it banged through acres of the of thatch of naked branches. A few more steps and they came to the cattle, huddled together around a feeding yard. Hay heaped high in feeder. Sydney made his way through the cattle.

"Dad!" Dad!" he yelled against the wind, yelled at the cattle, and yelled at the wind cows. His yells blended in with wind bellering and the bellering of the cattle until he felt trampled. He became more frightened. "Where is Dad? Has he frozen to death? Had the wind cows gotten even with him?"

As the red cattle reluctantly mooed and moved, wind tufting their red coats, Sydney saw the hayrack and team of

230

horses. Willows tangled its bed, and a pile of snow and hay covered one of the rack's runners.

"Dad!" yelled Sydney.

The pile broke open and Dad's head poked out.

"Syd," called his scratchy voice. "Oh Syd! I thought I was a goner."

Syd rode closer and saw that the sleigh had slipped down an embankment. A mound of packed snow locked the runners from moving forward. Sydney also saw his father's leg pinned against the rack's runner.

"Did the sheriff come?" asked Dad in a distant voice.

"Not today," said Sydney, drawing closer. "What shall we do?"

"Put that rope on the rack, then tie it on your saddle horn," said Dad in a weak voice. "Whip up those useless nags and drag us out." Sydney pulled off his mittens and fumbled at the rawhide tie on the lariat. The wind bit his numb fingers that he couldn't work. He began shaking again. His fingers got hold of the leather tie and he looked closer and saw that Robin Neeter tied the lariat with a bow knot.

He tugged at the tie and the lariat came off in his hands. He knotted the lariat to the rack. He wrapped the lariat twice around his saddle horn.

"I'm ready," he called.

"Take those reins and wallop that team as hard as you can hit them," said Dad in his scratchy voice.

Sydney looked at the rack, the sweaty, tired team. He could not see his father, but the wind pummeled without a break. He hoped Mom still prayed.

231

He pulled the lariat taut, and shouted with all his strength: "Geee uppp!" He whipped the free end of the lariat across the hard, aged black leather straps on the rumps of the team. Mostly he hit leather but all three horses knew what to do. They lunged forward in ragged succession until they found their unison pull; their muscled backs bent low and their hooves slipped and slid and dug against deep snow.

The rack inched up the bank and deeper into the packed snow. The rack rose high as the front runners crested the mound and leveled.

"Hold it, that's good. I'm out," shouted Dad's weak voice. "Whoa, whoa there." The team thrashed and pranced in weary agony. Sydney pulled hard back on the lines to hold them.

"I'm out but I can't get up," said Dad. 'I'm just too frozen."

"See if you can slide," said Sydney. He held the team till they settled down, then he tossed the lariat onto the wagon and rode around to his father. Dad slid out from the wagon, and lay on the heap of hay that had covered him.

"I know," yelled Sydney. "We'll string a rope through the wagon, tie it around your shoulders and I'll pull you up with the palomino." He hurried to untie the lariat but as he did so, his father began to move. Dad pulled himself up on one leg, took hold of the rack and hefted himself to standing. He fell forward, groaning and rolled onto the rack that sank beneath his weight.

"That worked," said Sydney.

"The thought of being dragged five miles over the snow by a runaway palomino worked," rasped Dad.

232

He slid under the tangle of willows and pulled hay over him like a blanket. As soon as he moved the hay, wind huffed it into the sky. Dad rolled over with his back to the blasting force. He rested for a minute. "You sure surprised me to show up," he said.

"Mom prayed me out here," Sydney replied. "Now she's praying us home. Let's go."

"I have already fed for two days," said Dad. "We can leave now."

He lay back exhausted on the bit of remaining hay and looked helplessly at the surrounding whiteness of the willows, rack and sky. Sydney took the reins of the team and dropped them over his saddle horn, tugging and coaxing them. They pulled the outfit forward. Cattle bellowed as it drove through their herd. With the wind at their backs, the team began trotting through the field and out the gate. The sleigh's runners whisked soundlessly forward.

Without bothering to close the gate, they heaved up the incline to the highway. The team's tired, muscled haunches shook as they trotted over soft snow.

Ironically, the blizzard began to die down. Wind drifted a low covering of snow over Dad's legs. As they glided into town, the wind died down more to reveal huge drifts massed along and over the road. The team pulled through the drifts, snow blasting downwind, until they reached home.

Sydney lost the reality of his eyes working in the real world and transferred to a world of his imagination. The horse beneath him now also felt unreal. Numb from head to foot, he felt part of some make-believe tale soon to vanish into the nothingness of fantasy.

The team no longer needed guiding and pulled into the lot by the house. As soon as the sleigh came near, Mom ran out with her coat fully buttoned and her boots buckled and a scarf on her head. She ran hunched over to Dad, who slowly rolled across his snowy blanket, and slid off one side, landing in a coaty lump. Mom caught him in an instant and, despite her weakness, dragged him through a flurry of snow to the porch. Sydney watched her struggling, barely tugging Dad into the house.

Sydney more fell than unmounted. As he unhooked the tugs from the wagon, surprisingly, like a fairy godmother, Robin Neeter appeared in her yellow storm coat, stocking hat, and took over. She vigorously pointed him to the house.

"Feed them the good stuff," yelled Sydney. "The alfalfa." As an afterthought, he added: "And oats in the corner of the milk stable."

She nodded and pointed again to the house and led the horses away toward the barn. The wind had almost stopped.

He felt to be someone else, somewhere else. Half his body didn't work. His feet, hands and face felt no cold but every movement brought pain piercing into his all-over numbness.

He turned to walk to the house. His pain vanished, even though the wind stilled. He couldn't move. He couldn't walk. He couldn't think. He leaned against the lowered wind for a long minute and fell over. He began to crawl through the snow. Snow felt suddenly so warm and friendly. He felt so safe here in the snow. He tried to stand, but fell again into the comforting snow. So, he crawled. He thought about sleeping for a while and then going into the house later, after he rested. But he crawled on. About to the house, he struggled to his feet and found the swing. He held to the ropes for what seemed like an age. Then he fell prone into the welcoming snow.

"Sydney! Sydney!" He heard Prielle screaming at him. He rose to a crawl and saw his little sister bundled in coats, standing on the steps looking desperately for him. When she saw him, she ran to him and began tugging his arm. He pulled away, but she kept jerking him. He lifted up and with superhuman effort crawled up the steps into the porch. Prielle opened the door and he rose high enough to collapse into the kitchen in a pile of cloth and whiteness.

"There's Sydney!" shouted LaMar.

LaMar tugged at him and Prielle slammed the door behind. Inside, the heat felt thick, like a furnace. He saw Mom giving Dad a hot bath. LaMar began unbuttoning Sydney's coat. Prielle unbuttoned his boots with her small fingers. He sat watching without moving as she pulled off his gloves. He weakly kicked until his unbuckled boots fell from his feet. Then he sloughed off his coat like a thick shell of hard, dead skin. He looked down, and Prielle urgently handed him a cup of hot Postum. He took the cup but couldn't feel it in his hands. He sipped it; the heat ran into his mouth and he rinsed it around on his cheeks. He could feel its exact width as it rinsed in his mouth, and as it scalded down his cold throat.

LaMar moved a chair nearer the open oven of the cook stove. Only then did Sydney realize Mom called orders to him from the bathroom. He saw hot towels around Dad's neck. Dad gazed vacantly at the ceiling. He looked half dead.

"God has the strangest ways of answering prayer," mumbled Dad. He said no more for an hour. Sydney wondered if he had passed.

Prielle appeared again with a bowl of snow. "Rub your hands and nose in this," she ordered. Sydney absently looked at her. Somehow, Prielle wore mittens as she began rubbing snow on his nose and fingers, which he could not feel.

"When they start to hurt, you can stop," called Mom.

As the numbness wore off, shooting pain took its place and Sydney begged Mom to let him stop with the snow. She shook her head and kept working on Dad, rubbing snow on his nose and fingers. As he slowly warmed, Sydney noticed that the coal warmed the whole kitchen – a thick, velvety, rich and everywhereness warm.

But Sydney stayed back from the stove. Sydney cried and rubbed, and rubbed and rubbed and cried and pains grew worse. "The snow is making it hurt," he shouted. Mom paid no attention, but kept working on Dad, now wrapped in quilts near the stove. She put a hot water bottle on his chest.

"I guess I had it coming," mumbled Dad.

Mom began to weep. "I thought we'd lost you," she said. "Thank the Lord you were found."

"Ohh!" moaned Dad. "Ohhh!"

Mom handed Dad his tin cup of Postum that had been sitting on the corner of the stove. This time he drank it by himself and spilled small spurts over the quilts when it burned his mouth.

By evening, Sydney's fingers' pain changed to pinpricks and then tingling. Dad still sat, still stared at the stove.

"We've saved the farm," Dad said without believing his words. "Garth Orr is coming on Monday."

After dark, Nat and Madge returned from school. About that time, LaMar started to hold his stomach. He crawled on the couch beneath his blanket and went to sleep. Dad left the kitchen, dressed, and returned near the stove, next to Sydney.

"I almost froze to death," Dad said to Sydney. "You saved my life."

"Mom made me," said Sydney. "Mom prayed me." The coal heat felt like heaven in the kitchen. He leaned back and took a deep, grateful breath.

"The Lord saved you both," said Mom. "The angels saved you. The blizzard angels."

"The Angels Neeter," said Sydney.

Chapter 17

"It's Merry Christmas and nobody will wake up," said Prielle urgently. "It feels like Santa Claus came."

Sydney rubbed his eyes. "They have come to take the house," he thought incoherently. "How can we sell the cattle in the middle of the night? How can we find all the cattle in the darkness? Where will we go?"

"Nobody will wake up," repeated Prielle.

Sydney hurt all over. "I know better than this," he groaned as he climbed out of bed and pulled the chain on the bare bulb, flooding the frigid bedroom with light. His toes and fingers still felt pinched and his nose hurt from yesterday.

"Hey," moaned Nat on the other side of the room. "It's the middle of the night. Turn off that light."

"Get him," ordered Sydney. "Sic 'em."

Prielle and Bartholomew scrambled over to Nat's bed and bounced to him. Nat reared up in bed and began tickling them. "Top it, top it," screamed Bartholomew. Prielle giggled and couldn't stop.

Nat finally ceased. "I will stop if you will go in and wake up Madge."

He dove back into his covers. The two padded off to attack Madge.

From the other room, Madge called, "It's too early."

Prielle and Bartholomew padded back with solemn faces. They hopped up on Sydney's bed to warm their feet.

"She won't get up," said Prielle.

"We'll see," said Nat. He reached under his bed and pulled out his trumpet case.

"Wait," said Sydney. "The old viola in the attic. Aunt Dru's viola; I'll get the viola." He hurried clumsily, as his snow-pinched toes didn't work well, to the attic door and shinnied inside. In a few minutes he returned with a one-stringed instrument with a dent in the back, and a case. He found a loose nut of rosin, and buffed it against a mostly hairless bow. He tightened the single string with all the pinch strength he had. "I shall play 'The Serenade'," he announced. "But," he added, "I haven't practiced for a while."

Sydney and Nat and Prielle and Bartholomew crept into Madge's room. The floorboards squeaked as they reached her bedside. Nat reached up and pulled the light switch chain.

"A-one, and a-two," said Nat. Sydney's bow sawed howlingly over the viola string. Nat's trumpet hooted a coarse reveille. Madge bolted up, but whatever she said fell beneath the ruckus. She promptly dived back under the covers and buried her head. Prielle and Bartholomew clapped their hands over their ears and fled. Their footsteps down the stairs sounded distant. Nat stopped, unable to blow into his instrument from laughing. Sydney's raucous whee-wheeing continued, drawing shrieks from the tortured viola and convulsions of laughter from Nat.

"Hey," boomed Dad's voice from downstairs. He sounded entirely recovered.

In a final glass-shattering finale, Sydney ceased.

"Where is that lousy cat?" shouted Dad through the hall door. "Take that critter out and shoot it."

"Humph," said Sydney. "Nobody around here appreciates classical music."

"We liked it," said Prielle, coming timidly back into the room. "It woked everybody up."

But LaMar remained asleep as the family gathered in the kitchen. "Let him rest," said Mom. "Last night he hardly ate supper."

In long family tradition, Mom cooked breakfast and they washed the dishes before going into the living room to celebrate Christmas.

"I'm worried about LaMar," said Mom. "It is not like a child to sleep through Christmas."

Dad picked up LaMar, who rubbed his eyes while Mom tried to get him to eat. He took only a few bites of mush, just enough to prepare him to have Christmas.

"Okay," said Madge. "Let's line up."

They lined up youngest to oldest. Bartholomew and Prielle were first, then Sydney as LaMar watched from a chair. Next came Madge and Nat, and then Mom and Dad.

"I wish we had taken a picture of this," said Mom. "Every year I wish that."

"Sure," said Dad. "Next year, for sure. Things will be better next year."

Dad slipped away to turn on the Christmas tree lights, and then he pulled the door open from inside.

Everyone surged forward. Bartholomew made a wide half circle and returned to hug Mom's knee.

"Here," called Nat. "You got a present, Bartholomew."

"Shall I open it?" pleaded Prielle.

"You have a present of your own," said Madge.

"Do I?" asked Prielle.

Madge handed her a small present. Prielle's small fingers carefully tore away the wrappings to find a mirror. Her delight showed in her reflection as she gazed into the glass. She clutched it in her hands and every few minutes stopped to look at her image in it. Soon each of the children opened a Christmas present. Bartholomew received a toy truck, LaMar a toy tractor and Sydney a new pocketknife, one with two good blades. Madge received a box of curlers and Nat a new white shirt.

"Look on the couch," said Mom. Eight oranges lined up in a row. "I know what those are," said Prielle. "Oranges." She bit one and soured her face. "They aren't very sweet," she said.

"You don't eat the skin on oranges," explained Mom. "It is called a rind."

Prielle laboriously tried to peel her orange. Nat helped finish peeling it and showed her how to pull off sections. She bit off the end of the first section and sucked it dry.

"Mmmm," she said smiling. "Just mmmmm!"

She looked around as she ate so no one might take her remaining sections.

They didn't bother opening their boxes.

LaMar walked to his box under the tree. He looked very pale against the tree and its decorations. He stood next to the tree without moving. He began to sway.

"Catch him," yelled Mom. "He's not well." Nat reached and Sydney jumped from the far side, but LaMar swayed more. His eyes rolled back and he plunged

241

downward, right into the Christmas tree, snapping tinsel and pulling the tree over on top of him.

"LaMar!" screamed Madge.

Dad reached into the tree and Nat lifted the tree and its wires off LaMar. Dad pulled him up and stretched him out on the couch immediately unoccupied.

"He just fainted," said Mom. She applied the cloth to LaMar's forehead and he stirred. She rubbed the cloth over his face and he moved his head. He reached down and pressed his stomach and screamed. His face looked more yellow in the flame light of the fireplace.

Mom looked at Dad. "We'll ask the bishop to hold a fast for him"

Dad's hard look softened and he nodded.

Sydney did not see graves in his mind. Instead, he felt certain his younger brother would occupy one. He remembered the wind and felt its relentless press against his side, and thought about its inescapable force changing the landscape.

Sydney walked slowly back. His insides felt numb and his skin contracted. Something in his mind snapped and he saw again the crash: what happened, and what would happen. He remembered the feeling of dread leading up to the crash, he remembered the terror of the crash. Then he remembered the flitting scene of the cow butchering, and how he tried to save Inca, and how he'd caused Mom and Dad to almost have a divorce. He remembered the graves, the open graves, and felt hopeless and worthless and damaged and knew two graves waited irrevocably in the future.

"Now they fast,' thought Sydney. But fasting and

prayer can't change the future, Sydney reasoned. Nothing is powerful enough to change the future. He remembered again the wind-swept open graves that he knew for a fact he would see again. He thought about prayer and his fighting the blizzard. He could not reason through the complicated texture of how fasting could change the future. He wasn't sure about prayer, though he believed it helped. But he felt certain about the future. The future could not be changed.

Yet one of the graves did not have to be for LaMar. Maybe that is how the future could be changed. But now that Dad is safe, who would the two graves be for?

He realized that if he hadn't seen the graves, he never would have gone into the blizzard for Dad. Dad would certainly have been in a grave. But now, how did it all fit together? He couldn't answer. He shook his head.

In the kitchen, Sydney put two more lumps of coal into the stove. He listened for the wind, but in the post-blizzard calmness, his mind instead heard Mom's scream for LaMar. The eyes of his mind saw over and over the pair of graves beneath the snow and gusts. That evening, as he lay alone in the double bed, coming sleep muddled his thoughts and melded with remembering cattle bellowing for their calves, with the yesterday's wind howling and thundering, with all acts against nature protesting against the Federal Land Bank taking away their farm. For a second, Sydney wondered if God really watched down on them, if He would really take care of them, all in a huge rush of oppressive silence, silence worse than the wind.

Next morning, a Sunday, LaMar lay motionless on his cot in the corner of the kitchen. Mom sat next to him,

243

bathing his yellow face with a damp wash cloth. Nat, Madge, Sydney and the children were about to leave for Church when Dad came into the kitchen.

"Your mush is on the stove," said Madge. "We are leaving for church."

"It is a fast day," said Dad. "For LaMar." He nodded his head toward the corner of the kitchen. "He's a little better this morning."

"Thank goodness," said Sydney. He turned to Dad. "What did you say?"

"I said LaMar is a little better."

"I heard that," said Sydney. "But what did you say?"

"I said it is a fasting day," said Dad, more loudly. "No food for us big kids."

A flood of futility and disbelief crossed Sydney's discouraged mind. "Yeah," said Sydney. "One of these fast Sundays, all the kids in the church are going to starve to death."

"It is for LaMar," said Dad quietly. Sydney looked at his father and thought he saw desperation. "He knows," thought Sydney.

"Don't see how fasting will help," he said aloud. "The future is already set. We just don't know how, that's all."

"We have one stew bone left," said Mom. "I am staying with LaMar, so we will have it after the fast ends."

Madge looked coolly across the kitchen like she didn't hear. "We will be leaving in five minutes," she interrupted. "Nat, are you ready?"

"I have to leave right now," Nat said. "I have to help prepare the sacrament, and bless it."

"We'll all go now," ordered Madge.

"I will put some gas in the car," said Dad. He followed them out and poured a little gas into the Plymouth from a can. Dad returned to the house. Nat drove the Plymouth.

Madge took Mom's seat.

"'Bout out of gas," Nat said. "We may not make it to church."

"Have some faith," said Madge.

"Druther have some gas," said Nat.

The Plymouth pulled in at the square-steepled yellow brick church. At church, Sydney waited behind the others, standing in the entry. He walked over to Voyle, who also stood waiting for the last minute to go inside.

"Sorry, Voyle," said Sydney. "I am sorry we beat you up. I hope you will forgive me."

"It's okay," said Voyle. He stood next to Sydney.

"Firm as the Mountains Around Us," began sounding. In the chorus, Sister Mister's powerful soprano lifted above the rest, "Carry on, carry on, carr-eee onnnn!"

At the first sound of music, Voyle quickly entered but Sydney stood at the chapel's back to look things over.

Even looking from behind, Sydney knew all the people who nearly filled the chapel. He saw Nat, seated at the sacrament table beneath the pulpit. Nat frowned at him, to signal him to take his place at the deacon's bench on the front row. Nat never came late. Sydney always came late. When he heard the sound of people coming behind him he walked quickly to the front.

Brother Perkins approached the podium to announce the prayer he'd forgotten to announce earlier. He sort of paused for the Warpels, who rumbled in behind Sydney. They were always tardy at exactly the same time. Brother

Warpel, in loud cowboy boots, herded his family toward an open bench near the front, and Brother Perkins waited for them to sit. Brother Perkins looked over the congregation and settled his look on Brother Petersen, who, he announced, would give the opening prayer.

Startled, Brother Petersen stood and made his way out of his crowded bench and walked to the pulpit. He folded his arms. He glanced up at the door and stopped. Everyone with his or her eyes closed stayed bowed, waiting.

Sydney and everyone else whose eyes weren't entirely closed turned their heads around to look at the back door, too. Sure enough, standing at the door in a light yellow shirt and bolo tie cinched up so tight it made wrinkles in his neck, stood Dad. Looking around.

Brother Petersen hung motionless at the pulpit with his arms folded and Dad also stood still. Even people with eyes closed began peeking around. Sydney felt the air around him warm up. He turned and half stood to wave to Dad, to tell him to sit down, for heck sake. Dad saw Sydney and walked with heavy steps down the sloping aisle all the way to the front and sat next to him on the deacon's bench. A ripple of eyes followed, penetrating the thick air. Brother Petersen began to pray, and all through the prayer, Sydney smelled Dad's red Brilliantine hair oil.

Brother Petersen gave a prayer much shorter than usual, but he still repeated himself twice. Brother Perkins stood to conduct the business of the meeting. He looked at Dad, raised his eyebrows, gestured with both hands toward the ceiling, shrugged, laughed inwardly. An uncertain ripple crossed the congregation. Dad half-smiled in return. Sydney stared at the floor. He studied Dad's trousers. They

246

were black wool and formless. Two of Dad's fingers remained in bandages. Frostbite showed in the swelling of his face. He looked at Dad's hands—big, rough and dirty under the fingernails. Dad didn't fit in here. Beneath the Brilliantine hair oil, he still smelled faintly of gasoline. Sydney felt his face growing red.

When the singing of the sacrament song started, Dad took the book and found the place.

"What's the matter?" he whispered. "Don't you boys sing?" He began singing in his toneless way.

"You sit here when we pass the sacrament," Sydney whispered to Dad. "For heaven's sake, don't stand up when I do."

Because they'd moved Fast Sunday for LaMar, today was testimony meeting, which started after the sacrament.

Sydney watched his father's big hands squirm on the formless black trousers. Sydney wondered what trunk held those trousers, and whether any mouse had ever lived in one of the pockets.

Sydney noticed his father's hands lay flat and start patting his knee. Sydney saw his father's hands reach up and take hold of the back of the bench in front. Then he felt Dad stand up, and millions of eyes poke his way. Civilization, as he knew it, was about to end.

"I don't rightly know how to begin this here talk," said Dad, turning to face the congregation behind him, without letting go of the bench in front of him. His hand clung to the wood as if to wring acceptance from it. He paused to look all around at the people, at each one.

"First I want to thank Bishop Lutty for his interest in our family. We've been through a tough few months

starting with our accident, and it looks like very soon we
will be leaving for the city." Dad paused and swallowed. A
low murmur of displeased surprise crossed the open room.
Sydney studied the wood grain that flowed like a canyon
creek across the back of the benches.

"I've learned a few things," Dad said, trying to sound
like Mister with a teacher voice. "When you build with
aspen, you spend your life trying to keep a weak thing from
being weaker. When you build with cedar, you can spend
your life making a strong thing stronger.

"I reckon I have built with aspen when I should have
built with cedar."

Dad coughed a little. "I owe a few apologies. I reckon I
acted plenty rude a few times. I don't hold no grudges and I
ask you not to either.

"Norda asked me to thank everyone for your faith and
prayers, and we are sure that LaMar will be all right. He did
suffer last night, and he's having a very tough time of it,
however. I 'spose your prayers just might get a little higher
than mine will, but I want you to know that I will be
praying, anyway." Dad stopped. He had no idea how to
properly end. "Amen," he said, and sat. Once seated, he
wiped sweat from his face with his wrinkled yellow sleeve.

Like new water flowing over an old stream bed, the
meeting continued with testimonies down a known course,
fresh as a spring yet predictable to the last eddy. Again,
Sydney wondered what good it would do for all their prayer
and fasting. He saw the graves; the future can't be changed.

He remembered feeling strength from Mom's prayers.
But dark thoughts grew in his mind as he considered how
easy LaMar could go. The idea of it expanded in awfulness.

"It can't happen, it just can't happen," he thought. "It won't happen." He looked around and realized that his thoughts were like the thoughts of everyone else in the chapel. But they believed fasting and praying would make a difference, if they just fasted long enough and prayed hard enough. Sydney desperately wanted to believe. He looked at Brother Reich. He looked at Sister Pourgette. They showed so confident. He decided to try to believe, even though it seemed impossible. Then it hit him. That is what faith is! For when something looks impossible.

He studied Dad. His face did not reflect the same faith expression as the others, but he looked different than he did a few days ago. Dad didn't act as angry, for one thing.

"Maybe almost dying changed Dad," thought Sydney. "Maybe almost dying is like fasting. I know that fasting is like almost dying."

After the prayer people pressed around Dad, shaking his hand and saying kind things. But after the people left Dad's hands kept shaking on their own. He hurried past to get outside in the cold where he could relax and feel at home. The family gathered to the Plymouth, nearly out of gas, and it motored them home. As they rounded the last corner to their house, everyone sat up with a jolt. There, in front of the house, parked the sheriff's car with its light rotating red stripes over the snow and highway, and behind it, H. Beesley's two-tone Chevy hardtop.

"Oh, oh," said Dad. "Here it is." He paused a Moment before muttering, "So this is what I get for going to church."

Chapter 18

H. Beasley and Sheriff Houghton paced on the porch, looking around and clapping their hands against the cold. Bright red eviction signs showed under Beasley's arm.

"Come in," said Dad from behind, looking down, resigned and utterly beaten. "I guess it is your house now."

They walked into the kitchen, Sydney followed by Madge leading Prielle, Nat carrying Bartholomew.

The bathroom door opened and Mom, steadying LaMar, looked at the visitors and wilted. She shuddered, walking to the chairs by the stove. She made a show of helping LaMar sit down and arranging his quilt so that it covered his shoulders. She pulled another fold over his head so that just his yellow chin showed.

Both visitors stared at him, warming their hands, looking. Dad politely added a few lumps of coal through the stove's front burner lid.

"No," said Sheriff Houghton, his left eye squinting. "It ain't. Not just yet."

"Oh?" asked Dad, still beaten.

"Do you have the check for me?" politely asked H. Beesley, stepping back from the stove and laying down his eviction signs on the imitation marble table top.

He avoided looking at LaMar.

"Tomorrow by noon," said Dad. A look of hope showed in his eyes. "If you can wait. Our boy needs to be in the hospital right now."

"Paid in full?" asked Sheriff Houghton. "Paid in full?"

"Yes," said Dad. "Garth Orr of Evanston is coming with a semi and several cattle trucks. He's buying the entire herd. Paying much better than the Preston market. Hay, too. But he couldn't come till tomorrow."

"That was very shrewd of you to wait!" said Sheriff Houghton. "We'll be back tomorrow to collect the check."

Dad looked hopefully at the sheriff, then at H. Beesley.

"Not so fast," said H. Beesley. "My boss is after me to get this place taken care of. We need to proceed right now. Garth should have come last week."

Dad's gaze dropped again. LaMar stood up and touched his middle. An agonized moan escaped his lips, silencing the visitors.

"Let's see the papers," said the sheriff.

H. Beesley handed him the papers. Sheriff Houghton looked them over.

"This date is last Friday," he said.

"Blizzard pinned me in Wyoming," explained H. Beesley.

"No excuse," said the sheriff. "Why weren't you here when you were supposed to be?"

"I told you," said Beesley. "The blizzard stuck me in."

"This is only good on the date of the paper," said the sheriff. "You'll have to go back and get new papers before I can enforce them."

"That is nonsense," said Beesley. "I told you I was stuck in the blizzard."

"There," repeated the sheriff. "There for you. The blizzard, an Act of God storm. That delayed you, and it delayed everything else until Monday. We don't do business in this valley on the Sabbath."

Dad stepped back and placed one hand on the coolest corner of the stove. He quickly lifted it off.

"I don't think a blizzard is a true Act of God," said Beesley. "Doesn't it have to be an earthquake or something like a natural disaster?"

LaMar leaned toward the stove. "I feel like I am passing," he moaned.

The visitors were silent.

"Could you get through?" asked Sheriff Houghton, growing angrier. His left eye nearly closed. "Who caused it? Did you?"

"No," said Beesley. "The worst blizzard in a decade."

"There," cried the sheriff, re-asserting his local authority. "And we around here don't enforce against Acts of God," he nearly shouted, one eye completely closed. "Especially on the Sabbath! Do you understand me!"

H. Beesley looked at the sheriff. Sheriff Houghton took the trusteeship papers and made a "4" out of the 1, changing Dec. 21, 1957, to Dec. 24, 1957. Then he wrote on the top of the white onionskin sheet of paper: "Delayed by Act of God." He signed next to it: Tavon J. Houghton, County Sheriff.

LaMar swayed back on his chair and Mom leaned forward, barely catching him.

"There," Sheriff Houghton said. "There." He looked at H. Beesley. "That will protect you against your boss, too."

Dad nodded. He looked to see what Beesley would say.

"Doesn't change anything," said Beesley. "Let's get

252

this paperwork signed, the eviction notices nailed up in prominent places where everyone can see them, and I need to get moving to Logan." He glanced at the pan of stew simmering on the back of the stove. He took a deep breath.

Mom stopped holding LaMar for an instant. He swayed beyond her reach, falling to the kitchen floor, and sobbing, then he slipped into unconsciousness.

"We've got to get this young man to the hospital," exclaimed Sheriff Houghton. "We'll take him in my car."

Dad scooped up LaMar and Mom rushed to cover him with the quilt. Nat held the door open and into the winter Dad carried the large quilts burying LaMar. Mom and Sheriff Houghton followed. A minute later, Sheriff Houghton's siren pierced the cold air, loud at first, soon growing distant. Dad returned to the kitchen.

"I can still proceed," said H. Beesley, glancing again at the pot on the stove, then at Dad.

He took a black fountain pen from his shirt pocket.

"Have you eaten lunch?" interrupted Madge sweetly. "We will have some delicious stew in a few minutes."

H. Beesley stopped. He looked at the stove where the pan emitted its own authority. "Maybe I will," he said, holding the pen mid-air. "Just a taste." He paused, then admitted, "Thank you. I haven't eaten anything since yesterday."

"Oh," said Madge. "Just a minute." All stopped to watch as she took a loaf of whole wheat homemade bread and sliced two huge slices. Beesley especially stared with his mouth slightly open as she buttered each slice and spread raspberry jam thickly on one and smeared honey liberally on the other slice. H. Beesley's head moved slightly up and down with her movements. She pulled a tall glass from the cupboard and poured it full of very cold milk.

H. Beesley followed her like a child to the corner of the table where he sat, pushing the eviction signs to one side and replacing his black fountain pen in his shirt pocket. She set the food in front of him. He bit into the first slice as a corner of heaven.

"Ohh," he said. "This is so delicious." Then he bit into the other slice of heaven.

"Oh," he said. "This is indeed delicious." He turned to Madge. "I felt so hungry I couldn't wait," he said, his mouth not completely empty. "I was trying to get to Logan before their restaurants closed." He turned to Dad. "I am not in such a hurry now." He ate a few more bites. "Let's do that paperwork tomorrow."

"Have some soup," said Dad, his voice thin and cracking. "Have all you want."

"Certainly," said Beesley, his mouth now crammed with bread. "I thank you for your hospitality."

Sydney, Nat and the children stood by the stove happily watching him devour their bread.

"Garth will bring his small army first thing, if I know him," said Beesley, mouth still full. "I will drive over with him." He looked at the food. "Speaking of Acts of God, this food is delicious as manna."

Dad caught his breath. He took another breath, deep like all the air in the universe suddenly returned. He put his hand again on the stove but on the wrong place and jerked it back. He rubbed his hand watching Beesley, who had nearly finished his bread and paid attention only to his food.

Dad took another deep breath, and put his hand on the back of a chair to steady himself swaying in hyperventilation.

H. Beesley didn't look up from his bread. Madge placed a big bowl of stew next to him. He looked at Madge. He smiled luxuriously at her, as he would at a bowl of raspberry tartish.

H. Beesley stayed to eat with the family, consuming even more stew than Nat, explaining once again that all the restaurants between here and Rock Springs remained closed after the blizzard.

"I nearly starved to death," he said. "I just kept thinking what would happen if my car slid off the road, or got stuck."

"I know that feeling," said Sydney, ladling stew into his emaciated torso.

"You can have these," H. Beesley said, handing the eviction signs to Sydney. "We'll never use them again." Sydney left them lying on the table.

After eating, H. Beesley put the papers in his calf hair briefcase, and excused himself. Madge insisted on sending a sandwich with him.

After the door closed, Dad took the eviction signs, folded them tightly, and fed them into the coal burning stove.

Sydney broke the silence. "Time is like wind," he muttered, looking at the door where Beesley left. "It flows past, touching everything, and everything touches it. You can't see it, you can't stop it, but its touch changes everything. And like wind, it can't go backwards. It can

255

only go forward, and it can only change things so nothing ever stays exactly the same."

Nothing was exactly the same.

"We're going to see LaMar," Dad said. Dad put on his coat and went to pour the last of the gasoline from the gas can into the Plymouth. Sydney followed.

When they walked into the hospital-smelling foyer, Doc Mooley stood talking to Mom. Doc's face carried the expression of a child with a broken favorite toy that couldn't be fixed. He just shook his head. He started to talk again, but he shook his head again. After he swallowed, he said, "We've given that kid so many shots of penicillin that his natural defense system has shut down. Now he's got more infection that neither the penicillin nor his natural defense system is stopping." He shook his head again. "It is very serious – the worst," he said. "I wish you had let me transfer him to the Primary Children's Hospital."

"You are doing everything they could do," said Mom. Dad stood next to her and slipped his arm around her shoulders.

Doc Mooley continued: "I drove up to Salt Lake on Saturday as soon as the roads cleared, and drove right back today. I have the new medicine – they call it an anti-biotic – they flew it in to Salt Lake City from Chicago. "It is still very, very new, and I started with low dosage. It may work and it may not. I gave him a shot, but so far, it hasn't done much." He rubbed his hands against his face. "So far, it hasn't."

"Let's give it some time," said Dad.

Doc Mooley nodded. "We have no other choice."

Dad turned to Mom. "They will wait until tomorrow for the check," he said.

Mom looked at Dad. She said nothing. The news didn't change the overwhelming pain in her eyes. She looked sadly at Sydney. Dad and Doc Mooley left together. Mom slowly rose and followed them.

Sydney knew what they were doing. They were talking that LaMar might not make it. That he might pass on. Mom knew it, too, and hurried to catch them. Sydney already secretly knew it in a way they couldn't.

"It doesn't mean LaMar has to go," he thought fiercely, his body filled with rebellion at the inner image. "The graves might mean something else entirely." Then he thought, "We fasted. We went without food. That must mean something."

He stepped quietly down the hall to LaMar's room. Hospital doors are heavier and wider than most doors, he realized as he pulled it open. The antiseptic smell of alcohol filled the room. LaMar slept unmoving beneath a white sheet. Sydney looked at his brother's face, yellow from the light bulb in the hall. He couldn't see LaMar breathing. He remembered the blizzard and all the white mounds outside.

"LaMar could just become just another mound out there," he thought. "He could die, and they would put him in the ground and a stone with his name on it would stand in the snow and never even change the color covering him." He thought about the family moving away and he thought about the selling of the cows tomorrow.

He thought about Mister, and how he'd tried to fight him. He thought about once being friends with Bleu and Melvin. "It is too much for one brain to swallow," he thought. "I can't think about all this anymore."

He stepped next to LaMar's bed.

LaMar writhed in his white covers.

"Are you awake?" whispered Sydney.

"Yes," said LaMar, opening his eyes. He looked very yellow and weak in the low light. "Are you here?

"Yes," said Sydney.

"Am I still here?" LaMar asked. "Did I die?"

"Nope," said Sydney. "You are still alive."

"I'm very tired," said LaMar. "I feel sort of dead."

"Does it hurt?" asked Sydney.

"Uh huh," said LaMar. "It always hurts. I used to not cry, but now I always do. The hurting wakes me up. I start thinking. Do you suppose I am going to pass through, Sydney?"

Sydney saw his younger brother's eyes searching his.

"Naw," he said, feeling exactly like he did when he lied. "You'll just get sicker, and then you'll get better, just like before."

"I feel like if I get much sicker, I won't wake up. But I am not afraid to die," said LaMar. "Mister says it is just like changing rooms; that you are exactly the same but in another room with different people. And you don't have your body, anymore. I am getting tired of my body. All it does is hurt."

"I think about it, too,'" said Sydney. "I don't know what would happen. It's like a scary dream you don't know how will end. I hope you don't die. All the people at the meeting said so, too. I have never seen them so sad. They are fasting for you," he added. "They are praying very hard."

"They think I will die," said LaMar. "But I might not."

"Nat and Madge are sad. Even Bartholomew is sad."

"Oh well," said LaMar. "But I might not die."

258

"We would all be very sad."

LaMar shook his head slightly. "But Sydney, I have one more thing I want you to do for me. To make me very happy."

"We're having a Christmas Valentine's Day party tomorrow. You can think of that. That will make you very happy."

"But one more thing."

"You know what happened the last time I tried to save something for you," said Sydney. "That made everything so much worse. It might not work this time, either."

"At least you tried," said LaMar without lifting up his head. He grimaced and doubled in the middle, holding his stomach. He began to cry and pressed harder. "It hurts so bad," he said. "So bad." The pain gradually subsided and he turned to Sydney again.

"Pray for me," he said. "That is what I want you to do for me. Pray to Heavenly Father for me to get better."

The boys looked deeply into each other's eyes. Slowly, Sydney began nodding. "Yes," he said, "I pray for you all the time. I just don't know how much good my prayers do."

"I know I won't die if you pray for me," said LaMar. "Really pray."

"I will pray for you."

"Have faith, Sydney. Have faith."

Sydney looked at his brother. He swallowed hard. He ducked his head. "I will try," he said.

From behind boomed Doc Mooley's voice.

"I gave him something to help him sleep. We need to let him sleep." Sydney reached over and hugged his little

brother and LaMar feebly hugged back. LaMar is always
such a good hugger.

Mom, Dad and Sydney left together. No one spoke on
the way home. The family waited for them in the kitchen as
they walked in.

Mom sank heavily into a chair. Prielle and Bartholomew
rushed to her. She hugged them a long time.

"Why are you crying?" finally asked Prielle, looking up
at Mom.

Mom pulled her on her lap, but Bartholomew began to
cry. She set Prielle down and pulled Bartholomew up. She
kept one arm around Prielle.

"LaMar is very, very sick," she said to the whole
family. She paused, struggling for control. "Doc Mooley says
there's a chance that LaMar might pass away in the next few
days." She sobbed. Madge and Prielle sobbed with her.
Sydney felt tears on his face.

"We must have faith that he can be healed," said Mom,
regaining her composure. "But we must prepare ourselves for
the worst."

"He might not," said Sydney. "But he might. We must
have faith."

Madge looked at him strangely.

Dad spoke. He spoke like he read words from a book
and had to study out each word before he could say it. "We
fasted today, and we didn't lose the farm after all. God works
in mysterious ways. At times, like this, we are in God's
hands."

He shook his head. "I don't pretend to understand it," he
said.

"His ways are indeed mysterious," Mom said, looking long at Dad. "Let's have family prayer."

As the family knelt around the stove, Mom took charge as usual. This time, she asked Dad to pray. His prayer wasn't like any of the others.

"God," he said, "You helped me when I didn't ask for it, when I didn't deserve it, when I didn't expect it. Now, I still don't deserve it, but I am asking, maybe not expecting, but hoping. Hoping a lot. God, our little boy, and all our children, mean everything to us. More than our cattle, more than our home, more than our farm. You found a way to save our home and our farm. God, our Heavenly Father, now we don't care so much for those after all, but our LaMar does mean everything to us. Please save our LaMar for us."

Afterwards, everyone hugged again and went quietly to bed.

Sydney prayed out loud at his bedside. "Please listen to me, Heavenly Father," he prayed. "You don't need LaMar up there just yet. Not just yet. Please leave him down here with us, so he can grow up." A sudden thought entered his mind. "Please" he said, "bless that new medicine to make him better." Sydney closed then, and he thought about what he'd said, and about the sudden warmth that flowed into all of him, into his whole self, as he prayed, and he could still feel it.

Chapter 19

On Monday morning, Christmas Eve, the day of the school party and closing of the school, Sydney walked along the highway between banks of snow higher than the cars – not that any cars drove on it – as he headed off to school. Shortly after he reached the ice-covered Highway 89, an approaching semi surprised him as it filled the road with its hugeness, and filled the silence with its loud rumblings. Sydney scrambled up a snowbank to let it pass. The semi surprised him more when it pulled over behind him and stopped at their house. Behind it, an assortment of other trucks following also pulled over, idling their powerful engines and smoking up the clear, bitingly cold air. Sydney watched as Dad came hurrying from the house, and climbed up the side of the truck into its passenger seat. The truck hissed as its brakes released and issued a deep and guttural growl and slowly began to move, followed by its siblings. As the truck passed, Sydney could not see Dad for the height of the square-nosed, boxy shaped truck. The trucks – other cattle trucks, grain trucks, a few pickups – passed slowly but relentlessly toward the cattle and the field. H. Beesley and his two-tone Chevy hardtop followed last. He waved to Sydney. Sydney waved back.

Sydney turned the corner to the school – no cutting cross-lots with this much snow, he thought, giving some relief to the needle wound of his mind. More relief came as the school's bell pealed, its rosy tones echoing across the snow-sheeted town. Today's bell rang, tones that lasted longer than usual. As Sydney listened, though, the metallic tones of the bell began to reverberate in his thoughts as a knell of doom, a warning, a tome announcing the coming silence. As he walked, Sydney listened to the prolonged resounding. Around the school stood no one; everyone else sat inside. Sydney realized that the bell rang for him. He hurried inside, where Onga stood, toward the door and flag, with her back to the class.

Draped across the room hung red tinsel streamers suspending red valentines that swayed and vibrated in heat shimmering from radiators. Red foil valentines taped to windows also vaguely diffused in shape at the heat. Like a Mrs. Valentine, Sister Mister in a red dress with white rabbit fur trim sat in a chair next to a smiling Mister at his desk. Mister wore his black suit, not even taking off his suit coat. The entire room glittered in the union of good will of the blending of the two red holidays. Mister presided over it like a stake president.

"This would make LaMar very happy," thought Sydney. "I will remember carefully so I can tell him everything." Sadness welled within at that, as he sat, Sydney forced his thoughts back on the classroom around him.

Mister nodded to Onga.

She held her hand over her heart and faced the flag, leading the Pledge of Allegiance. Onga smiled at Sydney. He half-smiled back. He noticed for the first time the thinness of her winter clothing.

She looked over her shoulder as Sydney sat.

"Ready?" she asked, still looking back. A hopeful smile crossed her lips. "I guess you are," she said. "I am, too." She smiled again. She nodded. Melvin and Bleu entered then in the midst of the pledging.

Onga stopped. She smiled at Melvin. "I guess we will have to start all over again, again," she laughed, drinking in the attention of the entire classroom but savoring that of Melvin. The pledging began a third time and continued to its finish. Onga stood still before taking her seat so she could walk next to, but slightly behind, the pair as they swaggered to their seats, final victors gloating over the ruins of local education. Or perhaps they now understood the mystery of X in algebra. Or because Mrs. Clonerson's sister liked them. Melvin ignored Onga.

Mister waved his arm. "I will remain seated today because I am not feeling well," he said. "I believe all of you know this is the final day of school in this building, and probably in this town. What is happening will impact all of our lives. I mention this only so you will appreciate your time here. My wife will now conduct the party."

Sister Mister began by leading Christmas carols, mostly soloing in her high soprano.

"I wish someone would write a Valentine's song," she said as she led the pupils in games that erased the sternness of half a century of strict discipline. Even Melvin and Bleu played with abandon, laughing, mocking the jailer now dressed in black on this, the last day of their incarceration.

"Now," Sister Mister said later in the morning, pleased her obligation to Christmas was now fully paid, and the real climax of the celebration arrived. "We shall open the Valentine Box," she said. The Valentine's Box, with a slot in top to accept valentines, glistened with new heart shapes pasted to its sides. Icicles, and even an improvised

264

valentine angel, decorated its top. A false panel opened to access its innards.

As pupils rested from their games, and as a prelude to passing out valentines, she uncovered a large bowl of red punch, and heart-shaped cookies frosted redly next to it. She began fussing around the Valentine box, as to relish the soon-vanishing experience, as to add to the memory. She straightened the valentine angel, reminding Sydney of his valentine. He started to feel as red as the box, wondering what Melvin would say if he saw his valentine to Addie. He thought of any other word he should have used: "Your pal." "Your friend." "Your good ole Sydney." But no. It would say "love" tiny as anything. "I'll tell them Madge made it," he thought in a panic. They he realized his handwriting would give everything away. "Love," he thought. "That is a word boys don't ever use."

Sister Mister opened the heart bank through its secret side panel that swung out. She reached through it to take each valentine one by one. Savoring each moment, she slowly read the name on each card: "Melvin Klaybill. That's a nice card, Melvin." Melvin walked up and took the card from her.

"Ann Bakewell." Ann, the apt eighth grade girl with dark hair, took the valentine with an expectant smile on her thick lips.

"Oh," Sister Mister said next, pulling out a large envelope. "Surprise! This one is addressed to me." She opened the envelope, withdrew the handmade valentine, showed it proudly to the pupils and read the inscription:

God smiles down in care supernal,
Remember dear, my love's eternal.

265

Alf

"Thank you," said Sister Mister. She leaned over and kissed her husband, right in front of everyone. Mister colored, red around the grayness of his face. They looked at each other, and Sister Mister patted his shoulder and kissed him a second time. Both their faces colored as she returned to passing out valentines, reluctant to let go of him.

"This is a nice one," said Sister Mister, a little louder than usual to change the focus. She held up the layered hearts valentine Sydney made. "Addie Lutty. Addie just had her tonsils removed. Would someone care to hand this back to her?"

Melvin stood up to get the valentine to take to Addie. Sydney slid lower and lower in the desk.

"I'll come myself," said Addie in her new, lower voice. Sydney perked up.

"I'm almost there," said Melvin. Sydney slunk again.

Addie hopped from her desk. Melvin reached up and took the card from Mister. But before he could read the signature, Addie deftly collected it from him.

"Thank you," she said, turning her back.

Both Melvin and Bleu eyed her young womanly form as she returned to her seat. She ignored them and studied the valentine. Sydney felt himself becoming valentine colored.

"Uhh . . . when is your voice going to get better?" asked Sister Mister. "You know, from your tonsillectomy?"

"It is better," said Addie. "I am better, too. My cold is gone, just like Doc Mooley said it would be. I guess this is how I am going to sound from now on." She smiled and shrugged. "This is the real me."

266

Sydney sort of smiled and she looked a jet shot at him. Their glances touched briefly. Sydney swallowed and studied the ink bottle hole on top of his desk. His neck felt hot. He shot a quick look back at her and she met his gaze easily and grinned at him. One of those feely grins that went deeper than a "hello, how are you doing grin" or a "Good job" grin. She had such a way of looking into eyes.

He studied the ink bottle hole again – a hole too small for him to crawl inside. He looked back and smiled. She reached over and put her hand on his for a touch. He felt like their eyes kissed, with the whole world watching.

Sister Mister read cards for everyone, saving and enjoying each as if it were for her. Valentines covered the tops of most pupils' desk with hearts of one size or another. The biggest pile, stacked on Mister's desk, had LaMar's name. When he came to one for LaMar, Mister read who sent it. Everyone sent a valentine to LaMar, including Melvin and Bleu.

LaMar's sickness changed the whole town. What happened before no longer mattered. All that mattered now is for LaMar to get better, a brother, a child of every family in town. Yet each card prompted another welling up of sadness, and each time Sydney forced himself to look away, to change the thought.

"They will be so sad," something said in Sydney's mind. He looked away again. "I can't think that."

"This is a nice card for LaMar," said Sister Mister, holding another card. "From Onga."

Sydney glanced at Onga. She sat half covering her desk with both hands on her chin. "I wonder why she is covering her pile of valentines?" Sydney wondered. Sister

Mister read a few more valentines as pupils sorted cards around on their desks by pinks and reds.

"Here's the prettiest card of them all," said Sister Mister. "The very last one." She pulled out a large valentine. "To Onga," she read. Everyone turned to gape at Onga. Onga stood up from her empty desktop. "Where are all your valentines?" asked Ann.

"I put them inside my desk," said Onga. She walked to the front and took the card. She didn't wait to return to her seat to open it, but stopped in the aisle in front of Melvin's desk. Real velvet and lace glued on the front of the fancy store-card valentine. Onga opened the card and Melvin half-stood to see.

"It says 'love,'" said Melvin. He leaned closer. "Love from a secret ad--, secret ad—, . . . secret admiral, I guess."

"Wow," said Ann from her front seat. "An admiral?"

"It's a general who sails boats in the ocean," said Sydney. "Do you know a general?"

"Admire," corrected Onga. "A secret admire."

"Oh," said Sydney. "That could be anybody."

Onga glanced around, her look hungry for her secret admire. Melvin and Bleu both looked down and Sydney saw Onga's look linger on them.

"I want to thank whoever sent this," she said. "I'll find something nice to do for my secret admire."

"That's the last one," Sister Mister said, looking at Mister and sitting down. Sister Mister remembered the refreshments and stood again, delighted to extend the event. "Now," she said. "If you will all line up for punch and cookies." Half the class stood and scrambled toward the front.

"No, no," said Sister Mister. "Instead, I'll bring the cups around to you."

Everyone sat down.

"That won't do, either," said Sister Mister. "Half of you come up and half of you wait."

Everyone stood again.

"Oh dear," she said. She sat in her chair again. "Why does everything get so complicated?"

Mister took over from his chair.

"Let's have the older boys serve the older girls," he said. Melvin and Bleu shuffled forward and helped themselves to refreshments. Onga smiled at Bleu when he served her. He slid into his desk without smiling back. Her book fell to the floor. Bleu leaned over and picked it up and slid it on her desk. Onga smiled again. A low monotone startled the pupils: Onga hummed. She inspected her valentine and hummed louder. She looked at Bleuford, but her eyes settled on Melvin. She smiled at him. Standing there, she looked almost pretty.

"Take all your books home," said Mister. "They won't do anyone any good left in this building."

Melvin and Bleu stacked all their books on top of their desks and left first. Sydney watched them as they hurried from the cloakroom and out the door without looking back. Onga quickly rose with her usual stack of books to follow them out. And when she left, Sydney noticed, she didn't even look in her desk for her other valentines.

"Look, Sydney," said Mister, pointing to the window.

Through the foil valentines taped to the windows, Sydney saw trucks passing, all piled high with hay roped to the racks. He didn't see the cattle trucks – they'd already gone. He'd wanted to see the cattle go. Cattle were the soul of the farm, giving it life. Without cattle, you lost reason for doing anything on the farm. In the winter, you fed the cattle, in the spring you calved them and then branded. In the summer, you turned them out on the range so you could hay. In the fall, you rounded them up, and sold the calves. You always moved this bunch or that bunch to this or that pasture or those calves to the corral, or the bull somewhere away. And fixed fence to keep them in. And cleaned ditches to water the hay to keep them fed. Brush-rubbing the field after they wintered to spread the fertilizer. Without the cow, you didn't need the horse. Without the cow, you don't need a farm. Without the cow, well, you're just another city dude with some land on your hands.

"That's what we are now," thought Sydney. "City dudes."

As the trucks passed, a needle, a needle of dread, pierced his thoughts; selling the entire herd of cattle right now will bring very bad luck. In his mind he saw again the two open, snowy graves on the cemetery hillside, blasted by a wind.

"A very bad time for bad luck," he thought. He shuddered deeply and tried again to have faith.

"It can't be," he reasoned to himself. "We've saved the farm. The bad luck is that the school is closing."

The last truck disappeared behind a stand of trees along with their winter of farm despair.

Addie stopped at his desk. He looked up at her standing so close her skirt brushed his side.

"Thanks," she said. "I got the prettiest card in the entire school." Her hand brushed over the top of his and she

270

looked right into him with that look of hers. She squeezed his hand and turned gracefully to her desk.

Mister hummed a little and dropped a stack of papers on the floor. The sixth and seventh grade girls finished gathering their things from desks and helped him pick up the papers. Then they left as a happy, talking group, Addie in the center, taking Sister Mister's arm, to walk her to her home. He could hear them singing a carol, Sister Mister's soprano rising above the others.

Mister shuffled his papers. Then he gazed at the room where he'd taught school for the bigger part of his life.

"Sydney," he said. "Could you wait with me? I don't feel a bit well."

Sydney nodded. "I hope you are not catching cold," he said.

"No," said Mister. "What I feel is deeper than that."

No one remained in the school room but the two of them. Mister walked slowly to the closet and took out a cardboard box. He began taking pictures off the wall and putting them inside the box. "I don't think I can last the year," he said. "You know, I will go to my grave wishing I hadn't left early the night of the accident. Somehow, maybe, I could have prevented all this."

"It wasn't your fault," said Sydney. "At all. We just should have gone home earlier like you told us to. No sense splashing about it. What's done is done. You can't run the wind backwards."

"I just don't know what will happen now," said Mister. "The world is turning inside out. There's nowhere to step but something changes. Some days I feel that nothing will ever be the same again. I feel so extra, so useless."

Mister returned to his desk and sank into the chair. He began stretching and rubbing his left arm.

"Times like these try our faith," said Sydney. "Maybe that is what time is for." And then to himself he thought, "I wasn't going to say that. That sounded just like Mom. Maybe I will get me one of those testimony things."

Mister brightened. "You're right." He pushed himself up from the desk and walked to the closet where he pulled out another cardboard box and began filling it from the shelves.

"This is so hard," he said after a few minutes. "I don't know if I can bear it."

Sydney came over to hold the box. Mister didn't answer. He kept putting pictures and books into the box. Then a surprised look crossed his face. "I feel very odd," he said, with a cough. He held his hand against his chest and walked to the desk's chair. He thumped down into the chair. He rested, and after a minute, picked up the can of pencil stubs and held them for a long time.

"I don't need to save these anymore," he said, and turned the can gently until the stubs slid rattling into the tin waste paper basket. His head dropped. He did not move until great sobs began to wrack his body. He held the empty can as though it were his empty life and its meaning fled with the pencil stubs into the waste paper basket.

"It is hard to leave something you love. It is so very hard," he murmured. "I don't have anything left, now, you know. Nothing but Alicia."

Sydney had never seen an old man cry before. He didn't know what to do. He reached over and hugged Mister, and stepped back.

Mister glanced up and tried to smile. A surprised look returned to his face that turned instantly to pain. He grabbed his chest again. His breathing became rapid. He breathed loudly and his breath sounded like snores. He held his chest tighter. His iron-colored hair hung down. His face turned more gray. His lips blued. Sydney watched with a growing horror, not knowing what he could do. He felt a rescue car slipping out of reach. Mister's eyes rolled back and half shut. He slumped lower, hunched over, still holding his chest. His head grew darker and dropped to the desk. He began to shake and breathe louder with his voice – sounding like a tractor that couldn't start.

"Huuuuuh! Huuuuuh!" he breathed.

"Help!" shrieked Sydney backing away in horror. "It's Mister! Something is wrong!"

He ran to the door and crossed the hallway. He found Mrs. Clonerson turning toward him from the far corner of her room, near a box she'd filled with books. Sydney lingered in the hall waiting for her to go back into the room first.

"Wait there," she said to him. "Don't come in." He looked into the room. Mister's feet and legs showed on the floor behind the desk. Sydney felt his skin quiver and then his insides caved and broke into little pieces. Even at his age, he began sobbing loudly. Mrs. Clonerson kneeled behind the desk, beyond his view. She knelt for a long time and finally stood and turned to Sydney.

"He's gone," she said with tears streaming down her cheeks. "Mister's gone."

Minutes passed. Finally, Mrs. Clonerson stood and looked around the room. She searched the closet. She

273

returned with a neatly folded black felt cloth used to cover the bulletin board. She spread it out, and tenderly covered his body. A line of cutouts of children's figures pinned across the cloth. The children's cutouts held hands, ringing the teacher.

"We'll need to call the mortuary," she explained. "You need to go tell Sister Mister. Be gentle and kind in the way you tell her. I will wait here."

Sydney nodded and hurried out of the room. As he walked to the hall, he looked at the white cotton rope hanging from the bell.

"This town needs to hear," he said to no one but himself.

He reached up and grabbed the rope, hauling with his grieving might, and listened as it clanged once. Then he jumped and dragged on the rope a second time and clanged it once more. He jumped a third time and clanged it, the one last pull reverberated in finality. Then he hurried out, grabbing his coat but not his boots. Outside, his feet slipped over the icy surface as he rushed the block to Mister's house. There, he waded through a drift and knocked on the formal, front door. Inside he heard Sister Mister soulfully singing "God rest ye merry gentlemen," in high, sad soprano. He knocked again and heard her invite, "Come in, please."

Sydney walked into the elegant room with its dark wood furniture and faint odor of mothballs. Still wearing her red dress with its white rabbit fur trim, Sister Mister turned from the piano where she sat. Sydney saw her studying his face. He tried to speak, but instead he looked at the floor. Sister Mister walked over to him. "Whatever is the matter?" she asked. "What has my husband done now?"

"He's passed beyond all that," said Sydney, struggling to speak. "He's gone now, gone into the other room."

Sister Mister looked at Sydney.

"What are you saying?" she cried out. "What has happened to my husband?"

"He's gone. Passed on," said Sydney, sobbing lightly. "I am so sorry."

Sister Mister collapsed on to an embroidered couch with its carved feet nestled in a plush rug, her head sinking into her hands. She wept. After a few minutes, she stopped and looked to Sydney. She reached out her arms and Sydney stepped reluctantly closer. Immediately she enveloped him in a hard but soft embrace, sobbing all over again. Sydney reached up and patted her shoulder. She sobbed more, and he patted her shoulder again. When the weeping subsided, she said, "I knew. I knew it. I knew he would go any day now. Closing the school destroyed him. We knew he didn't have much time left at all."

The sobbing began again. Sydney didn't know what to say, so he listened.

"Doctors told us a long time ago that his heart suffered badly from disease. We've known, we've known." She looked at Sydney and wiped her crimson face on her red sleeves. "This is sad, but it isn't a tragedy. He did what he wanted, he lived his dream, and he did it very well. He lasted till the school closed."

"He isn't really dead," volunteered Sydney. "He's just in another room, where we can't see him, that's all."

275

She looked at him. "Wait here," she asked Sydney. She stood slowly and walked to the table where the black telephone rested with its clothish cord running to a beige plastic box on the wall.

She opened a small paper book and carefully dialed a number from it. He heard her tell her name and ask to speak to Doc Mooley. He heard her say, "Hello, Doctor. This is Alicia Prate." She paused and replied, "I'm sorry. He passed away this afternoon. That is what I called to tell you."

He heard them talk, and she often said, "Thank you – that is so kind."

After she returned the receiver to the telephone, she turned back to Sydney.

"You don't need to go back to the school," she said. "But wait with me a few minutes." Sydney remained on the couch.

"Mister had a strong spirit," ventured Sydney.

"I should tell you," she said, interrupting him. "Doctor Mooley said LaMar didn't respond to the small doses of medicine. He's giving him a full dose, but he is awfully sick. He's in a tremendous pain." She began sobbing again. "He said," – she couldn't go on for a minute – you . . . we . . . we all. . . need to prepare for the worst."

"Oh," she added. "Maybe Alf is waiting to take him. Maybe they will be together." She began a new round of sobbing and Sydney felt himself subsiding, caving, disconnecting, hopeless in an agony of grief, an agony of twin graves. The boy and woman clung to each other.

Then Sister Mister stopped. "I need to be alone now," she said. "The veil is very thin at these times. I think I felt his presence while singing."

Sydney stood and walked slowly out of the front door into the cold. "Mister is gone and now LaMar is about to go also," he thought. As he passed the school, he walked back to put on his boots. Already coolness touched the building. Mrs. Clonerson sat at the desk, still as a headstone. A bit of black showed through the door.

"The station wagon for the dead will be here soon," he called.

"A hearse," taught Mrs. Clonerson. "It is called a hearse." Sydney pulled on his galoshes and snapped the buckles shut. He tromped out of the cloak room, steps echoing against the silent walls. He glanced one last time at the patch of black on the school room floor. Then he turned along the wide hallway, fighting the cold and silence that would soon prevail here, glad for his loud boots.

"Thank you," called Mrs. Clonerson, as an afterthought. "You were brave to do that."

Chapter 20

The next day, Christmas morning, the family gathered at the breakfast table, soaking inwardly in the pond of grief that covered them at the threat of what had and what might happen. Mom's eyes ringed with redness. Madge also cried. Dad talked about anything else. In a husky voice, he told about the cattle.

"Garth Orr said, over and over, 'I don't want any dropped calves,' 'I don't want any dropped calves,' 'I don't want any dropped calves,' " Dad mimicked insincerely as the family faced their daily wheat mush topped by thick cream. "Huge operation he has," continued Dad. "They came in like grasshoppers and took everything. You should have seen them cleaning up the stack yards."

Nat guided him along. "What about Old Lopp?" he asked. "Did she give them trouble?"

"They loaded every cow out there, the bull into a horse trailer. Old Lopp paced, watching her fellow citizens disappear by the cow. She lingered to the last, walking along the chute they set up. They waited – Garth Orr doesn't want no dropped calves, especially big ones – as she tossed her head and switched her tail and paced back and forth like she does. Finally, she had no cow followers. She eased closer to the ramp, cattle mooing. They scooted her in and shut the tailgate."

Dad took another spoonful and sat back. Today, he raised hay to sell by the stack and cattle to sell by the herd.

Deep silence followed.

"How did we do?" egged on Nat.

"Most money I ever saw in my life," Dad said. "He paid 28 cents a pound on the hoof." He took another spoonful. He looked gratefully at Mom. No one spoke, so he continued:

"Beesley drove me to town and collected his money. They drew it into a cashier's draft. He shook hands, told me what a fine daughter I had, and left. I guess that is the last we will see of him."

"I hope," said Madge. "I hope it is the last he sees of me."

"Did you get everything else paid?" asked Nat, uncomfortable in the silence.

"Paid the hospital, the bank, and we have about $700 left. Waiting till Monday made all the difference."

Again, he looked at Mom. She dabbed at her eyes. Silence built up. No one wanted to mention LaMar.

"Now that we can stay, where will we go?" Nat asked.

"Sister Klaybill's brother is head of school maintenance in Davis County, in Utah," said Dad. "He hires school janitors. He hired Carn, and he may hire me. Janitors can have most of the summers off. Sister Klaybill told him we are coming. They do have openings for head custodians. We'll try that first."

"When will we go see LaMar?" asked Sydney. "It is Christmas. Christmas Day."

"Before we visit LaMar, we will pay our respects to Sister Mister." Silence around the table deepened as the subject finally came up.

"Remember," she said. "Mister is gone, but just into another room where we can't see him."

"He couldn't bear to leave his school," said Nat. "The

other room where he went is a classroom."

"Grandfather's clock stopped," said Madge. "Never to ring again. His time expired."

"I never, ever want to see anyone die in front of my face," said Sydney. "Just me and Mrs. Clonerson were there." He looked at Mom for help. "I can't get it out of my eyes."

Sydney stopped eating and stared down at his mush, an overfull emotional absorbent and he expected to put more into it.

"Let's go see Alicia," said Mom, by way of consolation. "Then we will see LaMar. Maybe we will have a devotional there in the hospital. That's what Christmas is all about. We so easily miss the true spirit of Christmas, and we have so much to be thankful for."

She stopped and struggled and started again.

"He couldn't even speak last night, being so tired," she said. "Doc Mooley gave him the new medicine, but it didn't work. We have no other plans beyond that new medicine. I thought we would give him a little more time, in hopes he is more responsive. We have no other choice."

The pond of grief around the table deepened.

"We should go see LaMar," said Sydney.

"We could go see him, but he can't talk," repeated Mom. "He just lays there, barely breathing, yellow as a crayon. We will go later."

No one spoke. "We must have faith," continued Mom. "Remember Mister's blessing. He will be all right. He has to be."

Dad took a last bite of mush and stood. "Let's go to Prate's," he said. "Alicia is there by herself."

"No," said Sydney. "Mister is there with her."

They looked at him. Dad shook his head.

"Do we have any gas?" asked Nat. "Nothing is open today."

"Don't know what's open," said Dad. "We've never driven anywhere on Christmas Day."

When the family climbed into the Plymouth, and Dad turned the key, the gas gauge showed no gas at all.

"Now's when we practice our faith," said Dad. "I have already drained the tractor's tank. But don't worry. We've got enough horsepower inside the car to push it to the nearest station."

"That's comforting," said Madge.

"There's one horse," said Nat.

The car started and soon they drove smoothly along the back streets to Sister Mister's house.

"We're going to make it," said Nat. Just as he said that, the car began to sputter.

"Oh, oh," said Dad. "We may be walking after all."

"Oh no!" said Madge.

The car sputtered again. It pulled only a short distance before it sputtered one last time and coasted quietly to the side of the road. No one moved until Dad said, "Let's get out. Maybe Alicia has a can of gas somewhere there."

Nat climbed out first, followed by Madge and Sydney. Soon the entire family walked in single file toward Sister Mister's lonely house.

"Look," said Sydney, pointing to the cemetery hill where a long yellow truck parked and a yellow backhoe labored. "They're digging Mister's grave."

From the distance the family could see the dark spot where a pile of earth heaped against the snow.

"They will dig another before they leave," said Sydney bitterly.

"What a thing to say!" said Mom, turning angrily toward her son. "Even if you think it, you don't need to say it."

"I've seen it over and over," said Sydney. "What I see always comes about."

Mom didn't answer. Again, silence overtook the family. They trudged quietly the last half block to Sister Mister's. Mom reached down and picked up Bartholomew, held him for a minute and weakly passed him to Dad. Nat picked up Prielle and carried her on his shoulders. When they arrived at the Prate house, they were surprised to see Arsle digging a path. They stopped and watched as he dug.

Balancing on his game leg on the slippery surface, he chipped at a snowdrift stretched along the front porch, punctured only by Sydney's steps from the day before. Icy snow crusted the drift. Ice nearly a foot thick formed near the house where snow from the eaves drained in the daytime and froze at night. Arsle struggled to stand in the slippery snow, but he doggedly hewed a path, shovelful by shovelful. As he came near the house, he set down his square-nosed shovel and used an ax to hack away ice.

The Speng family waited respectfully, standing in the skirt of snow along the ploughed road, until Arsle hacked a path wide enough for them to walk to the front door. They slipped off their boots on the ornate white porch and stepped reverently into the living room of dark wood furniture and embroidered couch.

282

Sister Mister welcomed them. "Oh, thank you so much for coming," she said. "I know Alf appreciates it so very much."

Mom hugged her and they both cried. Dad nodded from a way back.

"It is such a blow," said Dad from a distance. "We are so sorry for you."

"We knew he didn't have much time," said Sister Mister. "We've expected this every day for the last ten years. Every day came as a gift, and we enjoyed each one."

As they talked, other townspeople came to pay their respects, the Warpels, and Mafe Gill and his wife, and Bleu. Bleu nodded solemnly to Sydney. Sydney nodded solemnly in return.

"We expected this a long time ago," she told them. "Every day came as a gift."

More townspeople came in on the wide path Arsle dug, and spoke in low tones of sympathy to Sister Mister. She wept a little at each visitor and then smiled. "Thank you so much for coming, especially on Christmas day," she said.

Bishop Lutty came alone, and between visitors, tried talk about the funeral. He wrote down the opening prayer – Brother Reich – and the song, "Carry On," decided upon.

Dad sat in the corner and didn't look up at anyone. Then Bishop Lutty asked him to help plan the funeral.

Sister Mister again changed the subject at hand. "I do so pray for LaMar. How is he this morning?"

Mom shook her head. "We've going to his bedside in a few minutes. He is so weak and so sick he barely realized that Alf has passed."

"He hasn't shown any improvement?" asked Sister
Mister. "He experienced a lot of pain last night."

Mom forced a smile. "We needed to come. We're going
right back," she said. "Doc tried the last shot last night, some
new medicine. But we didn't see any change. We have
nothing else to try, nor where to go. We really don't know
how much time he has left."

Dad didn't answer. "I will think about it," he said to
Bishop Lutty.

More visitors came, and after sitting for a few minutes,
Dad stood. Then he looked at Mom. She nodded. Nat and
Madge stood. Then Sydney stood and the two children
looking around, finally climbed from their chairs. Mom and
Sister Mister hugged again and the Speng family filed out. A
line of townspeople formed outside waiting in the snow to
pay their respects. Sydney followed Dad, who shook hands
with each of them as he passed. He looked around for the car,
and suddenly jerked back.

"Just a minute," he said. Sydney followed him as he
walked back into the house. "Excuse me," he said to Sister
Mister. "Did Alf keep a can of gas around? Or even a gas
can? We're completely out. I could walk to the store to get
some."

"I don't think so," she said. "Here, just take the
Studebaker. Keys on the fridge."

"I can't do that," said Dad. "Maybe I could just take
some gas from it."

"Nonsense. I hardly drive, anyway. Just take the
Studebaker." She turned to Sister Warpel. "We knew he
didn't have much time," she continued. "Every day came
as a gift."

Dad looked things over. He walked to the refrigerator, and took the keys. He went out and waved to the rest of the family. They squeezed into the small, robin-egg blue sedan. Sydney followed, glancing at the yellow backhoe still put-putting on the hill, but, with the grave fully dug, steamed back on the lengthy yellow truck.

Nat, Sydney and Madge squeezed into the back seat with Prielle on their laps. Then Mom squeezed into the front seat, bringing lonesome Bartholomew to her lap. Dad rolled the window down, as if to acquire more space. He hunted down the starter button, the car whirred to life and backed over the snowy driveway, past visitors, and into the road.

"My laws!" said Mafe, peering in at Dad. "I thought I'd lost my mind!"

Dad smiled grimly.

The car stopped and its snow-tired wheels spun on the icy roadway. Dad let the motor slow and started again.

"Wait!" said Madge. "Someone is chasing us. Yelling for us to stop."

"I'll see what they want," said Nat as the car stopped. He opened the door. There stood Sister Mister, all out of breath, weeping.

"Doctor Mooley called on the telephone," she said with panic lacing her piercing voice, between deep sobs. "You have to get to hospital. It's about LaMar. Oh, dear Lord! They said that dear little LaMar has died. The telephone line stopped working. I couldn't call back." She began to sob again. "You better just hurry."

Mom gasped and burst into tears. Dad bowed his head. Madge wept, even Nat sobbed and Sydney felt his skin begin to quiver and familiar sobs overtake his consciousness.

285

"'Mar gone," cried Bartholomew. "'Mar gone."

"No!" said someone behind them. "Please no!" Mothers in the line, LaMar's Primary teachers, shook their heads and began weeping. All those in the waiting line melded into an extended family. Sister Klaybill came from nowhere and put her arm around Sister Mister and gently helped her back toward the house, both of them shaking. Nat finally pulled the back door of the Studebaker closed.

Sydney saw Mafe climbing into his car and driving toward the cemetery.

Inside the Studebaker, sobs came from everyone. Mom hugged Bartholomew. Madge hugged Prielle. Dad's deep sounds throbbed in misery and loss. He hugged Mom and their grieving flowed in union. Nat and Sydney cried individually. After a few minutes, wheels on the Studebaker spun and it moved uncertainly forward. The odor of spinning, warm rubber spread through the half-open window. The car slowly accelerated but the wheels spun again on the iced roadway and the car's rear end slid from the road into a bank of plowed snow. Wheels spun impotently on the frozen way, first frontward, then backwards.

Dad breathed a long sigh.

"Boys," he said. The rear doors opened and Sydney and Nat climbed out and began pushing the car.

"Madge," said Dad.

Madge climbed out and the three of them pushed the small sedan, inching it forward.

After twenty minutes, when it cleared the snow bank, they climbed back. Sydney, the last one, glanced back up on cemetery hill and noticed the backhoe reversed itself off the lengthy yellow truck, and the small, distant figure of Mafe

286

directing it where to dig a second grave, precisely where
Sydney had seen it in his mind. Its put-putting labored
distantly; its smoke billowed darkly against the white
hillside. A breeze sprang up lifting snow across the two grave
sites.

Sydney climbed inside, utterly defeated. Overwhelmed,
he wedged his head down to his knees and abandoned
himself to the drift of desolation engulfing them all. Anguish
prevented them from speaking. Dad drove slowly over the
packed ice road, minutes passing as hours. The Studebaker
crossed acres of white, passing marshes with black tips
spearing up, fences prodding up through frosty layers,
willows of naked black bark, trees of weathered silvery gray,
frozen rivers – the world in constant cold war, and the world
in constant war of cold.

"LaMar so enjoyed playing tiddledywinks," he thought.
He thought about never again sleeping in the same bed with
LaMar. He thought about never making LaMar laugh. He
could remember every one of LaMar's laughs. He thought
about taking LaMar to see the cows, about going to see the
cattle. He thought about changing sides, to be on Mister's
side. Everything he'd done had been right, and now, with two
of them gone, his choices meant so very much more.

LaMar gone left a huge hole in the middle of life that
nothing could replace. The precious presence of his younger
brother now missing hurt so much more than he'd ever felt.
No more talking in bed. No more mixing their clothes up in
the dresser drawers. No more blunt statements out of
nowhere. He felt pain pressing against him from every
direction.

"What of faith?" Sydney wondered. He changed the
subject. "So much white," he thought. "Winter is a sort of a
gateway into heaven."

He listened to the wind whistle over the car and
wondered if it would ever stop. He thought he could hear in
its moaning and lowing from the window. Selling the cattle
brought bad luck that even fasting couldn't halt. Wind cows
were everywhere in the valley now. He thought about LaMar,
and Inca, and wrecking. Then he thought of Mister, and the
vacancy left to the living by his departure.

After a drive that lasted almost forever, the Studebaker
pulled up in front of the memorial hospital. No one moved.
Then front doors of the hospital opened and Doc Mooley
looked out. He looked at the Studebaker, froze in shock,
looked twice, and returned quickly into the hospital.

"Scared him good," said Dad grimly. "He thought it was
Alf back from the dead."

"Where shall we go?" asked Madge.

"We better take you to Doc Mooley's office," said Mom.
"And then I want to go see LaMar."

"We all want to see LaMar," said Dad.

"Even the children?" asked Mom.

"We'll all go," said Dad firmly. "We are family."

Doors of the Studebaker opened and they climbed
slowly from the car, and up badly shoveled hospital steps.
They entered the glass doors. Sydney looked at the white and
blue tiles and smelled the hospital smell of alcohol. In the
corner sagged the undying Roscoe in his wheelchair. Sister
Mister must have come last week for both valentines and
tinsel hung on the wheels and along the hand rests. The old
man stared out the window with his head leaning to one side,

288

still cursed with life. As the family turned to the hallway, not one person greeted them. The family paused.

"I don't know where to go," said Mom. "I don't know where they have him."

"Maybe we shouldn't take the children there first," continued Mom, her voice breaking. "Maybe they are not ready for us yet."

"Let's go," said Dad. He picked up Bartholomew and circled his arm lovingly around Mom. They slowly moved up the hallway. Their footsteps echoed.

"LaMar would have recognized our steps," Sydney thought.

Mom stopped and took a deep breath. She could not keep back the sobs. Dad held her tighter. In that setting Sydney felt silence brood across the hall and he suddenly knew that it was silence, not the wind, not the passage of time, he should fear. Silence that ruled the school, silence that pervaded the fields, the dead trees, the silence that swept across the cemetery....

Dad's arm slipped from Mom as she pushed ahead with her mouth clamped and white in determination, pulling Prielle behind her. A hush that even toned the ever-present silence grew as they prepared themselves a last time to view the mortal remains of their dearest family member. Mom, braced from head to toe, her arms stiff as cables, led the younger children she'd brought into the world to see the end of the child she'd delivered just before them. She headed into the hospital room. Her hand touched the door knob and she quivered, unable to go on. Dad's big hand reached out and covered hers, and his other arm circled her shoulders. Together, they pulled the big door open.

289

"Surprise!" yelled Venna and LaMar in unison to their stunned faces.

His mustard-colored freckles bleached off, his hair bed-tousled, his fresh hospital clothing rumpled, up and chattering happy as a monkey, sat LaMar.

The family stood still in shock.

"LaMarrrr!" bawled Mom, running to him and hugging him. "You're all right!"

"LaMar!" cried Dad. He reached over to mess up his hair but turned away and even he began to sob. Then they were all hugging and crying, even Venna. Doc Mooley came in, only to walk out again.

"We thought you had passed through," piped Prielle, the only one who could speak.

"I am better," said LaMar. "We tried to tell you but the phone went dead."

Doc Mooley came in. "I'm sorry—the phone line sounded so bad; I told her the line died, and I guess she thought I spoke about LaMar."

"What happened?" asked Dad after pulling himself together. "How did he recover so fast?"

"It's a powerful new drug – brand-new this year – a broad spectrum anti-biotic called tetracycline," Doc Mooley said. "It worked all along; we just couldn't see it. Three shots of the full dosage finally did the trick." He beamed so that his face looked like a cup with a light bulb inside.

"We have our miracle," said Dad. "Thank the Lord!"

"And the doctor," said Mom. She turned to Doc Mooley. "We so appreciate you."

"And I guess it could be considered a miracle," said Doc. "A lot of miracles in this day come through medicine. That doesn't make them less of a miracle."

More steps echoed down the hallway, and Bishop Lutty, who had followed the Studebaker in his car, came into the room.

"Oh!" he said, when he saw LaMar. He, too, burst into tears. "Oh, thank goodness. Oh, thank you, Lord!" His voice sounded squishy and he, too, turned away. Then Addie peeped into the room. She saw LaMar and her whole body jerked. She ran right over to him like a grown woman and cried and hugged him. LaMar looked around, trying to understand.

Others, who also had followed them to the hospital, pressed into the room, each shocked; faces dripped like they were in a tear storm. Mafe, with his wife, and Bleu. Arsle with Sister Klaybill and Melvin. Then Robin and Brid Neeter. The Warpels came last, bringing Sister Mister. Everyone cried. The room continued to fill until packed. Haggard, weather-hammered expressions that held through storms, crop failure, dying animals, broken down machinery now melted in emotional release; men and women wept. Standing behind the press of townspeople, Addie still cried and hugged Sydney. He hugged her back and patted her shoulder. He knew that Nat would tease him for the rest of his life, but he didn't care. Addie slipped closer to him and suddenly turned to face him. He looked right at her, into her wet eyes. He kept his arms around her and she leaned forward and kissed him right on the lips.

He felt the soft press linger, and felt helpless, like a cow in a tournament of tiddlywinks.

Something warm happened inside him. It wasn't just Addie, but something more. Something about his prayer made him realize Someone very wonderful knew him, and made promises that He always kept. Now he knew what a testimony meant. It meant God loved him. God is wonderful. God watches over us, he thought.

Outside, a wind sighed over the hospital, but for Sydney, deep inside, the pressing, kicking and moaning of the wind cows forever ceased.

Sister Mister made a little fuss entering. She screamed when she saw LaMar and hugged and kissed him. She looked like she would scream and kiss him again but someone started singing and she joined: "Silent Night." Everyone joined: "Holy night. All is calm. All is bright...."

Made in the USA
Middletown, DE
14 December 2021